J. E. MCDONALD

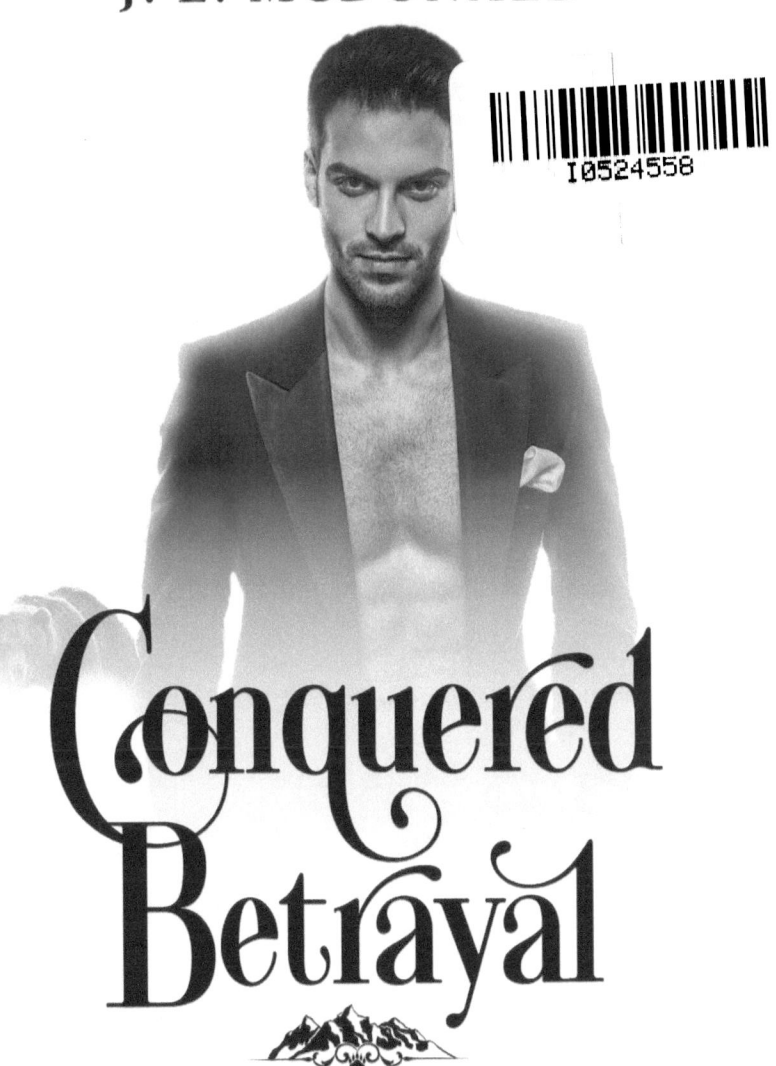

Conquered Betrayal

GOLDENLACH RIDGE SHIFTERS BOOK 3

MYSTIC OWL

AN IMPRINT OF CITY OWL PRESS

CONQUERED BETRAYAL

J. E. MCDONALD

MYSTIC OWL

CONQUERED BETRAYAL
Goldenlach Ridge Shifters, Book 3

MYSTIC OWL
A City Owl Press Imprint
www.cityowlpress.com

Cover Design by MiblArt. All stock photos licensed appropriately.

Edited by Heather McCorkle.

For information on subsidiary rights, please contact the publisher at info@cityowlpress.com.

Print Edition ISBN: 978-1-64898-382-5

Digital Edition ISBN: 978-1-64898-381-8

Printed in the United States of America

To Bevin,
For more reasons than I can name on a page.
But overall, because you're awesome.
I love you.

PRAISE FOR J. E. MCDONALD

"*Ghost of a Gamble* is a contemporary, gothic tale filled with sparkling wittiness, budding romance, thrilling suspense, and scary ghosts!"
— *InD'tale*

"Bree was funny, and quirky, but also independent, which I loved. I enjoyed the quirky atmosphere, the hauntings, and the hot romance between these ghost hunters. A great read for fans of paranormal romance!"
— *J. E. Hunter, author of The Torc*

"I adored *Ghost of an Enchantment*! Fun, magical, and romantic. Stella is everything I look for in a witchy romance heroine, and Wickwood is a delightful setting for these books. The pacing was perfect, and the magical mystery was right up my alley. Well done!"
— *Lisa Edmonds, bestselling author of the Alice Worth series*

"J.E. McDonald comes out swinging with *Captive Wilderness*, the first in a new paranormal romance series featuring shifters, plenty of spice, and forced proximity done right."
— *Gabrielle Ash, author of The Family Cross*

"McDonald's cast of supernatural characters are always impeccably crafted and leave you eager for the next installment of this delightful series."
— *Ashley R. King, author of Painting the Lines and Forever After*

"Bree is utterly charming right from the beginning, and her

dynamic with Zack makes for a wonderfully compelling story. *Ghost of a Gamble* is easy to sink into, with a supernatural plot that escalates all the way to the end."
— *K. Caine, author of A Study in Velvet and Leather*

"McDonald busts this worldwide open and brings it to new heights and dimensions. She easily navigates blending in all of the different plot points and relationships (romantic, family, and friendship) together into a fun and 'enchanting' story."
— *E.E. Hornburg, author of The Night's Chosen*

"A heartfelt paranormal romance about a skeptic teaming up with a paranormal investigator, *Ghost of a Gamble* is sure to make you smile. Bree and Zack have perfect chemistry and their banter is irresistible."
— *Kat Turner, author of Hex, Love, and Rock & Roll*

"Stella is a witch who doesn't trust cops. Unfortunately, Lucas is a cop--and the sexual tension between them is scorching hot, making *Ghost of an Enchantment* a fast-paced, compelling read."
— *K. Caine, author of A Study in Velvet and Leather*

"Transporting readers to a thrilling romance filled dimension, *Ghost of an Enchantment* is a breath-stealing page turner set in the magical town of Wickwood! With characters that provide touches of humor and a plot filled with mystical intrigue, readers will be enticed to move in and peek from their windows in anticipation of what will happen next!"
— *InD'tale Magazine*

"A fast-paced read with a tension-filled romance and high-stakes plot, *Ghost of a Summoning* is a paranormal love story you don't want to miss."
— *Gabrielle Ash, author of The Family Cross*

WORKS BY J. E. MCDONALD

THE WICKWOOD CHRONICLES

Ghost of a Beginning

Ghost of a Gamble

Ghost of an Enchantment

Ghost of a Summoning

GOLDENLACH RIDGE SHIFTERS

Captive Wilderness

Caged Fury

Conquered Betrayal

PART I

THE SCENT OF DECEPTION

1

JOLYN

Eleven Years Ago

I KNEW IT WAS WEIRD TO FOLLOW THEM, BUT I COULDN'T HELP IT.

Whenever I saw Kane, I had the urge to stay close, to see what he was up to, like he was some sort of superhero, and if I remained nearby, I'd finally get to see him change from his glasses to his cape.

Which was ridiculous because Kane didn't even wear glasses.

Ever since he defended me, stopping Tom Akins from beating the crap out of me when I was ten years old, I'd held him in high regard. And by "high regard" I meant "crush." I've had the *hugest* crush on Kane Baird for the past seven years.

Because he couldn't speak—some injury he'd suffered a few years ago no one ever spoke about—I'd learned ASL in secret. He'd been homeschooled for years now. On the rare occasions I saw him, a thrill went through me and I tried to prolong the sighting as much as possible. I'd take any excuse to stay away from home, to ease the tightness banded around my chest. Sometimes that meant following him.

Okay, so it sounded a little creepy. But seriously, what else was a girl supposed to do?

Skulking not far away, I followed him out of town. He was with his two friends Walker and Landon. They were always together, each a year apart in age. Walker, the youngest of them, would graduate in a month.

They made a handsome trio. Kane was the biggest, he'd only bulked up over the past couple of years. Landon, the most slender, always wore dress pants and a button-down shirt. Walker, shorter than the other two, was the most wiry in strength. His shoulders and chest seemed wider than they should for his height, like he wasn't done growing yet.

Deeper they hiked into the forest with me following. They passed the old trapper's shed, then the creek. Where were they off to? I could hear them talking, but not what they said, the wind carrying their voices away. I guess it kept my presence a secret too, because they didn't look back at where I trailed them, trying to keep just around the last bend so I could duck out of the way if they turned around. *Not a creeper at all.*

The trees grew closer together, the noise of town fading to nothing. My heart pounded while nervousness swirled in my stomach. I should probably head home and leave them to their day, but my feet kept following. What would I say if they discovered me? I'd daydreamed about being bold enough to ask Kane on a date. He didn't have a girlfriend from what I could see. But in that daydream, his friends hadn't been around.

They disappeared from sight. Picking up my pace, I puffed a breath of relief when I glimpsed them again.

A scream—a woman's voice—tore through the air. I froze, the fine hairs on my arms standing on end. A second scream followed, this one more masculine and primal. The three boys tore off in its direction, up a hill and away from the creek. I followed, running frantically through the bushes, branches scraping at my shoulders and arms. I cleared the hill, and the shallow valley spread before me. What I saw made my heart pound in my head. A huge grizzly bear dragged a limp woman by her foot through the layer of dead leaves on the forest floor. It let go when the three boys screamed at it, not twenty feet away. Were they crazy? That bear was massive and feral. Probably the one scaring campers at the local campground. But that was on the other side of town. These boys should be running in the opposite direction, not shouting at it.

In an instant, everything changed. The world blurred. Kane, the boy I fancied myself in love with, morphed into something else. He leaped through the air, skin changing into fur. He *transformed*. A gasp caught in my throat like a boulder. His clothes ripped from his body. Before I could scream, he'd turned into a massive bear, one whose growl stopped my heart.

I couldn't breathe, couldn't think, couldn't process what the hell I was seeing. A haze fogged my vision.

The fact that Walker also changed, turned into a cougar, was secondary. It hardly registered. All I could see was one bear attack the other. A roar ripped through the air. *Fur. Claws. Blood.* I didn't realize I'd grabbed hold of the tree next to me until I squeezed the bark so tight it cut painfully into my palm.

I couldn't look away. Every instinct in my body told me to get the hell away from here, but I couldn't move. Landon stood apart from the battling bears, yelling at them, shouting Kane's name over and over again.

But that wasn't Kane anymore. It was a monster. My infatuation with him shed from my body, fear and horror taking its place. The edges of my vision darkened. My head felt disconnected from my neck. The invisible band around my chest squeezed tighter. I forced myself to breathe. It came out strangled.

Landon turned, and I stumbled back, falling down the slight incline in my attempt to get away. I couldn't let him see me. If he could be friends with monsters...I didn't want any of them to find me.

Crawling on my hands and knees, I gulped breaths, then stood on jelly legs. I ran as fast as I could. By the time I reached the edge of the town, my lungs burned. I ran through Goldenlach Ridge to our property on the lake, ignoring the heads that turned my way. For once, I was grateful to see my brother. Emerson noticed me from his spot at the picnic table and stood up from the game of chess he'd been playing by himself.

"What's wrong?" He strode over and grasped my shoulders, steadying me.

Terrified, I shook my head, my entire body trembling. What I'd seen shouldn't be possible. It didn't make any sense. People shouldn't be able to change like that. Kane and Walker looked like normal boys, but they weren't normal at all.

"They're animals," I gasped between broken breaths. "They changed. The boys. They're animals." My words came out garbled. Would he believe me? It sounded insane.

Instead of dismissing me, a strange light entered Emerson's eyes, one I usually hated to see. "Changed?"

I nodded, panting for air, swallowing against the fear lodged in my throat. "I can't explain it." It felt like my tongue was made of sandpaper. "They were human, then they...weren't."

The hands on my shoulders tightened. I braced myself for more pain, but he let up, putting his arm around my shoulders in an oddly comforting gesture, and ushered me toward the house.

"Let's make some tea. Then you'll tell me everything."

2

LANDON

Present Day

I PASSED HIM THE TWO BEST PICTURES I HAD OF HER: ONE WHILE SHE'D been in service and the other from four years ago. Sitting on the beach, she'd been smiling at me when I took it, the necklace I'd given her glinting against the pink and red sunset. Wind made her hair almost stand straight up.

"I remember her," Walker said, turning the photos over in his hand, thumbing the worn edge of the smaller one. He gave them back, eyes narrowed.

"Then you'll track her down?" I placed them carefully in the top drawer of my desk. "I just want to know if she landed on her feet."

Walker stared at me, then withdrew toward the door. "Hey, whatever floats your boat, man. Your dime." He left my office with his eyebrows raised.

I stared out at the Vancouver skyline. It wasn't weird to find out what had happened to her, was it?

If her light, human scent hadn't twirled toward me on a breeze, she might have gotten away from me again.

I leaned against the concrete pillar of the DPM—Detroit People Mover—and listened as elevated train hummed and clicked its way above me, heading through downtown. There weren't a lot of places to hide on this moderately busy corner of Detroit, but I hoped the way I stared at my phone appeared inconspicuous—a regular guy waiting for his Uber.

Even though my eyes were trained on my cell, every other sense was focused outward, trying to pick up something, anything, that would tell me why my best friend went missing in this city over two weeks ago.

I may have sent Walker on a stupid job to track down Jolyn Mahn, the woman who broke my heart into a million pieces when she left, but now I didn't know what the hell was going on. Everything went even more sideways when Kane, who I hadn't seen in *years*, showed up at my office with a mate, a bobcat shifter named Brooke Covin. She'd been kidnapped along with her sister, Sabrina, the abductors using shift-suppressing collars very similar to the ones developed at *my* company.

If I could find Jolyn, maybe some of this would start making sense. Because she'd left Urick Enterprises suddenly four years ago, she was the only person I could think of who could have stolen the plans for the collar—and even that didn't track.

Jolyn. There wasn't a day that went by I didn't think of her, and I hated myself for it. Whenever I saw someone with naturally orange hair, my heart would squeeze in my chest, thinking it was her for a split second. Exhaling, I tapped my palm against my thigh. If I could just *get over her*, I could move on with my life, but the bear inside me wouldn't let that happen, moping and pining like a lovesick fool. I might have kept tabs on her, but I'd left her alone, respecting her need for space.

When I found out she might have stolen from me... *Well.* That changed everything.

If what Kane and Brooke had told me connected back to her, then she was into some serious shit. Not only theft, but human trafficking and God knew what else.

Had anything between us been real? Or had she been working for me with ulterior motives the entire time? Had she planned to sell off my intellectual property to the highest bidder from the start? If she'd needed money because she was in trouble, I would have helped her—which didn't make sense either because her family owned a billion-dollar pharmaceutical company. Why steal the collar Kane designed? As a human, she wouldn't have understood its purpose. If she'd learned about shifters, about me, then she would have said something. None of it added up.

What the hell am I doing here? This made day two of me staking out Mahn BioIndustries from across the street. The American headquarters of MBI took up the top half of the stone and glass building casting a thick shadow over the street. Its sister building was situated in Toronto, Emerson Mahn only expanding his empire to the states a few years ago. I'd read an editorial article hypothesizing he'd made the move because of more lenient food and drug regulations.

There was really no reason for me to be here except her family connections. If Walker, an ex-military private investigator, hadn't been able to track her down in Detroit, why did I think I could?

That brought me back to why I'd sent him after her in the first place. I knew the answer but didn't want to admit it, even to myself. She was the only woman I'd ever loved. Four years ago, I'd thought our relationship was perfect. Then she left me without a word and joined the army. The engagement ring I'd bought her still lay in its box on my mantle in Vancouver, a glaring reminder of our failed relationship every time I looked at it.

I ran a distracted hand across my jaw, contemplating the MBI building. That was when I scented her—vanilla cake mixed with nerves. If I hadn't known Jolyn so intimately, I would have missed it. My bear roared inside me, almost rabid in his need to get closer.

Her distinct fragrance came from a woman in a business suit with sleek, black hair, and big sunglasses, a brown leather satchel over her shoulder. I'd been looking for her signature orange hair, curly to the extreme. She'd always complained she could do nothing with it except what it wanted. I'd watched her try to wrestle it into a ponytail and agreed.

I might have dismissed the scent as my mind playing tricks on me if it wasn't for her body; athletic and trim, she could have graced the covers of yoga magazines. A figure I'd never forget—not after she'd haunted my dreams.

I straightened, clenching my fists. The anger I'd felt when I'd realized she might be involved in Brooke and Sabrina's abductions resurfaced. Now that I had her in my sights, I wouldn't let her go. It had been too long and I deserved answers, especially if she had stolen from me.

And Brooke's sister was still missing.

My feet propelled me forward. I crossed the road, between two cars turning onto Woodward Avenue. Adrenaline pumped through my system, warming my neck. She'd probably left Vancouver right after stealing from me.

She headed straight toward MBI's glass doors, a security checkpoint on the other side. I couldn't allow her to pass through. If I did, if she got away from me, then I might never track her down again. She would disappear like she had four years ago.

Each of my steps ate up two of hers. Twenty feet from the doors, I finally caught up with her enough to grab her elbow.

She froze, halting mid-step to whip her gaze in my direction with a quiet gasp, sunglasses blocking her eyes from my view. For a second, I thought I had it wrong, that this wasn't Jolyn Mahn, but her scent assaulted me again. My body tingled in awareness like it always had.

Her disguise was so good; I never would have recognized her by sight alone. She'd covered every freckle on her face and had to be wearing a wig. It pissed off both me and my bear—to cover her brilliant hair was a crime against humanity.

I ripped off her glasses and tore the wig from her head, throwing both on the ground before she could utter a word. And there they were: bright blue eyes. Her orange tresses were pinned to her scalp to fit the wig. A buzz of righteous satisfaction went through me at having exposed her lie. By the time the day was over, I'd learn every secret she kept from me, including a confession of her theft.

She froze in place, her wide eyes taking me in and her mouth partially open in shock.

"We need to talk," I said, my voice surprisingly steady for standing next to the woman who'd hurt me like no other.

My words seemed to break the spell holding her. She straightened, her eyes jumping to the building in front of us before returning to me. "Fucking hell, Landon, you have the worst timing on the planet."

I cocked my head to the side, frowning. That wasn't what I expected her to say. But when she tried to rip her arm from mine, I held fast. The flare of fear in her eyes, matched with the scent of it, was more effective than a splash of cold water. I let go and stepped away. It wasn't in my nature to manhandle women, but I didn't want her slipping away from me. Those answers I needed were way too important.

Movement out of the corner of my eye made me turn. Two security guards exited the building, big guys with bulges under their black suits like they were concealing weapons. *Bloody hell. They're going to beat the crap out of me for touching her, aren't they?*

"Okay, time to go." Jolyn's voice snapped my attention to her.

She seized my arm, pulling me down the sidewalk, away from MBI and the two guards. *What the...*

Her fingernails dug into my arm so tight, I knew they'd leave impressions. I tried to ignore the resulting goosebumps blooming across my skin. High heels clicked a staccato rhythm on the sidewalk. Faster and faster she walked until I almost jogged to keep pace. She kept glancing over her shoulder, and I did the same. The men followed us, closing the gap a step at a time, but trying to act casual.

"I know, I know," Jolyn muttered to herself, and I shot her a look. Except for the fingernails in my arm, she wasn't paying attention to me. "Just give me a damn second and we'll regroup."

I blinked., My earlier anger was replaced with a general sense of *what the hell*? After all these years, this wasn't how I'd envisioned our first meeting would go.

I cast another glance over my shoulder. The big dudes were still there. One spoke on his phone, but both of them had their eyes glued to Jolyn. I faced forward. Cracks in the pavement stretched out before us, interrupted occasionally by sections of sidewalk which appeared newly poured.

Why would Jolyn be running from MBI's security guards? Had she stolen something from her brother too? Was she a corporate thief? Was that what the disguise was all about?

We crossed against the lights on East Congress Street and cut toward an alley. I would have dug in my heels and found out what was going on if it weren't for the two guys trailing us. After a quick glance down the alley, Jolyn's grip on my arm tightened. She yanked me to the left, into the shadows between two buildings. A delivery truck sat parked on the right, but other than dumpsters further along, we were alone.

"Can you tell me what the—"

"No," she said, cutting me off. "Stay quiet."

My bear and I bristled at her tone. Screw the dudes following us. Even if her words held no heat, I didn't need this. I was the

CEO of a multimillion dollar tech company. No one told me to "stay quiet."

I yanked my hand out of her grasp and spun to face her. "You've got a lot of—"

"Quiet, I said." She gave me a light shove and I stumbled behind the delivery van, out of sight of the mouth of the alley.

Straightening, I flattened out the lapels of my suit jacket, trying to regain some control of the situation. "This has got to be the most—"

I didn't finish the sentence. One of the big dudes appeared from the other side of the delivery truck and gripped my shoulder.

"That's enough," he said.

Something metallic pressed against the side of my temple. *Click.*

Jolyn's eyes widened. *Shit.* Even as a shifter, there was no way I could dodge a bullet that close.

The dude's voice rumbled from behind me. "Mr. Mahn wants to talk—"

Jolyn took a step forward, but the other guy zipped behind her, reaching for her arm, a gun in his hand.

"No!" Not thinking, I lunged forward. Before I'd taken a half step, Jolyn spun around, low to the ground, and swept the dude's feet out from under him. His head knocked on the truck, *thwap*, and he crumpled to the pavement, unconscious.

My jaw dropped. Somehow, she'd also taken his gun from him and now pointed it at me. I raised my hands reflexively.

She cocked her head, eyebrows quirking at me, then stared down the dude at my back. "Let him go, and I might not shoot you."

The gun lifted away from my temple. "Like hell—"

Bang. Bang. The earsplitting sound sliced through my skull. My vision blurred. *Have I been shot?*

3

JOLYN

"IF SHE HAD ANY MORE FRECKLES, HER SKIN WOULD BE BROWN INSTEAD
of invisible."

The words halted my feet, my shoulders climbing up to my ears.
The group of boys laughed, all of them—Tom Akins and his gang of
friends. They were total assholes. Everyone knew it, but no one did
anything, including the teachers and parents because his father was on
the city council.

I should have kept walking, but my feet wouldn't move.

"A regular carrot top."

I'd heard it all before, but when it came from such an older, bigger
boy, my whole face heated.

"Now she's a beet. Maybe we should cook her up for vegetable soup,
tasty like." Tom smacked his lips together.

I fisted my hands. Why was everyone so scared of this guy?

"Is that what you want to be when you grow up? A vegetable in a
wheelchair like your mom?"

The words stabbed so bad, I didn't think. I spun around and
launched myself at him, my hands going for his throat.

Howling, Emerson's hired goon fell to his knees, his free hand covering his wound, blood seeping through his fingers. My heart beat incredibly fast in my chest. Landon stared at me with wide eyes, his hands still up in the air.

Could this day get any worse?

Shooting a real person was so very different from the dummies and paper targets of basic training. My bullets had done their job; he'd dropped his gun and was more concerned about his injury than shooting Landon in the head. But *fucking hell.* If the goon didn't quiet down, he'd bring all of Detroit to our location.

Ignoring all the questions swirling in Landon's dark brown eyes, I inhaled a deep breath, trying to calm myself. No one else came rushing into the alley, attracted by the noise. *For the moment.* I prayed Marley was already checking for video cameras. If I were recorded shooting someone, it would make this situation a whole lot worse, but at least the recording would show I'd been threatened first.

Squatting, I crouched beside the thug and reached inside my leather satchel for the hypodermic needle Alina had insisted I take with me. Looked like she was right.

"It's a flesh wound. You'll be fine." The goon tried to stop me, but I sunk the needle into his thigh and pushed the plunger. He fell forward, face to pavement, a moment later.

I snatched up his weapon and stood, tossing both guns in my satchel. Blessed quiet surrounded Landon and I as we stared at each other in an alley that stank of week-old food.

Holy hell, it had been four years, and how could he have become sexier? Neatly trimmed facial hair dusted his sharp jawline and upper lip, the hair topping his head just long enough to hint at his natural wave. Full lips, the cleft in his chin, everything was familiar but not. He'd hardened over the past four years. So had I.

The last time I'd seen Landon, he'd been a fresh upstart, the world at his feet, his business on the verge of exploding into an international contender. Now he was the epitome of a suave CEO. It looked good on him.

And there wasn't a guy on earth who could wear a suit like he could. Most men couldn't pull off black-on-black without resembling a gangster or a funeral home director, but not Landon. The top three buttons of his dress shirt were unbuttoned, revealing a light dusting of chest hair in the exposed triangle of skin. If I leaned in and pressed my face to the special spot at the base of his throat, would he smell the same?

I shook myself, snapping out it. This was not the time to reminisce about our year together—because Landon had stepped into a heap of shit so big, an elephant would get lost in it.

The urge to scream climbed my throat. *So fucked up.* After weeks of planning, finally on my way to exposing my brother and his under the radar sicko operation, Landon showed up and wrecked everything. I wouldn't have another chance to crack the servers hidden under the MBI building. The futility of it all made me question my choices over the past few days.

Scenarios ran through my head, ones where I left him here on his own. I did have another needle filled with the knockout drug. I had to figure out how to ditch him as quickly as possible. But each of those scenarios ended with him at Emerson's mercy with no clue as to what was going on. And that... I swallowed. No matter what I'd done to Landon in the past, that wasn't acceptable. Not when I knew what my brother was capable of.

I clenched my hands, trying not to dwell on the opportunity I'd missed. By afternoon, Emerson would have the whole building locked down tighter than a Regency virgin the night before her wedding.

"Jolyn," Landon said with a nod, lowering his hands to

straighten his suit jacket like he hadn't been witness to me knocking out one guy, then shooting and drugging another.

"Landon." My voice came out tentative and I wanted to kick myself for it. But I had to admit, he was taking this way better than a guy who spent his days in a boardroom should.

His next words undermined his calm exterior. "What the hell have you done?"

A breath huffed out of me, the urge to laugh coming out of nowhere. There wasn't time to even start to explain. "We need to go." I cast one quick glance at the goons on the ground. They'd probably already called for backup. We needed to get the hell out of Dodge before they arrived.

He swiveled away when I tried to take his arm again. "I don't think so." He scowled. "Start talking. Now."

I returned the scowl. "We need to move. Now." It was probably childish to imitate his voice, but I couldn't help it.

"Who's Lover Boy?" Alina's voice purred in my ear through my comm. One of my best friends, she might look unassuming when a person met her, but she was deadly as hell. "He sounds sexy."

Spinning on my heel, I headed toward the other end of the alley. "I don't have time for this." Like I'd hoped, Landon followed.

"Whoa. Hold up. You're just going to leave them like that?" he asked, catching up.

"Hell yes." And I hoped I never saw them again. I didn't have time to get arrested for attempted murder, or manslaughter, or whatever it would have turned out to be—especially because I wasn't a US citizen.

"They attacked us with guns. Shouldn't we call the police?"

"Hell no." With my luck, the whole Detroit police force was probably on Emerson's payroll.

"Who is this guy?" Marley, my other best friend and a tech

wizard, asked through my earpiece. "And why did he fuck up our op?"

The bigger question was, why Landon was staking out the MBI building. The fact that he was here, in Detroit, blew my mind. When I'd left Alaska and escaped my brother, Walker Hayles had told me someone was looking for me. I'd guessed it was Landon because he was our common denominator, but I'd hoped to hell I'd been wrong. *Guess not.* Sometimes I really hated being right.

I turned left out of the alley, heading toward where I'd parked. Landon blocked me with his body, the scowl on his face more intense than before. "You have some explaining to do."

What I really needed to do was get out of here, but I understood he would make it difficult no matter what I said.

Keeping my face blank, I nodded. "I'll explain whatever you want, just keep walking." The more time we spent in the area, the higher the likelihood Emerson would track us down. I wasn't sure if he was in Detroit right now, but I knew he was searching for me. I knew he wanted to kill me. If I'd had any doubts he understood the depths of my defection, what I'd done to his two thugs cleared that right up.

I skirted past Landon and kept walking, my gaze averted from those strolling down the sidewalk. Had anyone heard those gunshots? Or would they think a car backfired?

Landon matched my pace. Shoulder to shoulder, we trucked down the street. Tension climbed up my spine and nape as I waited for him to tear into me. I felt his eyes on me and kept mine forward. My skin heated, a flush spreading over my cheeks.

As we neared the corner, he finally spoke. "You stole from me."

"Yes," I answered without hesitation. If he'd figured it out, there was no point in lying.

He paused, like he hadn't expected me to be truthful, then

jogged to catch up. "The whole reason you worked for me was to steal?"

We crossed against the light, then headed south. "In a manner of speaking, yes." I couldn't give him more than that right now even if I wanted to. And I definitely didn't want to see the betrayal on his face I knew must be there. My hand clenched on the strap of my satchel.

"Everything." He cleared his throat and started again. "Everything between us was a lie."

That stopped my feet, my heart jumping into my throat. I met his gaze, finding his eyes the deepest of browns, almost black, my stomach squeezing at his wounded expression. "Not everything." I might have lied to him for a year, but what I'd felt for him, *truly* felt for him, was real.

The day I left Vancouver, left Landon, I hadn't thought I'd ever see him again and it had hurt more than I thought anything ever could. Physical pain, the things I'd endured at the hands of my brother, was nothing compared to how much my heart broke when I stepped on that plane.

And this was absolutely not the time to get into it, not out in the open. I needed to get Landon somewhere safe and regroup with Marley and Alina.

"Come," I said, jerking my head in the direction I'd parked the Fiat I'd borrowed from Alina. I'd left it close enough to the MBI building to grab it in a quick escape, but far enough away the plates wouldn't be scanned and flagged by Emerson's security.

Not that I really wanted to circle back to his building, but I didn't see an alternative right now. Landon fell into step beside me, and I glanced at him. "Do you have a car?" I should have asked that first. Maybe it had been closer.

I felt the pressure of his gaze with every step we took, the scrutiny of a CEO assessing his opponent over a conference table. "I walked from my hotel."

The Fiat it is.

"What's the plan?" Marley asked in my ear. "We're leaving for the van now in case you need backup."

I cleared my throat, keeping my eyes forward. "Understood."

Out of my peripheral vision, Landon whipped his head toward me, his brow furrowed.

"Are you going to ditch the guy? Because I can tell right now, he's going to be a problem."

Marley wasn't wrong. Having Landon here, him knowing what I'd done while working with him, only complicated everything. And I couldn't afford to be distracted right now, not when we didn't know the extent of Emerson's plans regarding the people who could shift into animals. The "beasts" as my brother called them. People like Landon's two friends, Walker and Kane.

In contrast, I don't think I'd ever met anyone more *human*, than Landon Urick. Even as kids he'd come off as the uptight one. He'd always worn dress clothes and loafers. When I thought about the day in the woods so long ago, Landon's civility stood out against the brutal backdrop like a smudge of red paint overtop a landscape watercolor done in blues. *How could he be friends with beasts?*

We rounded the last corner to Alina's gray Fiat 500. A relieved exhale escaped my lips to see it remaining where I'd left it, unharmed and untouched, four cars down. I picked up my pace.

"I'll do my best," I said to Marley, keeping my voice low. Even so, Landon heard and stopped me with a hand on my arm.

"Who are you talking to?" His scowl deepening, he tipped his head until he could see my left ear.

Now that he'd removed my wig, I had nowhere to hide my earpiece and I didn't want to shake my hair out of its net because it would make me more recognizable to Emerson's goons. Bright orange hair was hard to hide.

Quick as a cobra, he snatched the comm out of my ear before I could react. "What the hell?" he murmured, his eyes glued to the tiny device.

At a glance, a person could tell the little beige comm wasn't a run-of-the-mill wireless earbud. Marley had made some modifications to the top-quality earpiece, increasing its range, and Alina matched it to my extremely pale skin tone. She'd laughed heartily while adding a couple of freckles. Most people wouldn't have noticed it. Landon always did have good eyesight though, taking in every detail around him.

"This comes from Urick Enterprises," he said, his head tipped in confusion as his eyes hopped from me to the comm. "Latest model."

I held out my hand, unimpressed he'd recognized his own product, and that he'd taken away my only connection to Marley and Alina. I didn't have a phone on me, hadn't used one since escaping Alaska. Emerson was resourceful and connected, and only got more powerful as the years passed and his wealth grew. Long ago, I'd started a bank account on my own and he'd had it frozen. I basically needed to assume he had every aspect of my life monitored in his quest to find me, including any dummy accounts. Paranoia was my friend.

A screech of tires echoed down the street. Landon and I turned at the same time. A black SUV made a sudden stop past the intersection ahead and now reversed wildly to change directions—more of Emerson's men.

"Shit." I plucked the earpiece out of Landon's fingers, reinserted it, and ran toward the Fiat. Thankfully, I didn't have to tell him to move. The smack of his dress shoes against the pavement told me he followed.

"Get in," I said, unlocking the doors with a press of my thumb to the key fob. I kept my eyes on the SUV as it got itself pointed in the right direction. Throwing my satchel into the backseat, I hopped in and started the souped-up Fiat, complete with bulletproof glass. Landon squeezed himself in beside me, swallowing up the space in the compact vehicle with his height.

"Don't hurt my baby," Alina said in my ear like she knew I was about to put it through its paces.

"No promises." I didn't have time to make sure Landon was buckled in before I shifted in reverse, then changed gears again to shoot out of the parking space. Only a boulevard separated us from the SUV.

I sped down the street, giving the driver a quick glance: Emerson's head of security, Cliff. Out my side mirror, I watched him accelerate, then make a U-turn.

The traffic light turned yellow. I stepped on the gas, zipping across two lanes of traffic to make the left onto East Jefferson. If I didn't have shit to do in this city, I would have gone straight and taken the bridge to Windsor, disappearing into Canada like I longed to. I gave Landon a quick side-glance, noting how he braced his hand against the dash. Hiding wasn't an option now—if it ever was.

Passing under the shadow of the DPM, The Renaissance Center whizzed by on the right, the tree-lined boulevard blocking our view of offices on the left. I glanced in my rearview mirror. Cliff blew through the red light, making several cars lurch to a stop to avoid hitting him.

Was it too much to ask for him to follow basic traffic laws? I stepped on the gas, edging over the speed limit. "Any ideas?"

I asked the question to Marley, but Landon was the one to answer. "This isn't my city."

No shit. A glance in my mirror showed the SUV gaining on us. *Titty fucker.* "You're going to need to change your plates," I said to Alina through the comm. Those goons had probably already run them, already had her name. The last thing I wanted was for either of my friends to end up on Emerson's radar.

"I'll happily change my plates if you keep her in one piece."

"Who are you talking to?" Landon asked again, his angry voice dominating overtop of Alina's in my ear.

I didn't have any time to go into it. "Friends," was all I said, and focused on driving to keep us alive. The SUV continued to gain on us. I needed to get off this straightaway, to lose them somehow, but the further we drove, the more residential the neighborhood became.

I took another corner, then another. Even though I varied my route, I couldn't shake them. They matched my speed after every turn. There weren't enough cars to hide behind.

"Can you find me somewhere to lose these guys?" I asked Marley.

"Working on it," came her quick response. "I hacked into the live satellite feed. Take your next left."

I obeyed, and the traffic thinned significantly. "This isn't any better." We were sitting ducks out here.

Right on cue, a bullet pinged off the rear fender. Landon flinched, his head swinging around.

"Stay down," I ordered.

He ducked. "Are they shooting at us?" His voice was laced with disbelief. He turned his face toward me, lips parted. I had to ignore him in favor of keeping us alive.

"Take the next right," came Marley's voice.

I did. The street was almost deserted. The only advantage we seemed to have over the guys following us was our tight cornering.

"Another right," she instructed after a minute.

This street was wholly residential, the houses spaced out with tall grass and trees between them, more than a few boarded up or falling down. And no traffic to separate us from our tail.

"How is this any better?"

"Just keep going."

"There are kids playing on the side of the road, for fuck's sake."

"Keep going. I've got you."

Making a frustrated noise, I kept up my speed, hoping to hell no one stepped in front of the car. I wouldn't have time to stop.

"Next right."

"I don't see how this is going to—"

"Next right!"

"Fine," I gritted. The tires squealed as I took the next right.

"Immediate right."

"It's a back alley."

"I know. Circle the building, come out the other side."

Gravel sprayed behind us as I made the sharp turn. It was an abandoned service station, two garage doors boarded up, the white paint chipping off every surface.

The distance was short enough that the SUV hadn't followed us, overshooting the garage.

"This next bit is going to be tricky."

"Perfect."

"Think of it as one of those Humvee training exercises," Alina's voice cut in, way too cheerful for this situation.

"Not helpful." And the Fiat was the exact opposite of a Humvee.

"If you do it right, you'll be able to lose them," Marley promised.

"Fine." I followed her instructions, circling on our route. Each minute that ticked by made my shoulders climb toward my ears. I kept looking in the rear-view mirror, waiting for Cliff to reappear.

Marley's instructions took us past the same garage we'd driven around earlier. Farther along, we stopped behind an abandoned house, the overgrowth of trees hiding us completely from every angle. I shifted into park and let out a long breath, keeping my gaze trained on the house in front of us, not wanting to acknowledge my traumatized passenger.

After being chased for so long, sitting still made my skin itch, like I should be doing something, *anything*, besides staring out my windshield at a decrepit back door and leafy bushes. The sensation of being scrutinized crept over my body. I glanced at Landon. He stared at me with an intensity that created shivers across my skin. Shit, he was angry. He had every right to be. I didn't blame him. Adjusting my hands on the steering wheel, I returned my gaze to the house, its blue paint frozen in a perpetual descent. Wooden steps hung off the foundation at a forty-five-degree angle.

I would have given anything to be somewhere else, to not have him look at me like that. I'd been his personal assistant, fallen in love, then betrayed him. After all this time, he'd somehow found out that it hadn't just been me running from our relationship.

"How?" I asked, not sure what I specifically needed to know, and very much aware of my two friends listening in. How did he find me? How did he discover the truth about my theft? How could he sit beside me without shouting his head off? He could take his pick.

"I don't know what that"—he swirled his hand at the world around us—"was all about. And frankly, I'm too pissed to care. Where is Walker Hayles?"

Stiffening, my knuckles turned white on the steering wheel. "I don't know." The last time I'd seen Walker, the only time I'd seen him in the last ten years, he'd almost shot me. That was a few days ago.

"You're lying."

My stomach clenched. With Landon, my default seemed to be lying. I had to give him something. "Right now? No clue. Last I saw him, he was okay." A bit of a stretch. He'd been escaping my brother's Alaskan compound with a nameless woman in tow, another beast like him.

"So you are involved in his disappearance." His voice was low and disbelieving, like he spoke to himself. Then he squared his shoulders to me. "Saying 'he's okay' isn't good enough." Granite entered his tone.

I chanced a glance at him from the corner of my eye and noted the clenched jaw, the fists in his lap. "I saw him a few days ago and he was fine. Spunky even." There was a small chance Hayles had been recaptured, but after what I'd heard he'd done and survived while enlisted, I had faith he'd gotten himself and the woman out the same night I left my brother for good. There'd been enough chaos surrounding the compound, and I'd seen the damage they'd done to the security gate.

My eyes slid to Landon, then away. How could he be friends with someone who could shift their form at will? How could he trust someone like that to not rip off his face when they got angry? The questions sat on the tip of my tongue, but went no further—questions I'd had since seeing Walker and Kane transform in front of Landon that day in the woods.

Remembering the events of my last night in Alaska, my traitorous acts toward Emerson...I forced my hands to relax, twisting them against the smooth leather covering the steering wheel. It squeaked with the movement.

"Okay," Marley's voice came over my comm, and I straightened. "Your tail is doing a standard search pattern. You have some space."

"Let me know when we're clear."

"Can do."

I stared straight ahead, anxiety creeping up my spine with each silent second.

"I'd like to know more about these friends of yours," Landon said after a few minutes. "Maybe I can be friends too."

Alina snorted. "Marley pulled up his file. If a multimillionaire CEO wants to be friends with me, sure, I can suffer. Does friendship with him include borrowing his cabin on Vancouver Island? It's massive."

"Hold on, I'll ask."

After a full minute of waiting, Alina snorted again. "You're not going to ask, are you?"

"Hell no." Landon not strangling me was entirely temporary. I wasn't going to start asking favors from the man I'd royally screwed over.

The things I'd done for my brother... I leaned forward and pressed my forehead against the steering wheel, wanting to bang it, but managing to restrain myself.

"How did you find me?" I asked finally, needing the answer in case Emerson could use the same method.

Landon was silent for so long, I turned my head and met his gaze. That one, fury-infused expression was enough to make it feel like he'd punched me in the stomach. I'd hurt him. Badly. I'd gotten a job with his company under false pretenses. I'd slept with him, then stabbed him in the back after he'd given me the best parts of himself. And there probably wasn't anything I could do to fix my sins.

I didn't deserve a second chance.

I didn't deserve kindness.

Whatever he wanted to dish out in retribution, I'd take with a smile on my face. It was the least I could do.

"I'm going to need every detail you have on Walker Hayles's last whereabouts," he said, his jaw clenched.

I faced forward, my forehead pressing harder against the steering wheel, a physical reminder I was alive and free of my brother. I cleared my throat. "Of course." I'd give him information on the compound in Alaska, even if I knew Walker wasn't there anymore. Marley had confirmed its destruction with satellite imaging. "Let's get out of this situation first."

I straightened and leaned against the headrest, waiting for Marley to give us the all clear.

We were quiet for a while, when he said, "To answer your question, it was luck. Luck was how I found you."

Hopefully my brother wasn't so lucky.

"Are you bringing Mr. CEO here?" Marley asked in my ear after a while.

"No." Too complicated. Too much. Too...everything.

"Then you're going to need to figure out how to ditch him on your own."

"Fine." I gritted my teeth. "How about our friends tailing us?"

"Oh, they're long gone," Alina chirped. "We were just enjoying your heart-to-heart with Lover Boy there."

4

LANDON

I LEANED BACK IN MY CHAIR, MY EYES GLUED TO THE CONTENTS OF A file folder spread across my desk, the one the private investigator left behind. A copy of Jolyn's service photo lay in the center of it all. She'd corralled her hair into a ponytail, topped with a fatigue-patterned cap. Her bright blue eyes stared straight ahead, her expression serious. The other information told me she'd enlisted a year ago—right after she left me.

Picking up the photo, my brain raced to comprehend her choice, but I couldn't make sense of it. I placed the picture in the top drawer of my desk and rubbed my knuckles along my jaw.

What in the love of God had motivated her to join the Canadian Armed Forces infantry?

The string of muttered curses leaving Jolyn's mouth distracted me from the desire to strangle her—but only for a moment.

What the hell had she gotten herself into? Those people in that SUV had *shot* at us. I wiped my free hand over my face as she reversed the car out of our temporary hiding place. We bumped and rolled over the uneven ground of the backyard, tall weeds brushing the undercarriage to make swooshing sounds. Then we were on the pavement in front of the house, accelerating down the street at a zippy pace.

Only days ago, I sat in my office blissfully unaware I'd get myself in a car chase with the lost love of my life, who acted cryptic and slightly unhinged as she continued to have conversations with herself. And everything that had happened since Kane and Brooke had shown up was all strangely connected to her: two sisters abducted and Walker's disappearance.

When I'd started searching for Jolyn after Brooke and Kane's visit, I had no idea bullets were going to fly.

Sitting here, staring at her as she drove us out of the shabby neighborhood...a surreal sensation overcame me. The last night we'd spent together in Vancouver, where I'd asked her to move in with me, where I'd believed we were on the same page and taking our relationship to the next level—I'd thought I had everything I required in life at that moment.

Then it all came crashing down when she didn't show up for work in the morning and her condo had been cleared out.

Gone. Everything torn down in moments.

Not everything. That was what she'd said about our year-long relationship. I wanted to believe those words, but every time I thought of us together, I couldn't trust the memories. My burgeoning resentment at being used and tossed aside made it hard to remember what we'd shared.

She kept her gaze on the road and I took the time to scan her features—as beautiful and striking as the last time I'd seen her. She'd covered her freckles well, but a hint of them peeked out from the top of her blouse. I knew those freckles swathed her entire body. Though her hair was pulled back under a net and pinned, tendrils of orange were already escaping, framing her face.

I remembered what her lips felt like against mine, how every touch soothed not only me, but also my bear.

Furious at myself for those sorts of futile thoughts, I turned to stare out the window. "I could have you arrested," I said quietly, thinking about the crimes she'd committed against me and my company.

She'd signed an NDA the day she started working for me, and I hadn't understood the theft angle until Kane and Brooke's visit. Jolyn should go to prison. But from the guys chasing her, unafraid to shoot at us in broad daylight, it looked like she had bigger things to worry about than my legal right to prosecute.

When she didn't respond to my statement, I glanced her way. Lips pressed together, she white-knuckled the steering wheel, her eyes focused on the road.

Tearing my gaze from her, I took in the Fiat around me. Leather seats, shiny finishes, touchscreen, automated sunroof—this wasn't some starter model. Neither was the top-of-the-line Urick Enterprises communication device I'd pulled from her ear earlier, one so well designed I couldn't hear who spoke on the other end. I'd never thought my own technology would be used against me.

Who was she working for? And what did it have to do with her brother? She'd been trying to get inside the MBI building in disguise.

Fucking hell, Landon, you have the worst timing on the planet. What had I interrupted?

"We need somewhere to lay low for a while," she said, jerking me from my thoughts.

I narrowed my eyes. If we needed to lay low, then we would have time for answers. "I have a hotel room—"

"No." She cut me off before I could finish the thought. "Nothing under your name. They saw you. They probably know who you are now and will have your cards and phone monitored."

"*They*. Yes, of course." If I hadn't experienced the encounter with the two armed dudes myself, or been fired upon in broad daylight, I might have called her paranoid. It was obvious now I'd sent Walker into something dangerous. I'd only wanted him to track her down, see what she was up to.

The moment I'd found her, we'd been shot at. *What happened to him?* Shit, I hoped he was okay. If he got hurt because of me, and after all he'd been through, I didn't think I'd be able to forgive myself. "You're going to have to explain who *they* all are and how it's even possible for *them* to monitor my cards."

Her head bobbed in a nod. "Let's get to a safe spot first." Then she muttered under her breath, "Stop the commentary. It isn't helpful."

My brain rattled with memories. I'd had a crush on Jolyn since I was twelve years old. When she applied for the job as my personal assistant, something had told me it was too good to be true. Once she started working for me, when we became closer, all those initial concerns faded into the background.

Now I knew not to trust the woman who'd lied to me for a year.

Right after she left Vancouver, she'd been a ghost. If it hadn't been for her condo being emptied in one day, I would have thought foul play, but who emptied their condo before getting abducted?

Those first few days, weeks, had been the worst.

"Where are you staying anyway?" she asked, breaking into my thoughts. "I don't want to head back in that direction." Then, she snorted. "Actually, let me guess. You're at the Element."

"Fort Pontchartrain."

"Slumming it, are we? Rather pedestrian of you."

I narrowed my eyes, not liking the familiarity she'd slipped into. She didn't get to poke fun at my expensive tastes. Not anymore. I'd worked my ass off to get where I was. I hadn't been given a company on a silver platter like her brother. She should know. She'd been there during the beginning stages of Urick Enterprises.

We drove in silence, heading south. For a minute, I thought she'd drive to the border, then she changed directions, going east again.

"We could travel into Canada if we need to stay off the radar."

She shook her head before I finished speaking. "Then we'd have to clear customs and I have no idea if my brother has anyone on the payroll there."

I raised an eyebrow and watched her drive. She made it sound like her brother had people in every level of the government. And despite having gone through the past hour with her, I couldn't understand why she would fear her brother, the CEO of a prestigious pharmaceutical company, unless she'd stolen from him.

About to ask questions, I stopped when she stiffened, her scent spiking in alarm.

"What is it?"

"Our tail is back," she said, her eyes flicking between the rearview mirror and the road.

I turned around, and sure enough, a black SUV accelerated toward us from two car-lengths away. "How did they find us again?" I asked, facing forward, my pulse picking up speed.

"Don't know. Maybe live satellite imaging like us. But this time they mean business." She switched lanes and stepped on the gas.

And they hadn't before? I gripped the edge of my seat as she went faster, weaving between cars going half our speed. This lifestyle was going to get her killed. How many companies had she robbed? And did those "friends" help her with each theft? Had they been in Vancouver with her?

"Maybe you should return whatever it was you stole, pay for your crimes, and be done with it."

She tossed me a confused glance, then hollered, "Hang on!"

She braked, and turned the next corner way too fast. The tires felt like they lifted from the pavement.

Ping. Ping. Ping. Bullets bounced off the bumper.

"For the love of—" This wasn't how I wanted to die.

"I'm sorry!" she shouted, accelerating once more after we'd cleared the corner. "I'll buy you a new paint job!"

She wasn't even apologizing to me.

Ping. Ping. Clink. Clink. Clink. They hit the back window, bullets connecting, but not shattering the glass.

"And a window!"

More bullets followed, and she pushed down my head with one hand. "Keep low."

I couldn't see much except the floor of the car, but heard the roar of the engine of a vehicle close by, gaining on us.

"Quick. Grab a gun out of my bag," Jolyn said, her voice composed despite the life-and-death situation.

Reaching into the backseat, I grasped the strap of her satchel and yanked the bag into my lap. Inside, my hand connected to cold metal. I pulled out the gun she'd taken from one of the security guards. The make was similar to the ones I'd used with Walker at the shooting range when he wanted to relieve tension.

"Am I the only one who isn't carrying a gun in this city?"

"Probably," came Jolyn's quick response. "Do you know how to use it?"

I straightened my posture to give her a look.

"Stay down!"

Still folded in half, I said, "I've fired one a time or two."

The window beside me slid down. Roaring wind swept inside the car, doubling the noise level. I hesitated.

"Shoot them!" she shouted.

I didn't want to fire wildly in the middle of a city. Especially when I didn't understand what was going on. Maybe I should turn the gun on Jolyn, tell her to pull over so she could face the consequences of her actions. If she were part of a human-trafficking ring, she deserved every punishment the law could throw at her. My fingers twitched.

I peeked over the edge of the door, then ducked down. There were two SUVs, one of them right beside us. *Thud thud thud.* Bullets hit the door beside me with force, like I could feel them stopping an inch from my body.

Why am I not dead?

"Oh, my God," Jolyn said, slouched low in her seat to avoid the shots. "I'm so glad you reinforced the doors of this thing."

My relief was short-lived. Another barrage sprayed the door. The desire to keep out of the problem quickly faded. Jolyn might be on the wrong side of the law, but these guys were worse. If I didn't return fire, we'd end up dead. Maybe a few shots would get them to back off. From what I'd seen when I'd poked up my head, it looked like Jolyn had driven us onto a less-populated freeway.

"I told you I'd get you a paint job!"

I'd have loved to hear the other side of the conversation. Remembering the position of the SUV as best I could, I lifted the gun over the edge of the door and squeezed the trigger. The gun didn't do anything.

"Take the safety off," she shouted at me.

A quick glance and I flicked the switch, then braced myself as Jolyn took another fast corner.

"Shoot now! You've got a perfect angle."

Keeping low, I aimed at the SUV that had slowed to take the corner as well. *Bang bang.* The noise of the gun rang in my ears and the kickback jerked my hand toward me.

"Good hit! You got their window. Do it again," Jolyn coached from beside me. "But be careful."

With the SUV right behind us, I had to lean out the window a bit to get a good angle. The wind pressed against me, trying to throw me back inside. I pushed against it, aiming, and it suddenly felt like someone punched me in the shoulder. Shaking it off, I fired three times, then ducked down, wind whistling above me.

"You could drive faster," Jolyn said to whoever was listening on the other end of her comm. "We need some backup."

My arm throbbed and burned. With my free hand, I reached and touched my left shoulder. My fingers came away wet and crimson.

Oh shit. My vision fogged, stars swimming in front of my eyes. The gun's weight dragged itself to the floor.

"Landon? What is it?"

Jolyn's concerned voice reached me above the roar of the wind and the engine. I stretched out my hand to show her, the bright specks in my vision turning black.

5

JOLYN

I HUMMED SOFTLY, BRUSHING MY MOTHER'S HAIR. I DIDN'T KNOW IF SHE liked it, but she seemed to relax. Not that there was a huge difference in her demeanor. But I knew her well enough to feel the change. I always made sure to do the task before the nurse came. When she brushed Mother's hair, she was too rough.

"It's pointless, you know." Emerson walked into the room, making me stiffen. "She doesn't care."

"How do you know?" I asked without looking at him.

He didn't answer. I should have known better than to let my guard down. His hand snaked out to grab my wrist. Pain shot through the skin where a bruise faded from days before. I flinched from the anger in his gaze.

But his eyes weren't on me, they were on Mother. "One of these days, I'll find out who did this to her."

I yanked my arm out of his, twisting it even more, and returned to my task, my hand shaking. "The police don't know who hit her. I don't think they'll ever find out. That's what Dad said."

"Dad's too busy to care. It's my job to figure it out."

"They think she hit an animal because of the scratches. It was an

accident." *It didn't make me feel any better to say it, but there was no one to blame for her condition.*

"It doesn't feel like an accident."

Titty fucker. He'd been shot. I don't even know if Landon realized what happened. *Please let it not have hit something vital.* I couldn't stop to check. Not when I'd be killed execution style as soon as I parked the car.

These were some of Emerson's best, the ones he sent to do all his dirty work, and if I slowed down, gave them an opening, we'd both be dead.

"Okay, we're almost to you," Marley said in my ear.

"Hurry. Landon's been hit."

"Shit. Okay. Let's take care of the bad guys, then we can take care of him."

I bit my lip and concentrated on not putting us in a roll. My breakneck speed might be the end of us both. At least Alina's Fiat knew how to take a few hits and high-speed corners.

The sight of Landon's slumped form squeezed the band around my chest. It was my fault he'd gotten shot. I glanced in my rearview mirror, and noted the gray Mercedes van barreling up behind the SUVs. Relieved, I slowed a little for Marley to catch up, then watched as Alina leaned out the passenger side window, brown hair billowing out behind her, an assault rifle in her hands.

My breath caught in my throat as she balanced her hip and steadied her aim. Time seemed to speed up and slow down at the same time. *Bang bang.* Two shots and she hit the rear tire of the SUV closest to her. The vehicle swerved, then skidded, heading to the shoulder, out of control at the speed and trying not to flip.

"One down, one to go," I murmured under my breath. My

gaze skipped from the rearview mirror to my unconscious passenger, worry making my stomach drop. There wasn't a puddle of blood on the floor; I didn't think a major artery had been hit. It looked like the injury was near his shoulder, but any gunshot wound could be fatal if not treated.

Bang. Another shot and Alina had the second vehicle incapacitated. I watched as she disappeared inside the van.

"Good shooting," I said into the comm. Alina really was the best. "Thanks for the help."

"Always," she responded.

"According to radio chatter, cops are two minutes out," Marley cut in. "We need to get off the freeway before we're spotted."

"Taking the next exit." I changed lanes and got off the freeway, heading into a residential area. I didn't keep to the main road even though it slowed my progress. Getting arrested by Detroit PD would slow it more.

I kept an eye on the gray van until they turned off on a different street. We were well out of Metro Detroit now, and would need to circle back to our renovated warehouse.

"I'm going to stop for a minute to check Landon's wound," I said, searching for a safe place to park.

"Be quick, then drop him off at the closest hospital so you can get your butt home."

"No." The refusal was out before I could think better of it. "Emerson could get to him at a hospital. Landon has no idea what kind of trouble he's in right now." My stomach dropped further into my toes. In searching me out, he'd put himself at risk —another sin to add to my growing list against him.

Neither of my friends replied. I pulled up to the curb behind a sedan and jumped out, circling the front of the car to open the passenger door. Landon nearly fell out he was so slumped over. Thanks to his seatbelt, I was able to prop him up to check his pulse and examine the wound.

Blood coated his shoulder. Under my fingers, his pulse remained strong, rapid even. I couldn't see where the bullet went in, but I needed to stop the bleeding. I peeled off my suit jacket and wrapped the sleeves around the fleshy part of his biceps, my best guess at the location of the wound. That was good. It meant the bullet probably hit muscle instead of something important. But it didn't explain why he'd passed out. Could be shock, could be the sight of blood. I quickly checked him over for more holes, hands skimming over ribs and hips, and found none.

"Landon?" I patted his cheek softly, the light bristle of his facial hair tickling my palm. Even passed out and bloody, he remained the most handsome man I'd ever laid eyes on.

"What's happening with you, Jolyn?" Marley asked after a long minute.

"Just—" I pulled the sleeves into a knot. "Trying to—" Landon stirred and grimaced as I yanked it tight. "Stop the bleeding." Satisfied I'd done what I could and he wasn't in danger of immediate death, I straightened and closed the door, glancing around my surroundings to see if anyone had noticed us. The houses were spaced well-apart here. Not seeing any movement, I jogged to my side of the car, jumped in, and drove away from the curb.

"Hurry back. We're monitoring the police channels, and it doesn't sound like anyone is in your area. Alina needs to fix her baby."

For a second, I thought she meant Landon, and a dose of possessiveness speared through me, something I had no business feeling. Then I realized she meant the shot-up Fiat. I loosened my tight grip on the steering wheel.

Despite Marley's reassurance, I took a roundabout way to our home base, driving as fast as I could without drawing attention. There was no point in getting sloppy. After making sure I wasn't followed, I headed to the northwest section of Detroit. I reached our building and drove down the ramp to the garage underneath, screeching to a stop in front of the door. I rolled down my window and punched the six-digit security code into the keypad. The garage door chugged upward.

As soon as it was high enough, I floored it, driving to the other side of the wide, concrete space where our van was already parked beside the elevator access leading upstairs. Alina waited there, a gurney by her side. *We have a gurney?* When I told these two to equip our home base with everything we might need, I guess they took me seriously.

Stopping with a squeal of rubber, I tore off my seatbelt and jumped out. By the time I'd circled the car, Alina had sidled the gurney to the side of the car. I opened Landon's door. He slumped to the side. I unbuckled his seatbelt to slide my hands beneath his armpits.

"Look at all the blood on the seat!" Alina practically shouted. Back pressed against the car door, she reached for Landon's feet.

"Add it to the bill!" I shouted back. This was not the time to worry about leather upholstery. "Where's Marley?"

"Hacking as we speak." Alina lifted Landon's legs. "Making sure we weren't clocked anywhere, wiping our presence from the city cameras. You know, important stuff so she doesn't have to lift this heavy son of a bitch." The last part of her sentence was said with a groan of effort as we hefted him onto the gurney. "What does he have in his pockets? Rocks?" She pressed two fingers to his throat, and leaned down to check if he was breathing.

I wiped the sweat from my brow, panting. "Let's get him upstairs."

Alina already had the freight elevator waiting on our level, and we wheeled him in. The wide space had been handy for moving furniture, but was especially handy right now, fitting the gurney with miles to spare. Unfortunately, after getting the heavy outer door and the inner metal gate closed, the thing didn't move any faster than it had in all the previous times I'd taken it for a ride.

With clanks and groans of the mechanism, we trudged

upward one level at a time. I surveyed Landon in his unconscious state. His pale face contrasted with his dark hair. And were his breaths becoming shallower? My chest squeezed, and I started to second-guess my choice.

"You know I'm not a doctor, right?" Alina asked.

I brushed Landon's hair away from his forehead. "You always had an aptitude for field medicine. That's good enough." It had to be. "And I'll assist you."

"The guy probably requires surgery and a blood transfusion."

If Emerson got ahold of him, a bullet in the head would kill him faster than a bit of blood loss from a shot in the arm. "It's safer for him here." I wasn't sure if I was trying to convince her or myself. "Emerson could easily pick him up at a hospital."

"You don't know if he's on your brother's radar."

"I don't know that he *isn't*, either. The possibility is too great with how many connections my brother has."

We finally arrived on the level we'd renovated over the past month, and together we lifted the heavy inner grate, then the outer door. The squeak of the gurney's wheels echoed against the walls as we pushed him down the hallway and through a set of double doors into the first-aid room. Overhead lights shone circles on the floor. We parked him under the brightest one.

We worked quickly, cutting off his makeshift bandage and bloodied dress shirt. Alina shot something into his arm. I raised my eyebrows.

"Antibiotics." She injected another one, adding, "And sedative."

With Landon bare chested now, I watched Alina clean him up. "Went straight through," she murmured.

Whenever she asked for help, I assisted, and together we got both sides of the wound stitched up. Already the color was returning to his face and I was able to breathe easier.

"The bleeding has slowed," she said, wrapping up the last of bandage around his shoulder to keep it immobile. "Thankfully, the bullet didn't hit anything important."

I nodded, my throat tight. It could have been so much worse. I'd thought I'd made the right decision telling him to shoot out the window. But that bullet could have been eight inches higher and gone through his brain. *Done.* End of Landon Urick, the man I'd loved for the past four years.

Even if it hurt to do so, I could acknowledge that. I never stopped loving him the whole time I'd told myself to forget him.

I'd thought after I'd left Vancouver, my brother would leave him alone. I'd thought downloading the information from his secondary lab would be enough to cut off Emerson's interest. I'd thought I'd made decisions to protect him—from me as well.

And instead, he was right back in my brother's crosshairs. *I got him shot.*

Blinking the stinging sensation from my eyes, I ignored Alina's questioning stare. I needed to leave before I turned truly emotional.

Stepping to the sink beside the door, I washed Landon's blood from my hands. The sight of the red-tinged water swirling down the drain created a hard lump in my throat. I dried my hands on the white towel hanging on the wall, my gaze lingering on the crimson streaks in the bottom of the sink.

With one last glance at Landon, I left the first-aid room and searched for Marley. I passed their bedroom on the left, mine on the right. The armory door was open, revealing Alina's favorite spot in the warehouse. At any given time, multiple guns were laid out across the metal table as she cleaned them. She always said it relaxed her, put her in a place of zen, the same way as yoga. I didn't quite understand it. Cleaning guns was only ever required maintenance to me, but everyone had their quirks.

I paused at the next door, what Alina affectionately called "the cockpit," and surveyed Marley's domain. The description wasn't far off. Marley sat in front of a U-shaped desk with four computer screens. Her ergonomic chair might as well have been a pilot's seat. There was a second, smaller chair beside her for Alina. The rest of the surface of the desk was taken up by gadgets and things I had no clue about.

Beyond the cockpit was the galley kitchen, then further along, our living room. Sunlight contrasted against the cold of the concrete walls. Alina had done her best to make it homey, placing tropical plants in all the corners, and swathing the floor with overlapping area rugs. Two chocolate brown leather sofas and one armchair faced each other, piled with bright blue and lime throw pillows, a coffee table between them.

I leaned against the cockpit's door frame and crossed my arms.

"What happened to 'nobody gets into this place except us'?" Marley asked, turning to me. Her words were light, but her frown intense. Black, coily hair topped her head, tied loosely with a green band. Red glasses complimented her brown skin and eyes. Her bulky knit, gray sweater was rolled up to the elbows.

"I made an executive decision." Landon would like that phrasing. My stomach squeezed.

"Your decision could jeopardize everything."

I tossed my hands in exasperation. "Everything was jeopardized the moment Landon entered the picture."

My friend narrowed her eyes. "True. We should probably talk about that and his involvement in everything. You failed to mention him while we were planning this op."

"I didn't know he'd be there." I crossed my arms again, squeezing them tight against my chest to release tension. "I haven't seen or heard from him in four years."

"Yet you two seemed to know each other quite well."

I didn't want to go down this avenue of questioning. Not now. Not when all my feelings were being pulled out from where I'd thought I'd buried them. "Is there anything on the news about what happened on the freeway?"

After squinting at me with pursed lips, she turned toward her monitors. "The local stations are calling it gang violence."

I scoffed. Some gang we were, though it was a good description of Emerson's goons.

"At least," Marley went on, "it's better than them putting an APB out on all three of us and sending our pictures to all the media outlets. I've scrubbed what I could of our participation from accessible servers, especially the traffic cams."

"Thanks." I rubbed at my temple. "Maybe Emerson has less people on his payroll than I initially thought."

"We could hope."

Alina came up behind me. I raised my eyebrows at her. "He's sleeping it off. Seems fine. The easiest patient I've ever had." She shrugged.

"That's because he's passed out."

She grinned. "Yeah, but it doesn't make it less true." She handed Marley a phone and a slim, black leather wallet. "These were in his back pocket."

Marley took them and looked at me briefly. Wincing internally, I nodded. Landon would be so pissed we messed with his stuff, but we needed to keep this place secure—all our lives depended on it.

"And the sedative won't last forever," Alina added, staring at me with a too-shrewd gaze. "What would you like me to do? I mean, now we know he's going to be okay, we could drop him somewhere safe."

My stomach plummeted. Dropping him off somewhere, unconscious and unaware of what was happening with my brother, felt worse than what I'd already done to him, including getting him shot. Before we could cut him loose, he should be informed of the danger—without giving away what we were doing here. Because that would put my friends in more peril than they already were in for helping me.

I rubbed a hand over my face. There was no right answer.

"Just..." I pushed away from the door on a long exhale, knowing no matter what I decided, it would be a mistake. "Keep him under until I can figure out what to do."

6

LANDON

My feet wouldn't move. My brain wouldn't accept what I was seeing. Her condo was completely empty. I scared her away.

She'd sent a bullshit resignation letter to human resources. Hell. She was human resources. She was everything. I'd hugged her to me and kissed her forehead two days ago.

But this...it would have taken planning.

Despair cracked my chest open. My bear bellowed in anguish. I could hardly take a breath. What had I done? How could I fix it? Why wouldn't she have talked to me before doing this?

She left like this because she didn't want to talk.

This was permanent.

I shot up straight like a canon had gone off beside me, my head pounding, my arm smarting. It took me a second to orient myself, strange details seeping into my awareness. The scent of fresh paint and dust hung in the air. I was topless. Cold air brushed against my skin, a striped blanket pooling at my hips. An overhead light lit me up like a science experiment. I twitched. Achy pain speared through my arm. I lifted my other hand to touch the tenderness. A bandage covered my shoulder and biceps.

"Careful there," spoke a soft voice. "Don't want you to start bleeding again."

I zeroed in on the person, a human woman in a flowery, red sundress standing just inside a set of double doors. Her copper skin shone with vitality against the darker shade of her long hair. The room felt like a hospital, but also...didn't. For starters, there weren't any windows; all the walls were made of rough concrete. I lay on a gurney, but couldn't hear regular hospital noises on the other side of those double doors. And she definitely wasn't dressed like a nurse.

"Who are you?" I croaked, my throat dry. With a stroke of my hand, I felt the hair on my jaw, thick like I hadn't trimmed it for a while. "Where am I?" I tossed the blanket aside. My shirt might have been missing, but I wore the same slacks I had on when I'd found Jolyn in front of the MBI building. I tensed. "Where is she?"

"One thing at a time, Lover Boy." Her back to me, she fussed around on the counter beside the door. "I'm Alina Ramos, and you're in a secure location at the moment."

Must be one of Jolyn's *friends*, the ones she'd been talking to on her comm. "And where is this secure location exactly?" I clenched my hands, feeling the urge to lash out, my anger mounting. I'd found Jolyn. We'd been chased, and I'd been shot.

Alina turned, a digital thermometer in her hand, and with a quirk of her lips, walked toward me. "That's on a need-to-know basis."

"If I'm here, then I need to know." I knew the words came out harsh, but Jolyn had given me half answers, and now this woman was being evasive. If someone didn't tell me what was going on, I wasn't going to be able to hold on to the equally frustrated bear inside me. All this secretive bullshit was more proof Jolyn and her friends were professional thieves.

"I really didn't think you'd be up so soon," she said, not answering my question, and seeming unperturbed by my tone. She held the thermometer up to my forehead. It beeped. She frowned at the readout. "I haven't been able to get your fever down."

"I run hot." Being a shifter, I didn't have a normal human temperature, and painkillers and sedatives burned through my system quickly. But I wasn't about to tell her that.

God, how long was I out? What had I done while unconscious? My heart raced with dread—as fast as my mind sped with likely scenarios. My bear could have taken over and shifted to heal, but from the tenderness and heat radiating from my arm, that hadn't happened.

Her gaze bounced to the bandage at my shoulder. "So far, you're healing well."

I stiffened and watched her closely as she walked backward to the sink. Had I given myself away? But she didn't wink, or look scared, or give any other indication she'd seen more than a wound in my arm.

"The bullet went clear through your biceps, by the way." She set the thermometer on the counter next to a basket of bandages and glanced at me over her shoulder. "It didn't hit anything too important, just lost some blood. It'll probably be stiff for a few weeks. You should probably get a transfusion as soon as possible."

"Where's Jolyn?" Not that I wasn't thankful she'd patched me up, but I couldn't take being stationary, even if my shoulder felt like it had been through a meat grinder and the throbbing in my skull moved to a space behind my eyeballs. I needed a private place to shift and heal all my wounds, including the headache. It would restore the blood loss as well. My bear paced beneath the surface, wanting to be free, to stretch and move. It had been too long since I'd given him free rein.

I struggled with the locking mechanism of the gurney's safety bar, then swung my legs over the side. As soon as my feet hit the floor, the double doors opened. Jolyn stepped through, a blue dress shirt in her hand. She froze when her eyes landed on me. Her hair was how I remembered it from years ago. Freed from its net, it spiraled in every direction, wild like an out-of-control bonfire. She'd ditched her business attire for dark-wash jeans and a black T-shirt. With her face free of makeup, her freckles stood out in stark contrast to her pale skin tone. I knew what those freckles tasted like, both salty and sweet.

Suddenly lightheaded, I gripped the metal bar of the gurney behind me to keep upright. She took a step forward, like she was going to help me. I threw her a glare, daring her to get close. After everything that had happened since this morning, the strangling I'd been thinking about appealed to me like never before.

She stopped and crossed her arms over her chest, the shirt dangling from the crook of her elbow. We stared at each other like we were strangers, and I should have realized earlier that was exactly what we'd been from the beginning.

My fingers clenched on the bed. She'd thrown away everything we'd built together and I still had no idea why. Why had she stolen from me? What purpose did it serve? Did she understand what had happened to the design, that it had been used in two women's abductions? Who was her buyer?

"You're up," she said, then made a face like it was a stupid thing to say.

My bear twitched at the sound of her voice. I glowered, not wanting to share any of his reactions. "Where are we, Jolyn?"

"Our home base." Behind her, Alina slipped from the room. "For now. Until we accomplish all our goals."

What were the chances she'd go into detail about those goals? *Maybe it's better not to know.* "Are we in Detroit?"

She hesitated, then nodded, slipping her hands into the front pockets of her jeans, the blue shirt tucked over her wrist.

At least they hadn't taken me far. If I'd somehow ended up on the other side of the country, I wouldn't be able to keep my promises to Kane and Brooke. Shit, I needed to call them. Speaking of which...

"Where's my phone?" It wasn't in my back pocket where I last remembered it.

Another grimace crossed her face. "We wiped it, sorry."

"What the hell?" The acid boiling in my stomach grew in intensity. I straightened to my full height despite the ache in my shoulder.

She lifted her chin in defiance. "We don't allow outside devices in the building in case there's tracking software on it, and I'd consider that a pretty safe bet with you."

I clenched my fists, then forced them to relax. I wasn't going to get answers if I started shouting. "How long have I been here?"

Her eyes jumped away from mine. "A couple of days."

"What?" That would explain the gnawing hunger in my belly. "Why did I stay out so long?" The fact that I'd passed out from a gunshot wound to begin with was rather embarrassing. Walker would laugh when I told him—if I ever found him. But why had I remained unconscious?

A guilty expression crossed Jolyn's face. I cocked my head to the side. "What did you do?"

She swallowed, her throat bobbing. "We kept you sedated to allow for faster healing."

I saw through her lie. "You wanted to keep me immobile and at your mercy." She'd gotten me shot, kept me sedated, and messed with my phone.

The acid inside my stomach turned to molten lava. I advanced toward her, my bear rejoicing at my aggression. It should have worried me—that we were on the same page.

Jolyn's eyes widened, but I didn't stop. She took a step back, then another and another until her spine pressed against the wall beside the double doors. My hands shot out, caging her before she could escape, my palms pressed flat against the concrete. I ignored the burning in my shoulder in favor of impressing upon her the potency of my rage.

A memory flashed, one where I pinned her in a similar position and thrust inside her while she begged for *more...harder...faster.*

I gritted my teeth against the onslaught. "Where's Walker?"

"I don't know." Her face flushed, the apprehension in her scent heightening.

"Then you're lying to me like you always have been. You said you were going to give me answers. 'I don't know' isn't an answer. Where is Brooke's sister?"

Confusion furrowed her brow. "Who?"

Her reaction seemed genuine, but I couldn't trust my instincts around her. "Sabrina Covin."

She shook her head, confusion remaining. I also couldn't trust her enough to give her more details about the sisters if she wasn't already aware of them. Who knew what she'd do with the information?

"Why were those men after you?"

She shook her head again.

"Did you steal from them? Are you trafficking people?"

Her eyes widened. "What?"

"Why did you steal from me?" She flinched, but I wasn't backing down. "Why that lab? Why that particular design? What did you do with it? Sell it?"

Her chest heaved up and down, like she couldn't take a proper breath.

"It was all some payday for you, wasn't it? You used me like a cash cow."

"You don't know anything about me!" The words burst out of her like a breached dam. "You grew up with me and my brother, and you were totally clueless. Just like everyone else in that town."

A bitter laugh wanted to erupt from my throat, but I managed to swallow it. If she only knew how long I'd been infatuated with her, how I'd watched her from afar because I knew she had a thing for Kane, and I'd waited for her to act on her feelings.

"I know you fucked me with the intent of stealing from me. What does that say about you?"

A bruised expression crossed her face.

My chest twinged. I clenched my jaw in resolve. It might have been a low blow, but I wouldn't take it back. Not when my insides burned with all the lies she'd told me. Everything she'd done to manipulate me. Every soft touch she'd given me, every gentle word—it had all been to use me.

And now that I was on a roll, I couldn't seem to stop. I leaned in close, my lips grazing her ear. "Was it a bonus for you?" I murmured, the bristle of my jaw grazing her cheek. "A perk? Some physical compensation for all the corporate espionage?"

"Fuck you," she breathed.

This was a new layer to her, one that fought back. One who stared at me with defiance and promised retribution if I went further. I liked this new side of her. My bear liked it too. We wanted to see how far we could push her.

"You already have," I said, keeping my voice gentle. "You fucked me up so bad." I gave into the temptation and let my lips pass over her freckles, then closed my eyes in pain when she tasted as delicious as she always had. "Maybe it's my turn."

She raised her hand. I thought she would punch me, but she pressed her palm against the bare skin of my chest, right above my heart. I waited for the shove that would separate us, but it never came. She curled her fingers, nails scratching into my skin, eliciting shivers throughout my body.

Memories ricocheted through my mind, ones of us spending days together, making love, whispering secrets... My throat tightened, and my bear groped at the surface of my psyche. I fisted my hands against the wall and held completely still. My skin buzzed under her palm like she'd connected me to an electrical outlet. I wanted to roar at what had been lost, to growl, to get even somehow—

I pushed off the wall, needing to get out of there before I did something I'd really regret. "I'm leaving." No matter how enraged I was from her actions, I'd never hurt her.

Her hand fell away from my heart.

I swiped the shirt off the floor where it had fallen and gave it a shake. A little wrinkled, but it would do. My shoulder stiff, I gingerly swept it behind me.

Jolyn remained where she was, her arms hanging by her sides and her blue eye shining under the fluorescents above us.

I turned away from those liquid eyes. Her expression did something to me, something I wanted to deny. I didn't want to have feelings for this version of Jolyn, this one who felt like a stranger. Out of my peripheral vision, she lifted her hand and touched her cheek.

Swallowing against the lump in my throat, I slid the shirt over both shoulders and buttoned it up, Jolyn's eyes on me the entire time. My bear liked her undivided attention despite this messed-up circumstance. Sometimes I really hated my bear.

Jolyn cleared her throat and stepped away from the wall, pushing the door open wide enough for me to follow. The corridor had the same concrete walls as the previous room. To the right, an old freight elevator, big enough to fit that Fiat. To the left, more doors, then the hallway opened up into a living space.

"Where's my exit?" I asked without looking directly at her.

She hummed a contrary sound. "I don't think it's a good idea for you to leave."

"And I don't care what you think." Out of the corner of my eye, I saw the hurt pass over her face and lied to myself that it didn't affect me. "Unless you want to go into minute detail about your involvement in Walker's disappearance, and help me find him, then I have no further reason to be here."

When she didn't respond, I pressed my lips together before saying, "Didn't think so."

"But I did promise you this." She dug a piece of paper out of her pocket.

I took it: coordinates written in pen. I lifted an eyebrow at her.

"It's where I last saw him. The place has been destroyed, though. He won't be there."

More useless information. I tucked the paper in my pocket anyway.

A soft sound made me turn in the direction of the living room, my eyes landing on two women, one of them Alina. The other had dark brown skin, red glasses, and coily hair trapped in a green band at the top of her head. A bulky sweater topped faded blue jeans.

Alina slung her arm over the other's shoulders. "Hey, Lover Boy. This is my girlfriend, Marley, so keep your paws off."

Paws? I stiffened, but none of them had a knowing glint in their eyes, like she'd used the term in the literal sense. I forced myself to relax. "Noted."

Alina smiled. "It's good to see you so feisty after getting shot. How are you feeling?"

From Marley's impassive expression, it didn't look like she agreed with her girlfriend.

"I'm fine, but I've got to go, so..." I glanced at the freight elevator.

"Jolyn's right about it not being a good idea to head out on your own."

I swung my gaze back to Marley, the one who'd spoken. She walked toward me with my phone and wallet in her hand. "Your cell's been cleaned and set to factory defaults. You can use it again, just need to download from the cloud."

I raised an eyebrow at her, the one I reserved for CEOs who gave me trouble across the boardroom during a deal.

It was the first crack in her deadpan demeanor—she grinned. "You're welcome."

After checking all my cards and cash were still in my wallet, I pocketed it and my phone. "Which way is the exit?"

Both women looked at Jolyn over my shoulder.

I didn't have time for games. Sidestepping Marley, I strode down the corridor. "Unless you all want to disclose your involvement in Walker's disappearance." I passed an open door, my gait faltering at the sight of a table laden with numerous guns and other types of weapons. *That's a sure sign of illegal activity.* I kept going. "Or tell me more about this place in Alaska." The next open door revealed a room full of computers, monitors, and an assortment of Urick Enterprises tech. I paused to scan the setup, finding it professional enough to make me think these women were well-funded. "Then I suggest you show me the way out..." I forgot whatever it was I was about to say. "What is this place?"

No one said anything for a moment, then Jolyn spoke. "A person needs decent headquarters when they're trying to take down an empire." Her tone was disturbingly nonchalant.

"Ah," I said, not sure how else to reply. My heart double-thumped in my chest. She was willfully putting herself in danger, and I had firsthand experience to know it was life-threatening. Taking down an empire? I could only guess she meant her brother, but from the set of her jaw, I doubted she would tell me more. Thieving, guns, bulletproof Fiats... I couldn't be caught up in whatever storm she'd created for herself.

"Good luck with that." I needed to find Walker, and contact Kane and Brooke. "I'll leave you to it. But if someone doesn't show me the exit in the next minute, I'm going back for one of those grenades to make my own damn door."

For emphasis, I straightened the collar of my borrowed shirt. The effect was lost by the sheer number of wrinkles in the garment, and the fact I wasn't wearing a suit jacket or tie, but I'd mastered the maneuver when turning down pious CEOs. I knew it would still be effective.

None of the women appeared impressed.

"We have a bit of a conundrum," Marley explained. "We don't really want you to know where we are."

"That sounds like a *you* problem."

"Oh, it's your problem too," Alina said, then added, "Jolyn said we couldn't put a bag over your head and dump you outside city limits." The disappointment in her voice made the hairs on my arms stand on end.

"Definitely not," I asserted with a glance at Jolyn. She rubbed her temple with two fingers, a sure sign of stress—stress I didn't need to be a part of.

A thick metal door caught my attention on the other side of the living room done in browns, blues, and greens. I strode toward it. None of them stopped me. What did make me pause was the digital keypad beside the door, one that looked like it came straight out of last year's Urick Enterprises catalog. These women didn't mess around when it came to security.

"What if we blindfold you?" Jolyn's voice came from behind me, and with it a memory of me suggesting a game—to remove each other's senses one by one.

My heart banging in my chest, I turned to face her. From the high flush on her cheeks, maybe she remembered the same thing. "And do what with me?"

From behind her, Alina tittered. "Wouldn't you like to know."

Jolyn shot her friend a glare. "I could drive or walk you well away from here. Drop you somewhere you can get a taxi."

"Walk," I said immediately.

After a hesitation, Jolyn agreed with a small nod. "We can take the stairs." Around the corner was another heavy metal door complete with a Urick Enterprises keypad. She punched in a six-digit code. I didn't see enough of it to repeat the sequence. The metal door clanked open like a vault, revealing a stairwell. I hesitated.

"After you," she said.

I narrowed my eyes at her. "Why do I feel like if I walk through that door, I'll be stuck in there until I die?" After everything I'd seen in this place, I didn't think it was that much of a stretch.

With an exasperated huff, she stepped ahead of me. "It's just some stairs," she muttered under her breath.

"Wait," Alina said. "You'll need this." She passed Jolyn a black silk scarf. "It's light tight," she said when I stared at it. "I should know." Then she grinned. "Hey, do you use your vacation house on Vancouver Island very often?"

I paused inside the door. "Excuse me?" How the hell did she know about my cabin?

"Not the time." Jolyn's voice was as forceful as the metal door clanging behind us.

7

JOLYN

"*WHAT ARE YOU DOING IN HERE, JO?*"

I winced at the nickname, my chest tightening because Emerson was near. "Don't call me that." He used the name because I hated it. I hated it only because he used it.

"Why not? Then I can think of you as the brother I'll never have."

I'd heard it all before and did my best to ignore him as I closed the one brochure and opened the next. Since Mother died, I'd lay on her bed from time to time just to feel close, especially when I had a decision to make.

"What's all this?"

I wanted to hide all the info pamphlets under the pillow, but knew he'd take it as a sign of weakness. Staying the course was always my best option. I opened the next brochure. "None of your business." It was my life. I'd do what I wanted with it.

He picked up the pamphlet closest to him. "Veterinary school? Are you shitting me? You know dad wants you to go into economics and business."

"He said no such thing."

"If he gave you choices, then it was a test. Don't fail it and get cut

off from your inheritance. We have a family business to run, and messing around with animals isn't going to cut it."

"Go away," I said, my teeth clenched. I just wanted him to leave me the hell alone for a change.

His hand snaked out, gripping me above the elbow. I gasped as he squeezed, then closed my eyes trying to will the pain away. The more it looked like it hurt, the more he enjoyed it.

And he was always careful to never mark me where others could see.

I could still feel the impression of Landon's lips on my cheek.

Leading the way down the stairs, tension radiated off him in waves to crash against my spine. I wanted to hate him for the things he'd said to me, but couldn't. Because he wasn't wrong.

When we'd been together, I'd thought I knew him well, had him pegged. But since he'd found me, I'd never seen him so angry. Not even at a business deal where another company tried to royally screw him over and he told them all to go fuck themselves with a smile on his face. He always kept his temper. It was one of the reasons I'd felt safe with him.

Not for the first time, I asked myself how my life would have turned out differently if I hadn't run to Emerson the day I'd seen the beasts transform. My brother had been the only one home, the only one I could turn to. Since my father moved MBI from Vancouver to Toronto due to some regulations when I was sixteen, we'd rarely seen him.

Maybe I would have stayed in Goldenlach Ridge if I'd kept my discovery to myself. Honestly, I didn't know. My last year there, I had recurring nightmares of the day in the forest, ones that morphed into *me* getting attacked by the bear, of my screams silenced by its great, bloody paws. I jumped at shadows and couldn't interact with people I'd known forever. My senior year was spent with tutors at home. I hadn't complained the day my father told us to move to the penthouse in Toronto.

My brother used my fear as a tool against me, to make me more dependent on him in place of our absentee father, who was more interested in his rapidly expanding business than his children. Emerson never hit me outright, but left small injuries to remind me of what he could do if he wanted. None of the house staff knew or cared about what was going on. The woman who was supposed to be our cook and nanny disliked Emerson, probably felt as unsafe around him as I had. He knew that and exploited it. She'd been so preoccupied with him that she'd ignored me.

Emerson always hovered, ready to swoop in and demean me if I stepped out of line—something our father never cared to correct when he was occasionally home. We'd all needed "toughening up" after Mother died.

Maybe if I'd met Landon as an adult on my own, we could have started a real relationship, one where I wasn't lying to him every second of every day. There'd been moments where I'd allowed myself to forget what I was doing and lived in the moment. It was times like those I fell in love with Landon Urick: his drive for his business, his enthusiasm for life, his sweet and seductive nature both in and out of the bedroom.

When I'd left him, I'd known he'd be married within a couple years—he had to be, because he was that much of a catch. *The perfect guy.* Every time I thought of him with another woman, my heart felt like someone attacked it with a weed whacker. But even though I'd seen his name come up connected to some woman or another at special events, he'd never gotten married as far as I knew.

My chest squeezing tight, I hopped off the last stair to the ground floor. On a slow exhale, I confronted my former lover with the scarf in my hand. The look in his eyes made my heart pound. It was a mix of his earlier anger and something more poignant, a flare of memory perhaps.

The moisture in my mouth dried up. "I know you might not believe me, but I'm sorry. I never wanted to hurt you." I don't know if it was my imagination or wishful thinking, but I swore his granite expression softened slightly. Just as fast, it hardened once again.

"Then why did you?"

"Because at the time I didn't think I had an alternative." I swallowed. "This is my alternative. Right here, right now. I'm trying to correct my mistakes. It's my top priority." Not that he'd ever open up himself to me so I could make amends.

"And finding Walker is mine," he said, his eyes keeping me hostage, like he could will the answers he wanted out of me.

If I knew where Walker Hayles was, I'd tell him. But I didn't. I cleared my throat. "Please don't tell anyone about this place. We've invested too much to be set back again."

He didn't speak for a beat, then with his intense laser-focus, said, "I'm sure if this isn't some sort of larceny operation, you'll tell me more."

I shook my head, having no clue where he got his ideas, then grimaced at his expression. "It's for your own good. Stay away from MBI. Stay away from my brother especially. Return to Vancouver and forget all about me. And don't try to find us. Alina will probably shoot you if you do."

"And after she patched me up so nicely," he said in a flat voice. Then he straightened, becoming very still, his gaze on my throat.

I tensed. "What is it?"

He stepped toward me, and I sucked in a breath. This close, I inhaled the scent of him: crisp linen dried in the outdoors, a fragrance uniquely Landon, and one I'd never smelled on anyone else.

My heart picking up tempo, I peered up at him. His gaze skimmed from mine, downward, but I didn't realize what he stared at until he lifted a hand to touch the chain around my neck. Heat flooded my cheeks like I'd been caught doing something wrong. I held my ground as he tugged the chain out of my shirt until the pendant lay in his hand.

"You still wear it," he said quietly.

I didn't respond because there was no point. The evidence lay between us.

He'd given me the pendant a couple months after I'd started dating him. Made of ivory or bone, it was crescent shaped, polished down to a curved point like a moon, set inside a rose gold mount and attached to a matching chain.

Since he'd given it to me, I rarely took it off. The longest span was while I was in basic training. But it meant more to me than I could ever express to him—that he'd had something made specifically for me—and I never wanted to take it off again. It was a reminder of that perfect night on the beach a few days after our relationship turned a corner into something more physical and intimate. A night where I'd closed my eyes and pretended we were a regular couple with a future together.

Pretending was the only way I stayed sane that whole year.

He let the pendant fall on the outside of my shirt. When he stepped away, I shivered, the warmth of him replaced by the cool air of the stairwell.

"Why do you wear it?" he asked, a plea for the truth in his tone.

I met his gaze straight on. "I told you not everything between us was a lie."

He closed his eyes a moment, then met my gaze once more. "I don't think I can believe a word that comes out of your mouth."

Another punch to the gut I accepted with a thrust of my chin. I'd lied to him for a year. I deserved it.

Swallowing around the dryness in my throat, I lifted the scarf. "Let's get on with it, shall we?"

He stepped away from the staircase, closer to me, and for a

second I thought he meant to embrace me. Then I realized he was allowing me access to the stairs behind him because of our height difference.

My cheeks warm, I climbed two steps and stood behind him. The width of his shoulders strained against the wrinkled shirt, a little too tight, displaying his impressive back muscles. My stomach fluttered as I reached, my forearms brushing his shoulders. I made sure the scarf covered his eyes properly before swooping the silky material around to secure it tight to his head.

"Turn around," I said, cheeks burning more at the scratchiness of my voice. I didn't want to be affected by any of this.

He did as I asked, and I adjusted the material a bit to make sure his eyes were fully covered, my fingers sweeping against the soft skin of his cheekbones. I shivered. This had to stop. There was nothing between us except betrayal and bitterness. I needed to remember that, no matter how many good memories bombarded me in the process.

"All right."

He stepped back at my words. I hopped down to the ground and headed to the keypad on the wall. Six beeps echoed up the stairwell. The door clanked open to reveal a holding room made of concrete, the elevator door beside us, and another thick metal door on the opposite wall. Two cameras were mounted in each corner. I waved, knowing Marley and Alina watched from the cockpit.

Landon remained where he was, trapped in his forced darkness. There was no way I could lead him around without touching him. After taking a deep breath, I placed my hand on his forearm. He twitched.

"This way." I led him forward, through the holding room and to the door on the other side. "Stop." I punched the six-digit code into the keypad. The door clanked open. Bright mid-morning sunshine streamed inside. Landon tilted his head to the side.

Even if he couldn't see, he had to have felt the change in brightness and warmth.

I pushed the door open all the way. Fifty feet ahead, a chainlink fence enclosed a concrete yard. When first built, this place used to be a storage facility for a car-part manufacturer, but had since changed ownership a few times. Most of the factories and warehouses around us were deserted. The ones that weren't, Marley had vetted for activity that would conflict with our own, and Alina had made visual confirmations of each building's vacancy. A few artists had a collective down the street. More were used for storage by various individuals who didn't come by often.

Cameras recorded the property at every angle. With my hand on his arm, I led Landon across the yard. Weeds stuck up two feet high through the cracks in the concrete. Behind us, the warehouse didn't look like anything fancy, and my friends and I preferred it that way. We'd kept boards over some of the windows, even though Marley had swapped them out for bulletproof glass. The shabbier it appeared, the better.

I paused when we reached the gate, putting light pressure on his arm to make Landon do the same. The locking mechanism buzzed and I pushed the gate open, the metal rattling. I guided him through, then made sure to shut the gate tight behind us. He stood there, waiting, his face upturned toward the sun, looking like some shipwrecked victim with his eyes covered, his hair messy, beard scruffy, and the wrinkled shirt open at the throat showing a hint of chest hair.

Licking my lips, I turned away and closed my eyes against memories where we cuddled together and I sifted those short, soft hairs through my fingers. I gave myself a shake. *Quit thinking about shit like this.* It wasn't helping anyone. But I couldn't stop where my mind went, to those gentle spaces we'd created together whether they were a lie or not.

Swallowing, I opened my eyes to regard his towering form. That he could allow me to lead him blind like this said a lot about his character. I'd wronged him, and he had enough trust in me to allow it.

Or maybe it didn't have to do with trust at all.

"Jolyn?"

I'd been staring at him for too long. He reached up like he was going to take off the blindfold, and I grabbed his forearm.

"I'm here," I said, annoyed my voice went croaky. "This way." I tugged him to the left.

We walked, silent for a few blocks, me speaking only to tell him to step down or up on a curb, or when we were about to cross the street. The muscles beneath my hand were corded and taut. Landon might be a CEO, but he always kept fit. His morning routine always included a trip to the gym or laps in the pool of his building. When he'd been shirtless earlier, he'd appeared more toned than ever. *Not that I'd been staring.*

It took three blocks before we hooked up with a street with actual traffic. I stopped and glanced up at him. "I'm going to spin you around."

He cocked his head toward me.

"To mix it up a bit," I added.

He opened his mouth to say something, then closed it again. I took it as acceptance and used two hands to turn him. He didn't resist. After three revolutions, I stopped him, trying my best to ignore the body heat beneath my hands and the thick feel of his muscles.

"Are you too dizzy to continue?" I asked after a moment.

He shook his head. "I'm fine."

I guided him back the way we'd come for a block before turning left again. Three blocks later, I did the spinning thing again. Throughout it all, Landon didn't offer a word of protest.

It was time to take him somewhere he could hail a cab. My stomach squeezed. *And then I'll never see him again.* I aimed for a more densely populated neighborhood well away from our ware-house. If we received questioning glances from the people driving past, I ignored them. I'd seen stranger things in Detroit than a person being willingly led around by a blindfold.

Finally, I stopped on a corner I thought would be a relatively safe location, nowhere to indicate where we'd started our unusual walk, and spun him around three more times for good measure.

I let go of his arms. "You can take the blindfold off."

He took a slight step back and swept the black silk over his head, blinking rapidly through slitted eyes. He focused on me first, then whipped around, taking in the area. With his brow furrowed, he scanned the nearest signpost, no doubt noting the cross section of streets. It didn't matter. There wouldn't be a way to retrace our steps.

After taking in his surroundings, his eyes narrowed on me. I swallowed, bracing for what he'd say. If he shouted at me, called me names, maybe then I could get over all these lingering feelings.

He lifted his hand. For a split second, I thought he meant to cup my jaw like he used to, and I held my breath. But then he waved into the street. I turned to see a yellow taxi change lanes and drive toward us.

Panic squeezed air out of my chest. This wasn't how I envisioned saying goodbye forever, not a rushed event with a cab driver waiting for their fare. I didn't know what I expected— nothing on the side of a busy street. I could have said a million things on the walk here, and I'd lost the opportunity.

What should I have said? He didn't want to hear anything that didn't have to do with finding Walker Hayles.

The taxi stopped beside us. Landon lifted an imperious eyebrow and nodded. "So long, Jolyn." The silk scarf whispered from his fingers into mine. "I hope you find what you're looking for." He turned away like he would any old acquaintance who didn't really matter—a cold shoulder.

My chest ached as I watched him slide into the cab and shut

the door, the scarf clutched tight in my hand. His last words gave me pause. I'd never thought I was *looking* for anything. I only wanted to bring my brother's evil to a stop.

But I was searching for something, wasn't I? And always perceptive, Landon had picked up on that. I wanted redemption for my past mistakes, forgiveness. And he didn't appear willing, or able, to provide it.

The cab disappeared down the street.

How dare he? How dare he have the last word without giving me a chance to respond. I turned, searching the street for another cab, ready to chase him down before I realized what I was doing. A defeated laugh escaped me. Was I finally losing it? I scrubbed a hand over my face, inhaled from the scarf in my hand, and shoved it in my pocket. *Alina's not getting it back either.* Not when it carried Landon's linen-crisp scent.

I turned toward home. The twelve-block walk refocused me. I wasn't in Detroit to seek Landon's forgiveness. I wasn't in Detroit to see Landon at all. He'd been a hiccup, a speed bump, and I needed to push everything that had happened over the past few days out of my head. Landon was safe. Hopefully he'd listen to my warnings about my brother.

I must return to my main objective.

Arriving at our property, the gate buzzed open ahead of me. I jogged across the yard. After punching in today's code in the keypad, I took the stairs two at a time, renewed purpose in my steps. We had an evil empire to take down. *No more distractions.*

When I walked through the door to the living room, Alina was there waiting.

"I can't believe you mentioned his vacation house," I muttered.

She shrugged and led the way to the cockpit. "Those CEO types never use their 'cabins.'" Turning slightly, she put it in air quotes. "If we're friends with him, then maybe he'd let us borrow it."

"It's not likely going to happen when we're unwilling to help him find Walker Hayles," I replied, stepping into Marley's domain.

"And why won't we do that?" Marley asked without turning to us. Alina slid into the seat beside her.

I paused, a little stunned. "We need to focus on this mission, not hunt for a man who knows how to take care of himself."

"Yeeeaaaah," she said. "But the guy called Landon a half dozen times, and left about the same number of messages as Landon's secretary. Less than some other friend named Brooke, though."

An icy chill washed over me. We had information Landon wanted and we'd kept it from him. He was right to be angry. "Why didn't you tell me any of this?" Nausea swirled in my stomach. He'd mentioned a Brooke earlier too.

"You didn't ask."

And I wouldn't have. I wouldn't have wanted to invade his privacy like that, to hear his messages, but at least we could have told him people were trying to get a hold of him for the past two days.

I rubbed a frustrated hand over my face. "For fuck's sake, Marley." I didn't know what else to say. "It's like you're trying to get him to hate me more or something."

"Look," she said, finally turning to me with a placid expression. "It's no big deal. As soon as he connects to his network, he'll get his backlog of messages."

It would be pointless to try and track him down now. He'd probably already downloaded those messages. A faint ache buzzed behind my eye.

Alina frowned at me. "When you say 'Walker Hayles,' do you mean *the* 'Walker Hayles'?"

"Yeah."

"No shit." Alina's eyes sparkled with admiration. "That guy is legendary."

"I know."

"He had a stellar rep in the military, then he went into special ops and there were always stories about the amazing missions his team pulled off."

"I said I know." I never told my brother the stories I'd heard, the rumors within our ranks. It was the beginning of my rebellion against him, a small act.

Walker's team had a beast on their side. After seeing what a pair of them could do to a grizzly, terrorists didn't stand a chance. Had his special ops team known what he was?

I rubbed the sudden chill out of my fingers and came up behind Marley's chair. "You have Landon on your tracker program, right?" It was only a precaution. If Emerson got his hands on him, I needed to know where to send the rescue party.

"Yep," she said with a click of her computer keys. "He's coming in loud and clear."

I knew I should feel guilty about having the guy tagged, especially when I viewed listening to his messages as an invasion of privacy, but my anxiety concerning my brother's willingness to harm others was sky-high. He was a narcissistic sociopath through and through. If he perceived Landon to be a threat, he'd neutralize him. Knowing Landon wasn't in Emerson's clutches was the only way I could concentrate on the mission at hand.

The red blinking light headed toward downtown and I tensed. *Please don't return to your hotel.* I thought I'd made an impression there, that he'd take my warning seriously.

I pressed my fingers against the ache blooming across the bridge of my nose. If I had to go on a rescue mission to save Landon from my brother, I was going to be seriously pissed off.

And who the fuck is Brooke?

8

LANDON

"Have you ever wished you were someone else?"

Her soft voice whispered against my bare shoulder. I'd thought she'd fallen asleep, and I lifted my head to see her better. Shrouded in darkness, her eyes appeared haunted.

Worry tensed my muscles. I brushed my knuckles over her cheek, then squeezed her against me. "If I were someone else, then I wouldn't be here with you."

My answer seemed to startle her. She jerked, then blinked at me in the dark. Her body softened, her glazed expression dissolving into a smile. "I suppose that's true."

My hands clenched and unclenched in my lap as the taxi drove into Metro Detroit, the residential area Jolyn had taken me morphing into the more recognizable buildings of downtown. I needed an outlet for all my emotional turmoil.

I wanted to hate Jolyn Mahn but found I couldn't. And I loathed myself because of it. I allowed her to get under my skin, worm her way into my heart, and it had all been a masquerade—

an opportunity to make profit off my stupidity. For the life of me, I couldn't understand why my bear didn't want to attack her outright for all the emotional upheaval she'd sent my way, but he remained steadfast in the belief Jolyn and I belonged together.

I couldn't believe it any longer, not after what she'd done.

But she wore the necklace I made her.

Why? Why would she have kept it if it had meant nothing? When I thought of the lengths I'd gone to have it made—I'd ripped out one of my own claws to have it transformed into jewelry for her, so she could have a piece of me wherever she went. Of course, the next time I'd shifted it regrew, but now I kicked myself for the morbid sentimentality of it—melodramatic at the minimum. It had been my way, my first step, in telling her who and what I was. Back then, I'd seen a future together. She'd been it for me, a life partner until the day we died.

Ever since I'd known Jolyn as a kid, my bear had liked her. Maybe a little too much. Even when I knew she had a crush on Kane, my bear had wanted to lay claim to her. I'd only been twelve at the time, she was ten. It was at that point I knew my bear was completely ridiculous. What weirdo laid claim to a ten-year-old?

I pressed my fingernails into my knees, a technique I used to bring my bear to heel. He was in as much turmoil as I since we'd seen her in front of the MBI building. On top of that, he needed to run. If I shifted, then I could heal this god-awful burning in my shoulder. But I wouldn't risk even a partial shift until I was completely alone. I required a safe, private location. Something told me to heed Jolyn's warning about not returning to my original hotel. Which meant I needed to get Kane and Brooke out of there as well.

When I'd arrived in Detroit, it was already overdue time for my bear to have free rein. And since I'd been unwillingly sedated for days, he clawed to be let out. I'd never liked that side of me, kept a tight leash on it, but never ignored it either. I'd coined it "shifter maintenance" in my head. Living in a big city like Vancouver, I'd learned to listen when he told me he needed to run. Once a month, I'd either drive out into the middle of nowhere north of the city, or take a trip to my cabin on Vancouver Island. Either way, I let my bear do its thing, then I would return to work right as rain.

It was the opposite of what Kane went through with the animal inside him. During his shifts, he lost his whole sense of self. His grandfather and father had been the same way. It was why Kane moved to the wilderness to live alone, away from people, and why we'd developed the collars that could stop a shift. In the end it hadn't mattered. Brooke had stumbled onto the life he had built for himself in northern Saskatchewan, and now he was tentatively returning to society with her at his side.

Shit, I needed to call them. They were going to be so worried, especially with Walker and Brooke's sister missing for over two weeks. And since Jolyn wasn't willing to help, we'd need to find them on our own.

Ahead, a cell phone store caught my eye. "Pull over here," I said to the cab driver, an Italian man with a thick salt-and-pepper mustache. I slid him a twenty from my wallet. "I'll just be a moment." I didn't know what else Jolyn and her friends had done to my phone, and I didn't trust them not to have put some sort of spying software on it, especially after thinking there was a reason to wipe it in the first place.

It took a bit longer than I would have thought, but with my new phone in hand, I jumped back into the cab. I named a boutique hotel I'd heard of yesterday, different from the one Kane, Brooke, and I had already checked into. With a nod, the driver rolled away from the curb.

As soon as my new number connected with my old cloud, notifications started popping up. Text after text, message after message. I'd been unconscious for two days and it looked like anyone who cared about me started to freak out. There was just one call from my mother, but speaking with her only once a week wasn't out of character.

Relief spread through me when recent messages from Walker came through. He was alive. He was okay. But none of his messages told me anything. They were all: "Call me back, bro" and "Where the fuck are you?" then a few "WTF" texts, and "I'm going to beat the shit out of you if you've gone to an all-inclusive and turned off your phone."

The cab pulled up to the hotel as I was about to call Walker. Before I could press the green icon, a call came through with an unknown caller ID.

I answered. "Hello?" My phone tucked between my shoulder and my ear, I paid for my fare, including an extra tip, and hopped out of the cab.

"Landon!" Brooke's voice rang over the line. "Thank God you're okay. We were so worried. What happened?"

"Uh," I squinted up at the ten-story building, and strode toward the glass doors. "I had a bit of an altercation and just got a new phone."

"It's been days—hold on a sec. I'll put you on speakerphone. I have Kane here—and your car has been parked the entire time. We thought you were abducted like Walker. We were about to call the police, and then—" Her voice paused. "Kane wants to know where you are."

"A new hotel," I said, stepping through the glass doors. "We need to switch ours."

After a beat of silence, Brooke asked, "Why?"

"It's a bit complicated—for security reasons." I rubbed my face, moving away from the check-in counter to the posh lobby on the right. Tall windows were flanked with velvet drapes, lush sofas creating three independent conversation areas. I scanned the few patrons sitting there. If our first hotel was being watched, how could I get Kane and Brooke here without anyone noticing?

A resigned puff of breath escaped me. Now I was sounding as paranoid as Jolyn.

Brooke's next words stumbled me into an emerald green sofa. "But Walker and Sabrina were checking in."

I straightened. "Walker is here in Detroit?"

"Yes!" Her enthusiastic voice shot over the line. "Good news! We found my sister. Or I guess she found us. And Walker. They're together. Like, *together* together. They're mated."

"What?" My head spun.

"I know. Weird, right. I guess no less strange than Kane and I, but still strange." There was a moment of silence, then she said, "Kane wants to know if you found what you were looking for at the MBI building."

"Yeah, then some." I paced behind the sofa watching a couple cut through the lobby to the restaurant behind. "Is Walker with you now? I need to speak with him." He'd know how to get everyone here with minimal fuss.

"They're downstairs. Should be returning soon. What's going on, Landon?" Worry edged her tone.

I didn't want to get her worked up. She'd been through enough. "Just," I rubbed my newly pounding temple. I required a shift ASAP. "I need to talk to Walker first, then he'll fill you in, all right?"

From Brooke's protest, it wasn't all right, but I hung up anyway. Letting out a breath, I called the number Walker had left me. He was safe like Jolyn had predicted.

It rang three times before he picked up. "Hayles," he said after a beat.

"It's Landon."

"Fuck, man." There was a pause and a sound of movement. Background noise trickled through. "It's good to hear from you. After everything, I'd thought you'd been picked up by that fucking psycho."

I straightened. "Psycho?"

"Yeah, Emerson Mahn," he practically growled, making every fine hair on my body stand on end. "The things I want to do to that motherfucker would be too kind after the torment he put Sabrina and me through."

It was a stab to the solar plexus. *Emerson Mahn*. The name echoed in my head. Why hadn't I seen it before now? Jolyn's brother. We'd all lived in Goldenlach Ridge, and everything that had happened with my friends was connected too: Brooke and Sabrina's abduction here in Detroit, Walker going missing, and Jolyn almost getting herself killed.

I'd thought she was a professional thief, but she'd said she was taking down an empire. I should have asked more questions. I'd left the three people who could have given me answers.

"What happened to you two?" I'd put my friend in harm's way by asking him for a favor.

A loud breath huffed on the other end of the line, then he said, "A lot. It's too much to get into over the phone. Oh, and hey. I found Jolyn. She's in Alaska. You can send me my paycheck now."

I scoffed and continued pacing, my mind spinning. "Yeah, well, I found her too, so I'm not sure I owe you anything."

"Bullshit. I guarantee you I found her first." It sounded like he was trying not to laugh. Relief that he was okay and able to make jokes made the tension in my shoulders lessen.

"Are you returning to the hotel?" he asked. "Sabrina and I were about to get a bite to eat. She said something about wanting a salad for once."

"Yeah, so about that. We need to talk."

A stillness came on the other end of the line. "About what?"

"It's necessary to change hotels. I did something stupid— you'll love it by the way—and now I'm on Mahn's radar. Which means the hotel isn't safe for the four of you either." I quickly gave him a rundown of my last couple days, being vague when I needed to. "So you're going to need to keep a low profile while you change hotels."

"Look, man, we're already keeping a low profile. I don't want to go into it over the phone, but yeah, I'll get them moved safely. We'll be there by midnight."

The worry hovering in my chest dissipated. I could trust Walker to be careful. If he was mated to Sabrina like Brooke said, he would be even more cautious.

We hung up, then I hesitated a moment before calling my secretary, Nadine.

"Urick Enterprises."

"It's Landon."

"Mr. Urick." Her tone hardened. "I've been worried sick about you."

I tried not to smile. Looked like she was going into full-on mother hen mode. "Sorry about that. I ran into a few problems with my phone."

"Problems? You haven't returned my calls for days!"

"Yes, well. I'm fine, but I need you to do something for me."

"What is it?"

I could visualize her narrowing her eyes behind her wire-rim glasses. "You know the card we keep in case of emergencies, the one that's not attached to me or the company?"

"Yes..."

"I'm going to need it to book a hotel here in Detroit, but you're going to have to do it from your end."

Rustling filled the silence, then she asked, "What's this all about?"

"Nothing I can get into. See it done, please."

"Of course, sir."

"And Nadine?"

"Yes?"

"Thank you. You're the best." I'd give her an extra quarterly bonus for having to deal with me.

I stewed for twenty minutes, thinking about what Walker had told me and how Jolyn was involved, then strode through the entryway to the check-in desk. Three hotel staff were helping others. I spoke to the fourth, a man wearing the blue and gold uniform, a brass name tag pinned to his chest with *Mathieu* on it.

"Ah yes," he said when I told him who I was. "Arrangements have been made for whichever room you like, sir."

"Penthouse suite, please."

"We have three available at the moment. Do you know which one you'd prefer?"

"Perfect. I'll take all three."

9

JOLYN

I PAUSED MID-STEP, WISHING *I* HADN'T COME HOME AT ALL TODAY. *My chest tightened to the point where I couldn't take a breath. It was bad enough Emerson had returned, but to have Allan Croskey, our cousin, here as well made my skin crawl. The pair of them together... I'd found a pile of dead squirrels in the woods after Allan had left last time.*

They sat in the drawing room, a chess board between them. From their postures, it looked like my brother was winning, as usual.

Before I could turn around and leave, Emerson caught sight of me. "Jo. Come here. I have something to tell you."

I knew if I didn't obey, he'd make it worse for me later. Especially if I acted contrary in front of Allan.

"What is it?" I asked, stopping beside them.

"You've been accepted to the University of Toronto in business, finance, and management. Congratulations." He passed me a large brown envelope.

My stomach squeezed. "You're opening my mail now?" I pulled out the crisp sheets of paper. "Wait. I didn't apply for this program."

"Father approved of everything."

Could I have nothing of my own? Glaring, I turned away.

I should have expected it, but gasped when his hand snaked out to

grab me. I wore a short-sleeve shirt today due to the warm weather,
and his fingernails dug into the skin below my elbow, biting. I did my
best not to react, even when Allan's eyes were fixated on the spot where
my brother held me.

"You haven't thanked me." Emerson spoke in a mild tone.

I clenched my jaw, eyes stinging with tears. "Thank you."

"Set up the pieces. Watch them fall," Emerson said as Allan tipped
over his queen, his eyes crinkling in mirth when he let me go.

I should have been concentrating on the laptop in front of me,
but my mind kept drifting to the man who'd left in a taxi three
hours and forty-seven minutes ago.

While he was unconscious, I hadn't been able to resist
watching him sleep. He held the same magnetic force as when I'd
been with him, but he was also different. Laugh lines accented
the corners of his eyes now, a speckle of gray hair at his temples
that only made him look sexier, and he'd let his facial hair grow, a
light dusting of scruff along his jawline, instead of being clean-
shaven like he used to be.

No matter the differences, he was still one-hundred-percent
Landon, and irresistible as hell. There were moments while I
watched him sleep, the pleasure of having him near outweighed
the danger he'd put himself in to search for me. I'd stayed close,
affirming to myself that he was okay.

At least he seemed to take me seriously and not go back to his
original hotel. Marley had tracked his movements, noting he'd
stayed away from MBI and Fort Pontchartrain.

I would likely never see him again, so nothing I felt right now
mattered anyway. I needed to focus on destroying Emerson and
all he stood for.

But...what if it were possible for a second chance? What if

Landon found it in himself to forgive all the shitty things I'd done to him? *Like there's hope for that.*

"This is stupid," I said aloud, closing the laptop. If I couldn't read more than a sentence at a time, then I was useless to Marley. I might miss something important. Standing, I paced the room, trying to clear my mind. Maybe I should go for a walk, or a run, or *something.*

"Having trouble concentrating?" Alina asked from where she sat on one of the sofas, her own laptop balanced across her knees.

"You could say that," I muttered, unable to meet her gaze, embarrassed I was mooning over Landon *fucking* Urick like a teenager.

"Would this have something to do with Lover Boy?"

Scrubbing my hands over my face, I groaned and turned to her with a "what do you think?" expression she couldn't mistake.

She set her laptop on the coffee table and patted the space beside her. "Come here and talk it out."

I couldn't resist the offer, and dove at my friend, setting my cheek on her stomach to grip her around the waist in the hug I desperately needed. The scent of wildflowers swirled around us.

She waited, stroking my spine, not offering any words, just comfort. My throat tightened at the kindness. What did I do to deserve friends like Marley and Alina? Two women who'd dropped everything to move to Detroit when I told them what kind of trouble I was in and what I planned to do.

Growing up, I hadn't made many friends, even though Gold-enlach Ridge wasn't that big. A lot of that had to do with my brother. First, it was him telling me not to bring people home because it upset my mother, even though she never showed signs of being upset. Then it was the knowledge my friends would be at the mercy of Emerson's whims as much as I was if they were in his sphere. Call it a self-preservation instinct, but I stopped trying to make connections because of it. Everyone in school labeled me a rich snob. I used that label as a weapon, keeping people away. It was one of the reasons my infatuation with Kane Baird became a safe haven, an imaginary escape.

I'd never realized how lonely I was until I'd gone to university. By then, I'd already built solid patterns to keep myself distant from others. It wasn't until Emerson sent me to work for Landon that I opened myself up to someone.

God, I was so fucked up. It could have been another of my brother's manipulation tactics. Had he known how hard I'd fall for someone who showed me the least bit of affection? With Landon, I hadn't been able to keep my distance. He'd knocked down the bricks in my walls one by one. If it hadn't been him, but someone else, would I have fallen as hard?

No. There'd been other boys, other men. I'd dated in university and none had stirred me the way Landon had. I'd seen two guys while in the military, and neither had come close to the connection I had with Landon. It had been impossible not to compare any guy who'd shown an interest in me to him.

While I sorted through my thoughts, Alina stroked my arm, both of us silent. Only the quiet sounds of Marley moving around in the cockpit broke the hush now and again.

"He hates me," I said finally, admitting to the true crux of the matter. "He used to love me."

Alina didn't ask a question or make a comment, but stayed quiet with a supportive hand on my shoulder.

I finished the thought. "I could survive living with the fact he'd probably been hurt, probably didn't like me much. But now he knows the truth—that I went to work for him under false pretenses and stole from him—and I can't hide from the facts. I'm no longer blissfully unaware of his feelings. He hates me and he'll never forgive me."

"And it bothers you why?"

I already knew the answer to that, and Alina probably did too. Did she really need me to say it aloud?

She gave me a gentle shake when I didn't speak.

I sighed with a heavy breath. "Because I care about him. Of course it matters what he thinks if I still have feelings for him."

"And it would be so much easier if you didn't have feelings for him, but we can't turn off our feelings, unfortunately."

"Yes." I closed my eyes, remembering the coldness in his gaze as he slid into the taxi. If I didn't care, then it wouldn't have hurt so much.

"Hey," Marley called from the cockpit. "Both of you get in here."

The edge of her tone got us moving. I untangled my limbs from Alina's embrace, and we hustled to the cockpit. Two of her monitors were filled with code, the other two with what looked like forms and documents.

"What did you find?" I asked, moving to stand behind Marley's chair while Alina sat in the second.

"Something interesting. I made some leeway with the files you collected in Alaska. I've done a lot of keyword searches and have separated some important documents into categories. Most of the ones regarding the Alaskan compound I've filed under 'reprogramming.' There's something else that has a lot of documentation and it's called BDX-32. I didn't know what it was at first, but it might be some kind of drug. I haven't found anything about it online."

She glanced at me then, and I shook my head. "Haven't heard of it either."

Marley turned to her monitors. "Following that path, it's mentioned in conjunction with an abandoned and condemned warehouse outside of Detroit. Your brother bought the place using a shell company. I'm also seeing invoices for the same property. I don't think it's vacant."

"You think something's going on there right now?"

"Yeah."

"What?"

"Don't know, but it probably has something to do with this BDX-32 stuff."

"We could rent a plane to investigate," Alina said.

I turned to her with my lips pursed, knowing she suggested it only because she'd recently earned her pilot's license. "I don't think that's necessary if it's not far."

Alina shrugged. "Then we should send the drone."

I nodded. "Do it." She headed to the roof. "Did you find anything else?" I asked Marley.

"Yeah, I mean a lot. But nothing concise enough to give to our media contacts. They're going to want videos and images, not me in front of a map full of pins and strings telling them how things are connected. They'll want evidence they can turn into newsworthy stories, prime-time shit, for this to work."

"I know," I said, and tried to keep my bitterness to a minimum. We needed hard facts, irrefutable evidence, sent out all over the world at roughly the same time in order for our plan to work. Everyone needed to learn about what Emerson did to beasts for his own sadistic pleasure. It would put an end to his hunting parties at the arena—wherever the hell that was—and the experiments I'd seen at the compound in Alaska.

He had too much influence. If we only spoke to one media outlet or one law enforcement agency, then he'd snuff them out or pay them off before they could peep a word.

Across the globe, our contacts were ready for our story. Emerson couldn't silence every voice at once. We'd expose him for who he really was and destroy MBI in the process. All we needed was that sensational, newsworthy evidence we'd been searching for since I'd enlisted the help of my friends.

Alina returned, sliding into the chair next to Marley. "All ready to go," she chimed.

"Are we going to have any problems with the range?" I asked.

"It should be okay," Marley said, turning her monitors to the drone's feed. "It'll be tight, but it should make the round trip. If

not, we'll have to drive and get it. It is cutting-edge Urick Enterprises' tech, after all."

I barely resisted the urge to clap a hand over my face. "Why
do you two always sound like an advertisement for him?"

"What?" Alina asked as the drone lifted from our roof. "It's
not our fault he offers quality technology at affordable prices."
The scope of the image grew as it gained height. "If you two make
up, you should see if we can get some discounts."

I rolled my eyes at her as Marley flew it west, the cityscape
changing from industrial to residential, then sparsely populated
as it flew past Northville and beyond. It took about forty-five
minutes before she neared the location of the warehouse.

As the drone approached, details came into view. Floodlights
had been installed around a perimeter enclosed in an eight-foot
chain-link fence, barbwire curling along the top. Since it was
midafternoon, those floodlights weren't required to see a building
made of aluminum and wood. Two guards manned a gate on
wheels at the north end of the property, similar to the entry point
Emerson had in Alaska—only opened if a person had clearance.

Even more reminded me of the Alaskan compound: the large
yard with vehicles, the fence circling the property, the airstrip, the
guards patrolling the perimeter. Everything held Emerson's influence. It made it look like a mini Sing Sing.

"Keep back," I said, touching Marley's shoulder. "Don't let
them see the drone."

Marley nodded, easing off.

"It's definitely not abandoned," Alina said, turning to me.

"No," I agreed with a nod, my mind churning. I needed to find
out what my brother was doing inside that warehouse, but hesitated to involve Marley and Alina in a full-blown operation that
could turn deadly. The car chase on the freeway had been bad
enough. I may have asked for their help, but I wouldn't sign their
death warrants.

"What are you thinking?" Marley's voice cut into my thoughts,

and I found both my friends staring at me with similar speculative gleams in their eyes.

They hadn't been with me in Alaska and I was glad for it. My
brother's twisted experiments might not apply to humans, but
he'd have no qualms about hurting my friends to gain
information.

Like Alina could read my mind, she said, "You're not doing
this on your own."

Shaking my head, I dismissed Alina's comment. "Bring the
drone home," I said to Marley, and she nodded. The view on the
monitor shrank, then changed to foliage as she rotated the drone
in the direction of the city.

"We need to find out what's happening in the warehouse,"
Alina asserted, putting the emphasis on "we."

Of course they knew exactly where my mind had gone, and
from the set of Marley's jaw and the narrowing of Alina's eyes,
they wouldn't let me do this alone. I would do anything to keep
them out of harm's way, but I couldn't be in two places at once. I
had to trust their military training would be enough to keep them
safe.

I nodded, conceding. "Then we go there. Tonight."

10

LANDON

I RAN THE SILK SCARF OVER HER BODY AND SHE SHIVERED, HER PUPILS dilating in the low light, something only someone like me would notice. "I want to tie you up. To make you scream with pleasure."

She tensed, and I stopped my teasing, worried I'd gone too far. "What is it?"

"I don't like being helpless," she said quietly, then swallowed. "Don't like things on my wrists."

Interesting. We'd been together for a few months and I never would have guessed. Now that she mentioned it, I'd never seen her wear even a bracelet. I'd have to explore her statement more, her issues with trust, some other time when she wasn't panting and needing release.

I smiled. "Very well." I passed her the scarf. "Then you can tie me up."

"These sofas are velvet. I love it. I could roll around on them all day." Brooke's voice carried out into the hallway. "And a jacuzzi tub?" she screeched. "I'm never leaving this place. I've found my new home."

Kane tipped his head to the side, considering her statement, and I smiled. "Looks like someone should install a new tub at the cabin." His considering expression turned into a thoughtful smirk. "Come," I said, jerking my chin in the direction of my room. "They can find us once they're done exploring."

Both friends hesitated, their eyes glued to the suite where the excited chatter could be heard through the closed door. I paused at their almost-identical expressions, that need to see their mates, but also give them space.

"They'll be fine," I said, and both my friends stared at me with skepticism. "The only other room up here has an older couple. Only they and the staff have access to this floor."

After a brief hesitation, they followed me inside. Each suite was decorated a little differently, but all contained velvet and leather furniture done in earth tones. Tall windows were flanked with lush drapery, exuding a sophisticated but comfortable vibe. I'd spent the afternoon here on my own, waiting anxiously for my friends to arrive.

Soon after checking in, I'd locked myself in the spacious bathroom and let my bear loose. It wasn't an ideal space for him. He wanted to be out in nature for a long and hard run, but at least I was able to heal my arm. He'd enjoyed the jacuzzi tub quite a bit too. It only took twenty towels to clean up the mess. After that, I ate three trays of room service in human form.

While my mind raced with all the possibilities of how Jolyn and her brother were connected to my friends' disappearances, the rest of the afternoon was taken with trying to catch up on work I'd missed, mostly over the phone with my secretary. Nadine bent my ear with how I wasn't supposed to "do that to her again." Like being MIA for a few days was the end of the world. I guess when it came to the everyday operations of a business like

Urick Enterprises, it was. Luckily, I employed fantastic people to make sure everything ran smoothly.

Kane had packed up my belongings from my room at the other hotel, and the staff already set my suitcases on the bed, visible through the French doors beside the flat-screen TV. Sliding my hands into my front pockets, I leaned against the door frame and studied my two friends. I'd been so glad to see them both, I'd hugged each for a good while in the lobby, only letting go when Walker cleared his throat a few times.

On the other side of my room, Kane took in the view of the glittering Detroit nighttime skyline. Walker flopped backward on the sectional sofa, arms spread wide, letting out a breath like he hadn't had a moment to relax in weeks.

I'd seen Walker at his worst. When he'd returned from over-seas after being discharged from the military—after one of his closest friends had been murdered—he'd been a mess. Angry, combative, and continually half-deep in a bottle of the cheapest whiskey a person could find. I'd scarcely recognized him and thought him suicidal on more than one occasion. The only thing I'd been able to do was be there as a friend. And when he'd finally crawled out of the deep, dark pit of despair, I'd given him investigative jobs to keep him busy. After talking to the occasional military therapist, he had seemed to be returning to his former self.

This version of Walker, the one with a newly claimed mate and story to tell, was better than that post-military one. But trauma still existed there. I could see it in the tension around his eyes, even as they were closed, his face tipped toward the ceiling.

Mated to Brooke's sister? It was beyond strange. Growing up in Goldenlach Ridge, shifters were everywhere, and of course I'd heard of the term "fated mates," but it had honestly seemed like a mythical thing. Once in a generation.

From the way Kane and Brooke were together, I knew they

were meant to be. Could the same thing have happened to Walker? The unlikeliness of it made me shake my head.

At my request, the hotel staff had placed a decanter of scotch on the sideboard with five glasses. I strode to it, filling two fingers worth in three of them. I hadn't wanted alcohol earlier, alone, and with all the phone calls I'd been fielding with Nadine, but after the last few days I'd had, I needed a stiff drink.

Kane turned away from the tall windows, taking the glass I offered him. "Did you have any problems leaving the hotel?" I asked.

Using ASL, he signed a quick, "No."

Walker elaborated, his eyes remaining closed. "The others stayed at the hotel while I got us a new rental. Used the underground parking to swap out your trunk full." He lifted his head to meet my gaze. "Quite an assortment of gadgets you've got there, by the way."

"I like to be prepared," I said, passing him the second glass.

He nodded his thanks, set it on his knee, and returned to his previous position, eyes closed. "We checked out, but paid for an extra day so we could stay until nightfall. Left in the cover of darkness. Took two hours of driving to make sure we weren't followed, and poof. We're here. Like magic." Meeting my gaze, he lifted his glass in a salute and tossed it back in one huge gulp.

Then he gasped, sitting up straight. "Oh, shit. That was the good stuff. Fuck." He breathed through pursed lips. "Man, totally wasted that one." He lifted his glass for me to pour him another. "Sorry. I'll do better the next time."

Tsk-tsking, Kane sat across from him and sipped his own drink. I swiped the decanter off the sidebar, and raised an eyebrow at Walker while I poured the amber liquid into his glass.

"Last one. Promise," Walker said, responding to my unspoken question. "It's been a hell of a week." He took a large whiff of the fumes, then tossed it back too.

Kane set down his glass on the side table with a quiet smack to sign, "You drank it as fast as the first one."

Walker flashed us his teeth. "Yeah, but I smelled it first." He placed the empty glass on the coffee table and leaned back again. "I keep waiting for the shit to hit the fan."

It was a loaded statement, filled with more emotions than I could name. Exhaustion? Anger? From the tidbits I'd gotten so far, I knew he and Sabrina had been through something terrible.

"Tell us what happened to you." I sat in the wingback chair across from them. "And what Emerson Mahn has to do with it."

He rubbed a hand over his face and cracked his neck. "I told Kane some of it already. God, it's fucked up. You're to blame, really," he said, his eyes narrowed. Then he shook his head. "But if you hadn't sent me after Jolyn, I wouldn't have run into Sabrina, so I guess I should be thanking you for the two weeks of torture instead."

I straightened in my chair, stomach sinking low and fingers tight around my glass. "Torture?" He'd called Emerson Mahn a psycho, but torture?

"Yeah." He ran his hand over his face, as if to wipe away the memories. "I'm not going to tell you what they all did to me. It was sick and twisted, and they controlled me with a collar. The same kind Brooke had on when Kane found her. Sabrina was in one too, and they put her in a cage—were going to sell her off to some fucking hunter, put her in an arena. They could make you shift at will, or keep you stuck in human form to run their experiments."

My stomach churned the more he spoke. The collar was my fault. Not once while we developed it had I considered how it could be used as a torture device. We were making it to save lives, to stop rabid shifters from hurting others and exposing our kind. It was my breach in security and it had caused my friends real harm. Nausea crawled up my throat. Had Jolyn been an active participant in this torture?

She'd said she planned to bring down her brother's empire, but how culpable was she in my friends' abductions? My anger with her had cooled since this morning, but it began ramping up again.

"Was Mahn acting alone?" I croaked, the need to roar scratching up my throat. My bear itched to rampage in reciprocal suffering.

Walker shook his head and ice-cold dread of his next words crawled up the back of my neck. "Mahn employed this sicko named Croskey," he said. "Mahn got away, but Croskey's dead. I made sure of that." There was a grim sort of satisfaction in his tone when he said the last part.

"Son of a bitch," I breathed, my mind spinning. "Are you two okay?"

"We are now," he said with a nod.

"And Jolyn was a part of it," I stated, a question even though it didn't come out that way. I prepared myself to hear the worst and squeezed the glass in my hand, needing to ground my body as the world spun around me.

"Not of her own free will. She seemed trapped like we were, only she wasn't in a literal cage."

"She didn't help you." I clenched my jaw, ready for a renewed surge of anger.

"Dude. She was the *only* one who helped us." When I said nothing, he continued. "She burned every bridge she had in that place to do so. There was no way she would've been able to go back—not like the place is still standing, anyway—but it would've cost her everything."

My grip on my glass loosened as his words sank in. She wasn't part of it. She'd done what she could. It was all I could have asked in a place that sounded like hell on earth.

But she hadn't been truthful. She hadn't told me my friend was being tortured. What were her exact words? *I saw him a few days ago and he was fine. Spunky, even.*

Spunky. Yeah, a great description for Walker breaking out of that place and the hell he would have wrought on those who got in his way.

And she hadn't admitted to knowing Sabrina even though Walker had said they kept her in a cage. Maybe she hadn't known Sabrina's name.

And if she'd come to work for me to steal...and her brother used the collar to control shifters...

My stomach dropped again. "Then Jolyn—" I almost couldn't get the question out, cleared my throat, and tried again. "She knows what we are?"

Walker's emphatic nod froze the blood in my veins. "She definitely knows about shifters. Too many humans knew at that place. It was enough to make me want to rip off my own skin." He ran a hand over his head, exhaling. "My friends at Clyborne Inc. are looking into it. They're going to be combing through all of Mahn's connections who have excess knowledge of our species, trying to minimize the fallout and eliminating the more dangerous ones."

Internally, I winced, not wanting to delve deeper into the statement, but knowing if others were doing the same to shifters, they needed to be stopped. I'd heard Walker mention Clyborne Inc. before, knew Astrid Clyborne, the owner of the shifter-run mercenary group, had offered him a job with his old crew, but he kept turning her down.

He must have seen the question in my eyes, because he explained, "I called them for backup in Alaska. They helped destroy the fucking place. Emerson Mahn was apparently already on their radar."

"Why?"

He shrugged. "Wouldn't tell me because I'm not on the payroll."

I could tell from his posture it bugged him to be left out of the loop. Was he reconsidering Clyborne's offer?

But that wasn't what was making me feel queasy. Jolyn knew about shifters. It tipped my world on its axis. She'd stood in front of me and hadn't said anything. She hadn't looked at me with fear or suspicion because of what I was.

Maybe she doesn't know about me.

Neither her or her friends gave any indication they knew I was different. There was that "paws" comment from Alina, but it didn't necessarily mean anything, just a turn of phrase.

I set my glass aside and stood, needing to move, and walked to the tall window with its sparkling view of Detroit. At first, my own reflection bounced back at me, then I focused on the building across the street, lit up in the dark.

How long had Jolyn known about shifters? Was it recent knowledge, or had she known from before she worked for me? Was *that* the reason she applied for the job?

I crossed my arms, not really seeing what was in front of me, remembering how Jolyn looked when I woke up in their converted warehouse. Beautiful as always, but haggard, stressed. Too much weight on her shoulders. She hadn't wanted me to leave, citing her brother as the reason. Because she knew I was a shifter?

I rubbed my jaw, replaying our conversation. I'd been purposefully harsh. She'd betrayed me, hurt me, and I thought she'd deserved it. A sick sensation swam in my stomach. Emerson Mahn was the one using those collars. If she'd come to work for me, thieved because of her brother... What had she shouted?

You grew up with me and my brother, and you were totally clueless. Just like everyone else in that town.

"Bloody hell," I whispered, my breath fogging the window. What else had Mahn made her do?

I closed my eyes. I'd basically called Jolyn her brother's whore without realizing it.

And she meant to bring him down. All those weapons I'd seen...

A person needs decent headquarters when they're trying to take down an empire.

Whatever she'd done in the past, she was in mortal danger now. Maybe she had been her whole life and no one ever knew it. I'd rarely seen her father, and knew her mother had been in a wheelchair most of Jolyn's childhood. They'd lived in one of those houses with a maid, a cook, and a gardener. With her mother being a mentally impaired quadriplegic, and her father never home, what kind of life had she led at the mercy of someone like Emerson Mahn?

I owed her an apology—for the things I'd said to her and assuming the worst. She'd told me not everything between us was a lie, and maybe I could believe her now. I'd fallen in love with her for her quiet fierceness, her gentleness toward the weak, and her sharp wit. When we'd been together, I'd never felt more whole. If she felt a fraction of that...

Turning away from the window, I found Walker and Kane staring at me with furrowed brows. Before they could voice the questions in their eyes, I asked Walker, "How did Mahn pick you up in the first place?"

With a long exhale, he leaned forward and pressed his elbows against his knees. "After you sent me to find Jolyn, I stumbled across this warehouse her brother owned, but it was through another company and, I don't know, it got my spidey senses tingling, so I went to investigate." He shook his head. "The place was guarded like a prison with all the barbwire. I knew there was no way I could get inside without being seen. Not as I was, anyway. I needed gear. I was about to leave, when along comes Sabrina, pretty as you please and smelling as good as sin, and before I could get her out, we were jumped by three cougar shifters. Sabrina got away for the time being, but they shot me full of drugs, knocking me out, and shipped me to Alaska in a crate."

I closed my eyes. *Son of a bitch.* I'd sent him there. "I'm sorry," I said, meeting his gaze square on.

"It wasn't your fault. Not really," Walker said, his voice gentler. "You didn't make the sick fuck employ shifters to hurt people."

I shook my head, not accepting the rationalization.

Walker went on. "I don't know how he was able to do it. Mahn controlled them with these chips in the back of their necks." He rubbed his own reflexively. "Those collars they put on us... You'd almost beg to die they could make it hurt so bad." His hand dropped into his lap. "From the sounds of it, Kane took care of the one cougar at his cabin, and a few others of Mahn's shifters. Sabrina killed another one when we escaped the compound, and my old team killed the last. There's always a chance Mahn has more of those brainwashed fuckers up his sleeve somewhere, but at least the three who'd attacked us are gone."

That was a lot of bodies my friends were responsible for. Would legal repercussions follow? If they did, I'd spend as much of my money as was required to get them clear of it. They didn't deserve punishment for defending themselves and running for their lives.

"Clyborne is going to send a team to take out that place." Walker's voice might have been quiet, but there was steel in it.

"Which place?"

"Where they picked me up."

That was good. It meant no one else would fall victim if they went poking around. "When?"

"I don't know. Soon. Tonight or tomorrow."

Before he could say anything further, the sound of jostling at the door to the suite grabbed our attention. Both Walker and Kane were on their feet, heading to their mates in the next instant. The sisters had their arms slung around each other, bumping into the door frame when they tried to enter at the same time. They were a matching set of opposites, one blonde, the other a brunette, but both beautiful.

Laughing, the sisters headed toward their men. It had only been minutes since we'd all been together, but from the way my friends pulled their women to them, you'd think days had passed.

Two newly mated couples. I rubbed my knuckles over my jaw. I should have gotten them their own floor.

"These suites are amazing, Landon," Brooke said to me from the circle of Kane's arms. "Thanks for arranging them."

"My pleasure."

On the other side of the coffee table, Walker pulled Sabrina down with him onto the sofa, cradling her in his lap, his hand on her ass. With her wavy brown hair spilling over his chest, she tucked her head under his chin and hugged his torso.

I'd only just met her, but she seemed a serious sort, a contradiction to her more free-spirited sister. Maybe it was what she'd suffered at the hands of a madman that made her so stoic. I could hardly blame her.

While Kane and Brooke messed with the record player underneath the TV, and Walker spoke quietly to Sabrina, I stared at the amber liquid in my glass.

I'd thought Jolyn and her friends were corporate thieves. Now I understood they meant to take down Mahn—three people against a billion-dollar multinational corporation. *Not very good odds.*

When she'd said "empire" I thought she meant his pharmaceutical business, not a hidden agenda where people's lives were on the line. And now Walker's former crew were thrown into the mix. This spelled disaster to anyone caught in the cross fire. I should have gotten more information about Jolyn's plans before I'd left, but I'd been more concerned about Walker than what three women were planning to do with their day.

I needed to find their headquarters and let them know Clyborne Inc. was in the picture now.

An older-sounding jazzy beat filled the room, and Brooke gave a satisfied whoop. "I've always wanted a record player.

They're so retro." She pulled Kane against her, moving to the rhythm. The big guy only had eyes for his mate, his face glowing. "I think I promised you a dance, sir," she said, her tone suggestive.

I rubbed a hand over my face, mystified at what my life had become over the past week. "Hey, guys. If you're going to have that kind of dance, you need to head to your own room."

11

JOLYN

My heart felt like someone had stabbed it a million times. I'd covered myself with five blankets, and still shook. Kane was...I didn't have a word for it. Monster? Abomination? Kane, the boy of my heart, my kindred spirit...

Unable to finish the thought, a sob left my mouth. My eyes were opened to the truth, but my chest felt like a chasm.

I couldn't leave the house, couldn't do much except hide in my room and try to remove those screams from my brain. Every time I closed my eyes, I'd see the blood and carnage. I couldn't sleep.

How many of these ferocious monsters existed around me? If Kane was one, who else?

My hands were icy cold. I didn't know if I would ever be warm again. The only silver lining with this horror—Emerson was the nicest he'd ever been to me. Kept saying how we were in this together...

Another truck rumbled through the gate, a cloud of dust billowing behind as it turned on the highway. That was the second cargo vehicle to leave in the past thirty minutes. What I wouldn't give to know what was on those trucks. Maybe we'd find something inside to tell us.

Alina and I crouched fifty feet from the chain-link fence topped with barbwire. It was after one o'clock in the morning, and this place didn't seem like it was winding down anytime soon. With Marley doing support from our van, and only two of us out here, we needed to be as stealthy as possible.

We wore all-black tactical gear, knitted caps over our heads. Alina had insisted I darken my face and throat with makeup, because otherwise my pale skin "glowed in the dark"—it wasn't an unfair statement. Night vision goggles gave us a superb view of the area, bathing everything in a green glow. Already I didn't like what I saw: too much activity.

A cargo plane was parked on the tarmac. Guards patrolled the perimeter in pairs. All the windows in the warehouse were lit up like a holiday lantern. A third truck came out of the garage, and I flexed my fingers. How the hell were we supposed to get in there?

The night remained calm and cool, barely a breeze to ruffle the leaves. When it was this quiet, I felt like every one of our movements was as loud as a gunshot, signaling our position. But I had a right to be paranoid. We'd found two motion detectors in the trees along the fence line, and kept well back because of them.

One of the plane's propellers began to spin, the back of it brightening with orange from its internal combustion. My stomach clenched. Where was it headed? To my brother? To the arena? Its whirring sound reached where we perched, the volume increasing when the next propeller joined it in motion. Still as statues, we watched for long minutes. The ground crew removed the wheel chocks, cleared the area, and the plane taxied to the end of the runway. It sat there a while before the engine roared louder, then the plane sped forward. The front tipped upward, and the wheels lifted from the ground. Lights blinked in the dark as it flew farther away.

An artificial hush settled around the warehouse in the absence of its noise pollution. I looked over at Alina. We didn't speak—the motion detectors had made us extra cautious. She pressed her lips in a thin line. Just like me, she must have realized we might not be able to breach this place. There were only two of us, and we hadn't come here for a suicide mission. If it was too dangerous, we'd need to back out.

Still, we waited, looking for an opportunity. Minutes, then hours passed, and we remained in our concealed positions. Then, one by one, the lights went out in the building.

My heart rate picked up tempo. We hadn't seen a truck leave since the plane, but cars had thinned in the parking lot, each clearing the gatehouse one at a time. Now it looked like the guards on the perimeter duty were reduced by half.

I glanced at Alina, and she nodded. We could do this. We waited another thirty minutes before I spoke in my comm to Marley. "We're a go," I said.

"Roger that. One moment."

Not even a minute had gone by when the floodlights surrounding the property went out, submerging the whole area in darkness. Earlier, Marley had started some rumors about rolling power outages in the area.

"Electricity has been disabled. You may proceed. Over"

Alina and I stood. Through the green haze of my night vision goggles, I watched one of the guards on this side of the property speak into his radio. The pair of them waited a moment, then turned on flashlights before resuming their route.

My legs protested from holding still for so long, but I pushed through the pain to jog down the hill. We skirted the motion detectors even though they should have been ineffective with the power cut.

We paused a moment, waiting for the guards to pass. Using the thermal imaging on my goggles, I made sure no one was on the other side of the back entrance. We continued forward after the guards rounded the building. Crouching by the chain-link fence, Alina pulled her bolt cutters out of her pack and got to work. Glock in hand, I scanned the area, seeking threats. Everything remained quiet.

With a section of the fence cut on two angles, Alina bent back the wire. I squeezed through first; she followed. Taking a breath, I gave her a quick glance, then we sprinted across the grassy twelve-foot space, not stopping until we'd pressed ourselves against the building, hidden in shadows.

My breaths left my lips in short bursts, and I mentally talked myself down from the adrenaline rush. Alina looked as calm as ever. Having been deployed overseas for two years, she knew how to deal with these situations. I might have been in the infantry, but my entire military career had been spent in Canada, not anywhere close to combat.

Even so, this whole operation energized me more than intimidated. If I'd been allowed to, I would have stayed enlisted. Emerson hadn't permitted it, and I understood why. His reach hadn't extended to the military, and I'd been away from his influence too long—he'd been right to worry.

I took a breath and nodded to Alina. While I kept a lookout, she crouched by the door and used a lock picker to crack open the mechanism. This door appeared similar to the ones Emerson had used in the Alaskan compound, but with the keypad dead on the side, Alina was able to get it open. We sneaked into a hallway crammed with boxes. They towered in stacks like someone was moving in—or moving out. My mind returned to those trucks.

Alina closed the door behind us with a click. We waited, listening. When we heard no one nearby, we continued forward. The first two rooms were empty office spaces, the third a storage closet, the next a bathroom. The last door on the right was locked. We glanced at each other. I kept watch while she crouched to pick the lock.

Click. We were in. I shut the door quietly behind us and

scanned the space. It was exactly what we were looking for, a working computer where we could download as much data as possible onto a USB drive, and a connection to Emerson's servers where we'd leave one of Marley's invasive viruses as a parting gift.

While Alina looked around, I sat at the desk and plugged in the thumb drive. The monitor lit up, and I propped my goggles on my head. The computer whirred—a soft noise, but it sounded loud when we were trying to be so quiet. Time ticked by slowly. Alina pressed herself against the wall by the door, listening.

Fingers tapping on the desk, I waited for the prompt on the screen to signal completion. The white message popped up, and I slipped the drive out of the slot, swapping it for the one that would deploy Marley's virus. A minute later, I yanked it out, and slid it in my pocket with the other.

Joining Alina by the door, she glanced at me, and I nodded that we were good. Soundlessly, she turned the knob, hesitated, then stepped out into the hallway. I made sure the door closed completely, that we left no evidence of our presence.

We started back the way we'd come. Voices from far-off made tension crawl up my spine. I spun around to stare down the long hallway. Flashlights cut through the black, blinding through the lens of my goggles.

People were headed this way. I turned, ready to run to the exit, when one voice rose above the others.

"It doesn't matter. We won't need it anymore."

Emerson's words splashed over me like arctic water. I froze, unable to move. *He's found me.* Blood pumped in my ears. Every horrible thing I'd imagined him doing to me cascaded through my mind. My chest squeezed so tight, I couldn't take a breath.

A strong hand gripped my arm. I flinched, ready to lash out against my brother, to fight for my life.

But it was Alina. She pulled me into the empty office, closed the door, and locked it. My chest heaved up and down. Alina held her fingers up to her lips, a message for me to be silent, but I couldn't seem to breathe any quieter—not when it felt like I sipped air through a straw.

The closer the voices came, the more panic traveled up my spine. Emerson was talking to someone, snippets of their words reaching us. His tone remained even, calm.

He doesn't know I'm here. This sounded like a routine inspection, or something like it. But why in the middle of the night?

If I'd known he'd be here, I never would have come. My eyes went to Alina. Thank God she'd kept her cool enough to get us hidden, but now we were trapped. If she were discovered with me...there was no predicting what my brother would do. I couldn't allow him to find us. I'd kill everyone here before I'd let him get his hands on her.

The voices became louder, like they were right outside the door. My gun tight in my hand, I took a step back, out of direct line of sight if it opened. Alina did the same on the other side.

The doorknob rattled.

"Don't bother," said a different man's voice. "That one's already empty, everything's in the hallway here. I can take you back to..." The words faded, the light from the flashlights becoming dimmer. Slowly, my heart rate lowered. I took a proper breath, but kept my eyes on the door.

Titty fucker, I was mad at myself. I was a trained soldier, and I fell apart as soon as I heard my brother speak. My hand tightened on my gun. He didn't have power over me anymore. I couldn't let this happen again. I wouldn't break down, wouldn't freeze.

Even when we couldn't hear the voices anymore, Alina and I stayed put. Then Marley's voice came through the comm. "I have chatter on the power company's radios. Looks like they're close to fixing their end."

Not looking at Alina, not wanting to see judgment there, I placed a hand on the knob and opened it a smidgen. All was quiet. I opened it wider and crept out, listening for Alina behind me. When we got to the exit, this time she cracked it open, listened, then nodded that we were clear.

We paused briefly in the shadows for the guards to move farther off, then sprinted to the space we'd cut in the chain-link fence. One after the other, we shimmied through, then ran into the trees.

A *kerclunk* echoed through the air. Propping my goggles on my head, I turned to see the electricity on, floodlights blazing to erase the shadows we'd found so useful.

My chest squeezed. Emerson stood near the entrance, his arms crossed and strawberry-blond hair glinting in the glare of the floodlights. And he stared right at me.

My heart leaped into my throat. *There's no way he can see me from there.* But that didn't stop me from spinning around and running to our van as fast as my legs could carry me.

PART II

A TASTE OF FREEDOM

12

LANDON

Four and a Half Years Ago

IF MY BEAR BECAME ANY MORE OBNOXIOUS, I WAS TEMPTED TO SHIFT just so I could beat the shit out of him. I needed to do this sweet and gentle, not aggressive and dominant like he wanted.

The scent of lasagna began to take over the condo as it cooked in the oven. Jolyn sat beside me on the sofa, a glass of red wine in her hand. Soft music played in the background, and I'd lit a fire. The weather had turned cool again, windy, over the past week. It wouldn't last long, with summer just around the corner.

The light from the fire reflected off the curls of her hair, creating their own dancing inferno. She'd always seemed other-worldly to me, even when we were children. Her black blouse was open at the neck, giving a tantalizing view of her freckles where they disappeared in her cleavage.

Claim. My bear's essence reverberated through my head. It wasn't like he knew specific words, but that was definitely the point he was making. I felt his desires and emotions in my gut.

But dammit, in this instance I really needed him to shut the hell up. I had to keep chill. I'd already needed to tread carefully because of her position in my company. She'd started as my personal assistant. When she'd agreed to date me, I'd promoted her to HR director. Yeah, there'd been mutters of favoritism, but it would have been worse if I'd been in a relationship with my PA.

Staring at the fire, she tucked a curl behind her ear, and took another sip of her drink. She'd worked for me for two months before I'd asked her out, and it took her a couple weeks before she agreed, *after* I'd offered her the HR job if working too closely made it awkward. I'd known she was interested well before that because I could scent her desire.

Every time we'd worked in close quarters, her intoxicating fragrance would flare. On the outside she was calm and professional. But on the inside, she wanted me as much as I wanted her. I would have blamed it on my imagination if it hadn't happened all the time. My bear reveled in her reactions, and didn't understand why I never acted on it.

It was her hesitancy that gave me pause. A scent of nervous tension hung around her, almost continuously, one I didn't remember her having as a kid, but it was there. So even though I scented her desire when we were together, I never rushed things, always following her physical cues, not the fragrance that drove me to the brink.

I didn't need to scare her away by going all caveman. *Or cavebear, as it were.*

But since she'd arrived this evening, I'd been getting cues from her that she wanted to take our relationship to the next level. So did I. *Badly.* And my bear was already panting, circling, ready to mount her and bite her neck with the least bit of encouragement.

That's not how this works, buddy.

The guy did not understand the finer points of wining and dining. Good thing I was the one in charge.

Or was I? When Jolyn licked her lips, he practically roared inside me, scratching to get closer. I crossed my legs in the other direction, trying to obscure what those little movements of hers did to me.

Finesse, I told him. *We need to use finesse.*

It was quite apparent he did not know the meaning of the word.

I cleared my throat, and she startled, like her mind had been a million miles away. "How was your day?" We'd been apart until a half hour ago. She'd said she wanted the day to herself and that was completely fine.

My bear didn't like those kinds of days. He only liked the ones where he could see her in the office as much as possible, take her to lunch, then dinner after work. He wasn't too impressed by her transfer to HR. I kind of agreed with him.

Her eyes warmed at my question. "I did a little shopping, a little exploring, nothing fancy."

"Exploring?"

Her mouth lifted in the corner, and I wanted to lick that smile. *Lick. Bite.* I curled my nails into my thighs, trying to tame my bear.

"Yeah, I walked through Gastown for a bit—that's where I bought the cake—ate way too much food at this market I found, but it was nice, even with the weather being what it was." That lemon layered cake sat in its box on my kitchen island, waiting for the end of dinner.

My bear grumbled. He wanted to go shopping and exploring with her. I was kind of there with him, then I shook my head at myself. *Women need space too, my dude. Get a grip.*

Her explanation complete, Jolyn gazed toward the fire.

"You seem far away," I murmured, wondering at the change of her mood since she'd arrived.

"Sorry," she said, and smiled a little. "Just distracted." With a huffed breath, she set her glass of wine on the coffee table, and curled into my side, her arms wrapped around me.

My bear and I sighed at the same time. That improved things.

She'd been too far away, that was all. Everything felt ten times better already. I breathed a deep breath and sank into the hold, inhaling her vanilla scent. Then, her desire blossomed over top of the nerves.

My bear paced inside me. *She wants us. We want her. Claim.*

Her hand lifted, skimming along my abdominal muscles to my chest, her palm settling over my heart. Every touch she gave me felt like coming home.

"Landon?"

"Yeah?" I answered around the emotion in my throat.

"Do you want to make love?"

My bear became so excited at her question, fur sprouted on the back of my hands. I snapped them out of sight.

I cleared my throat again, adjusted my position beneath her, and said, "Um." *Play it cool. Play it cool. Don't freak her out.* "Do you?"

Instead of answering, she stroked my chest, down then up again, the silk of my shirt whispering beneath her palm. My cock stood up at attention. My bear growled with need. I bit my tongue to hold the sound inside.

Lower her hand traveled, this time pausing at the button of my trousers. When she started undoing it, I placed my hand on top of hers, relieved the fur had disappeared.

Tension stiffened her body, that scent of nerves returning.

"If we're going to do this," I said, and waited for her to look up at me. I took one of her curls and tried to tuck it behind her ear like she'd done. It bounced right back out. Giving up on that, I continued, "Then we're going to do it right."

Her brow crinkled in bemusement, her hand twitching on my fly. "What's the right way to do it?"

A smile grew on my face. "Ladies first."

Her eyes widened, and I took the opportunity to kiss her parted lips. *Perfection.* Every time I tasted her, it was like the very first time all over again. Her moan of pleasure spurred me on.

Keeping my mouth against hers, I adjusted our positions until I cradled her bottom in my lap. My hand dove into her hair.

Her tongue stroked mine, as enthusiastic for this kiss as I. My bear wanted to consume her. I wanted to make sure she was screaming in pleasure.

I broke our kiss, leaning her back to access her throat. I inhaled gulps of her scent, tasting her skin on the way down. Her hands squeezed my shoulders, fingernails biting into skin. Shivers cascaded down my back and up my scalp. I loved that. She could scratch me as much as she liked. I almost told her to squeeze harder, but bit my tongue. This wasn't about me, it was about her.

I looked up from the top button of her blouse. "I've always wanted to learn how far these freckles go."

She licked her lips, the scent of her desire spiking, and gave me a little nod.

Bracing on my elbows, I undid the top button, then the next, and the next, until her blouse parted, revealing a black lace bra beneath. My bear bashed against my psyche, wanting to rip that bra open to reveal the treasures beneath. Ignoring him, I trailed my fingers from her throat, through the valley of her breasts, then along her stomach. Everywhere I touched were more freckles, right until they disappeared into the waist of her skirt.

"One of these days, I'm going to count them all," I murmured.

Her face flushed red, her scent swirling around us. I altered our positions again, kneeling beside the sofa until I could glide her skirt down her hips and thighs. She lay there like an offering, a feast, in her black, skimpy underwear. It was all I could do to contain my bear.

I kissed her kneecaps, her inner thighs, and stroked the backs of her knees with my fingers. "You're so damn sexy," I said against the skin of her hip, enjoying her gasps of pleasure. I wanted to worship every part of her, show her how much I loved her with my touches.

I licked the inside of her elbow, her wrist, kissed the palms of her hands. She held my heart there.

Beneath a hooded gaze, she watched my movements. My lips grazed the freckles on her stomach, then traveled to her breasts. Cupping the globes, I left her bra where it was and nipped at the juicy flesh through the lace. I took my time, reveling in her responses, tweaking the hardened pebbles beneath.

One hand still toying with her nipple, my mouth searched down for another sensitive area. I wanted to pay homage to every inch of her.

"Stop."

I paused at the desperation in her voice, ice blooming across my heart. My lips hovered over her wrist and I met her eyes.

She licked her lips and continued, "Stop being so gentle. I can't take it anymore."

My bear roared. *Claim!*

"You make me feel too much," she whispered, and it sounded pained.

I leaned back to examine her face. Her scent had changed to something almost frantic. My bear liked it, took it as an invitation to show the aggression he held inside him. But I didn't think the same. I didn't want her desperate. I wanted her blazing with arousal.

"Jolyn," I said, keeping my voice even. My hand lay gently on her stomach. "I'm going to go down on you. I'm going to make you come so hard you see stars." I watched in fascination as her flush deepened, spreading from her throat down to where my hand pressed against her skin. "*After* you've come so hard you see stars, then you can tell me what to do, got it?"

For a few seconds she just stared at me, then finally gave me one little nod.

"Good girl."

She shivered.

Standing, I gathered her in my arms, and laid her on the rug in front of the fire. She watched me as I unbuttoned my shirt and slid it off my shoulders. Her gaze roved everywhere, heating me more than the fire.

I needed to taste her skin again. Starting with her lips, I savored her piece by piece. Her throat tantalized. Her cleavage made me salivate. She leaned up and I removed her bra, exposing perfect breasts to the light of the fire. I laved every inch of her, paying particular attention to her nipples and areolas, until she gasped my name, fingers flexing in my hair.

Roving lower, I ate up her freckles one at a time, then settled myself between her legs. The thin lace of her lingerie barely covered her. I ran my fingers over the strip of material, watched her quiver, then swept it aside. Her beautiful pink folds glistened in the firelight.

I licked her. Everywhere. Explored every crevice, needing to know her like no man had before. Her hands clutched my head, and both my bear and I growled our encouragement. I wanted to know every secret of her body and of her mind. I wanted to submerge myself and never surface.

After long sweeps of my tongue, I concentrated on her clit, another perfect feature of her amazing body. Her fingers tightened. I backed off, then returned for more, wanting this to last as long as possible.

"Landon, please," she moaned, and I smiled against her gorgeous center.

I would edge her another time.

Pressing my tongue flat against her, I shifted my weight until I could explore her with my fingers. Two sank into her depths. My bear roared. She groaned. My eyes closed at how good she felt, that I got to play with her this way, give her pleasure. I pumped my fingers slow and steady inside her, and flicked my tongue over her clit. Her legs shook. Her fingers gripped my head, showing me exactly where she wanted me.

I pinched her clit between my lips. She shuddered against

me, my name exploding from her throat. Her thighs squeezed my ears. I sucked every bit of her orgasm through her clit until she gasped for breath, her fingernails digging into my scalp. It only turned me on more.

In the resulting silence, the fire crackled, dying down to embers. Her thighs relaxed, and I lifted my head. Every part of her body glowed with sex flush. My bear approved. But we weren't done yet.

Allowing the fabric of her underwear to slide back in place, I crawled up her body, then leaned on my elbows to give her a kiss. A satisfied, bemused expression graced her features, like she wasn't sure what had just happened.

I stroked her cheek, her intoxicating scent swirling around us. "Did you see stars?"

Her mouth curved in a smile, and she nodded.

"All right." I smoothed one of her curls behind her ear. It sprang back out. "What would you like to do now?"

Unadulterated need consumed her features. She squeezed my shoulders. "I need it harder. I need you inside me."

Claim! Bite! Take her now!

My bear may have approved of my feast, but his desires weren't slaked. And in my aroused state, his roars were becoming harder to ignore.

I stood and extended my hand. She took it and I pulled her to her feet, didn't stop tugging until she was plastered against me. With her soft breasts squeezed to my chest, I kissed her again. *I'll never get enough.*

Keeping hold of her hand, I led her through my condo, past the kitchen to turn off the oven, then continued to the bedroom.

Before she could do anything else, I scooped her up in my arms, and laid her out on my bed, making quick work of her underwear. I feasted on the sight of her splayed before me, but she didn't let me stare for long.

"Too many clothes," she said, reaching for the front of my trousers.

She unbuttoned me, then rolled down my zipper. My pants pooled at my knees. She grabbed the waistband of my boxer briefs, then tugged them down. My cock jumped in front of her, buoyant. She grabbed me, warm hand wrapped around my cock as firm as a handshake, and I groaned at the sensation of her skin against mine.

And as though she were ravenous, she licked me from root to tip.

"Bloody hell," I moaned.

She smiled, and swallowed me whole.

Her mouth on me...oh God...I didn't think I'd ever felt anything so good before in my life. And the way she looked, taking me down her throat, her eyes glued to mine. *Fuck.* There were no words to describe it. I pumped my hips. Her cheeks hollowed. She drove me so high so fast, I almost spilled right then and there. But I didn't want that. I wanted to make everything last.

She backed off, swirling her tongue around my tip, then took me deep again. She did it again. And again. Pushing me close to the brink, then backing off.

Oh hell, she was edging me.

Guess I deserve that.

My calm, professional girlfriend had a devious side. I couldn't have been happier.

Just when she pushed me back to the brink, I pulled out. Leaning down, I gave her a kiss and spoke against her mouth. "I want to fulfill your wishes, take you hard."

"I want that too."

Her husky voice created shivers across my skin. I reached into the bedside table and grabbed a condom. I kept my eyes on her as I tore the package with my teeth, then wrapped up my cock. She licked her lips and scooted back on the bed, spreading her legs open in invitation.

Holy angels above, I never wanted to forget this instant, because it was erotic as hell and felt like the most profound moment of my life.

This wasn't just sex.

It would never only be sex with her.

Taking a deep breath, her scent infusing me, I crawled up the bed, tasted her pussy for a few lazy licks, then kissed my way up her stomach. Her fingernails bit into my shoulders.

"Landon," she murmured against my mouth. "Please."

"Anything for you."

My cock nudged against her. She tilted her hips. Little by little, I entered her. My eyes rolled back in my sockets.

If I'd thought her mouth was perfection...

What word meant better than perfect?

I couldn't hold back, and plunged into her tight heat. My bear roared, and the sound that emerged from my chest wasn't that far off. I think fur might have sprouted across my shoulders.

"More," she groaned, thrusting her hips into mine.

I stopped holding back and gave it to her like she wanted. Her legs wrapped around me, flexing, urging me to go faster. I captured both her hands, held them above her head, and pounded into her. She moaned, arching her back, her breasts jiggling with each pulse of my hips, nipples brushing my chest.

Keeping her hands captive in one of mine, I slid my free one between us, finding her clit. It brought my face to the crook of her neck. I inhaled, filling my head with her scent.

"Yes," she panted.

I stroked the space between us even as I pushed deeper inside her. God, I wanted to bite her. No other woman had done this to me before. I agreed with my bear. I needed to claim her. My teeth grazed the spot where her shoulder met her neck. I salivated, my bear turning rabid inside me.

Still rocking inside her, I closed my eyes and pressed my lips together. *I can't.* She didn't know what I was. I couldn't claim her without being truthful. And now wasn't the time for truths.

Her body tensed, a groan erupting from her lips. Inner walls spasming around me, her orgasm spurred my own. White light shot behind my eyes. I soared through the clouds. Nothing existed in my mind but pleasure. My bear roared, scratching the surface of our bond, trying to seal the deal.

"I love you," I groaned, falling over the edge, capturing her lips in a searing kiss.

For long moments, we existed in a cocoon, just the two of us. Then sounds crept back in: the traffic outside, the music playing in the living room, our gasping breaths.

Supporting my weight on my elbows, I stared down into Jolyn's bright blue eyes. I brushed my mouth against the freckles on her cheeks, then rested my forehead against hers.

"I think the lasagna's done," I murmured.

She laughed and pulled me tight against her. "I guess we did work up an appetite."

"Need to keep up our strength," I agreed, trying and failing to tuck one of her curls behind her ear again.

"Then let's eat."

We did. But it wasn't lasagna. And it wasn't enough to satiate our desire.

I knew then, I would never be able to let her go.

13

JOLYN

I FOUND *E*MERSON *WATCHING* TV, *A LIGHTER IN HIS HAND.* I*T WAS* Father's lighter, engraved with his initials, but neither of them smoked. Emerson clicked it open, then closed, then open, then closed, the sound loud even with the news showing the recent multigovernment summit.

"These beasts, they're everywhere."

My heart leaped in my throat. I stared at the TV, not understanding what he was seeing. "What do you mean?"

"That guy, dictator in the Middle East, he's one of them."

"How do you know?"

"I just know. They give off...an energy I can see."

I swallowed, not having any way to dispute his claims.

"I understand it all now," he went on. "They're the ones responsible for Mother's state. And her death."

"How?"

"The marks on her car and body. She hit one of these beasts, and either it, or its friends, attacked her." He looked at me then, cold determination in his eyes. "No one is safe with them around."

The overhead light buzzed, making the throb in my temple intensify. After the night we'd had, and being up so long, I should take a nap, but I couldn't turn off my brain. The words on my laptop screen blurred into nonsense. I touched my phone and noted the time: eight thirty in the evening.

Alina sat across the dining room table from me, a laptop in front of her as well. She didn't look any better than I felt. We'd been too electrified from last night's mission to relax.

It wasn't like I slept well anyway. Chronic insomnia had plagued me since I was a child. The only time I'd ever experienced a full, uninterrupted night of sleep had been when Landon held me tight to his chest. I rubbed at the sting in my breastbone, shaking my head so I wouldn't think about it. Right now, my fatigue was worse because the ebb of adrenaline was taking effect.

I flicked my gaze to Alina. She hadn't said anything about the way I'd frozen last night. There hadn't been reprimand in her tone after we'd gotten to safety, or censure in her gaze. I deserved both, but appreciated the lack. *It won't happen again.*

If—*when*, the moment came to face my brother, I wouldn't hesitate. Lives depended on it—and not just my own.

Not counting the near miss, the mission had been flawless. We deserved a win after the debacle at MBI. What we had now was a whole heap of intel that needed to be analyzed on top of the stuff Marley was trying to sort through from Alaska—and only three of us to do it.

And I could admit I was shit at going through data. Plan an op, no problem. Boots-on-the-ground mission? I had that covered. Read through pages and pages of files? You'd only get a couple hours out of me before I wanted to stab something. I think it had to do with my brother forcing me to go into the business program. I hated being in front of a computer.

"Um, Alina?" Marley called from the cockpit, and both Alina and I straightened at the strange tone in her voice.

"Yes?" she asked, standing.

"You swept the place for bugs and trackers after Mr. CEO left, right?"

Alina and I glanced at each other, eyebrows raised, then headed to the cockpit together.

"Yes," Alina replied.

We stopped inside the door to see one of her monitors with a view of our property. My heart sped up. In the rays of the setting sun, Landon was at the gate, bolt cutters in hand—a contradiction to the fancy gray suit he wore. He broke his way through our fence to access the empty yard where I'd escorted him blindfolded only a day ago.

Titty fucker.

"It seems your safety measures to keep our location a secret were insufficient," Marley said in a droll tone.

"Impossible." I'd walked him out of our way for over an hour. Even if he roamed the area aimlessly searching, we were one warehouse among many, no distinguishable characteristics to announce our presence.

"Nothing's impossible," Alina piped up in a too-cheerful voice. "Just highly unlikely. I would have agreed you'd done enough, but obviously not. He probably has an incredibly good sense of direction, or an eidetic memory."

"He was blindfolded."

"Maybe eidetic can translate into sounds and scents too."

I shook my head, but her words made the hairs on the back of my neck stand up. There was having a good sense of direction, then there was the uncanny knack of knowing where you'd been before without trying. I gripped Marley's chair.

"What do you want me to do about him?" she asked as we all watched Landon skulk across the empty concrete yard, the bolt cutters now hidden in the small duffel bag over his shoulder. He looked good, like he hadn't been shot a couple days ago. His movements were full of lithe grace, no indication he felt pain in his shoulder.

Theoretically, we could do nothing. He wouldn't get inside. Not with just bolt cutters. Or we could let him in through the first door and trap him for as long as we wanted.

The last option churned acid in my stomach. It was something my brother would have no problem doing. I wasn't my brother. Could I ignore Landon as he tried to find a way inside, knowing he was out there? *No.* Not when he was so close, and he must have come back here for a reason.

Do I want to know that reason?

As we watched, he knelt on one knee by the door, dirtying up his fine suit. He dug something new out of his bag. Big as a brick, it resembled one of those first cell phones invented. Next came a screwdriver. With a deft hand, he popped off the casing of the keypad.

"He's messing with my stuff," Marley cried, indignant.

"Well, isn't it kind of his stuff too?" Alina offered. "Most of the tech in this place is made by Urick Enterprises."

"Unhelpful," Marley gritted out.

I narrowed my eyes at the screen. Could he get inside? We all held our breath as he attached the brick-phone thing to the keypad with two wires. The longer he messed with it, the more we relaxed. Marley's security measures were solid.

Then the door clicked open.

"Holy smokes," Alina gasped. "I have to admit I'm impressed. I thought he was one of those guys who only knew how to schmooze, golf, and shake hands with other boys like him. He's resourceful when he needs to be, isn't he?"

"Yeah." I exhaled a slow breath. "I'll go get him. You two wait here." I uncurled my fingers from the leather of Marley's chair.

"Are you sure you don't want backup?" Alina asked with a hopeful tone.

I narrowed my eyes at her before making my way to the stairs.

Punching the code into the keypad, I opened the door and jogged down. My feet hit the ground floor and I took a deep breath.

Landon was on the other side of the door. I'd resigned myself to never seeing him again, the likelihood that I'd fail in my mission to take down my brother and die in the process being pretty substantial. Now Landon was *right there*. All those second chances I'd thought about could be a possibility—*if* he'd ever forgive me my sins.

That was about as likely as me shooting rainbows out of my ass.

I took another breath and punched in the code for the door. Pushing it open, I found him with his device attached to the keypad for the elevator. He froze when he saw me. My stomach swirled in appreciation. He'd cleaned himself up, his facial hair trimmed, and his suit looking like it came directly from the dry cleaners.

Straightening away from the wall, he smoothed his lapels and gave me one of those looks he thought impressive in the board-room. "I was beginning to think this particular panel was impenetrable."

"Likely," I said, knowing to say anything else would be disloyal to Marley. We'd all thought the outside keypad was impenetrable too. "What are you doing here, Landon?"

He leaned against the wall and crossed his arms over his chest like he had all the time in the world to chat with me between two thick blast doors. "I realized, belatedly, I should have asked more questions about your operation when I was here."

I swallowed. "It's better if you don't know what's happening. Safer."

"Possibly," he allowed. "But even if it puts me in danger, I need answers to what happened to my friends." *And your involvement.*

He didn't say those words, but I heard them anyway.

"*They* deserve answers," he added.

So we were at an impasse—him not leaving, me not wanting him to sink deeper into the clusterfuck that was my life.

But this was a different Landon than the one who left in a cab yesterday. He wasn't staring at me like I'd kicked his dog, or drove over his grandma with a tractor. He was looking at me like he used to, like I was the most important person in the world and there wasn't anywhere he'd rather be, while staying laser-focused on the things I was going to say.

I'd taken those moments for granted when we were together, hated them, really, because those times were always filled with lies.

Now it could be different. I didn't need the lies between us, didn't want them. And for the first time since he'd found me in front of the MBI building, it seemed he was willing to openly listen to my side of things.

I stepped back and cracked the door wide enough for him to enter the stairwell. "Would you like to come up?"

If he was surprised by my offer, he didn't show it. As elegant as always, he swept his duffel bag off the ground, stuffed the brick-phone inside, then slung it over his shoulder.

The stairwell echoed with our footsteps. A couple stairs ahead of him, I cleared my throat. "So I take it you got in touch with Walker Hayles?"

"Yeah."

"And he's okay?"

When he didn't answer, I stopped on the landing and glanced at him over my shoulder. Emotions flickered behind his dark brown eyes, ones that made my chest ache. Was Walker not okay? Had something else happened after we'd parted ways? I'd made light of how resourceful he was when Landon had found me, but I would have done more for Emerson's captives if I could have.

Besides, those captives were both beasts. Wouldn't they have been able to survive in the wilderness indefinitely if they had to?

They'd already gotten their collars off and could change into their animals.

I turned away from his intense stare and punched the code into the keypad. The heavy metal door clicked open, and we found Alina and Marley waiting on the other side. The former had donned a gun-belt over the dress she hadn't been wearing when I'd left to retrieve Landon. She always did like to make a statement—fashion and otherwise.

"Oh hey, Lover Boy," Alina said, her voice chipper. "Nice to see you again. We're going to inspect your bag for trackers, et cetera." She held out her hand. "Fun trick finding us. Like to explain that one?"

"Not especially," he replied, reluctantly handing over the duffel. "Am I going to get that back?"

"The bag?" Marley asked. "Sure. Just not sure about us returning any of the fun stuff you have hiding inside."

"I could use another set of bolt cutters," Alina interjected, dropping the bag on the table beside our laptops.

"And I could use whatever the thing was you hacked my keypad with," Marley added.

He scratched the bridge of his nose. "It's in the prototype phase, a bit bulky."

"For a prototype, it worked fucking well," Marley muttered, her brow furrowed as she held it in her hand, turning it over. "I can't tell you how many safeguards I put in our doors, and it was like you had ten mini hackers in here or something."

"I'll need that back," Landon said, his voice firm.

"No problem," Marley responded without missing a beat. "Just expect it in pieces." And off she went to her cockpit, blocky brick-phone in hand.

He closed his eyes briefly, before focusing on Alina.

"Write it off, Lover Boy." She slung the bag over her shoulder before following Marley. "Isn't that what you CEO types are best at?" she called, then disappeared into her armory.

From his irritated expression, he'd been insulted.

"Pay them no mind," I offered. "They don't know you."

He turned to me then. "And you do?"

The dig hit where it was supposed to, right in the gut. Trying to cover the hurt, I tipped my head in acknowledgment. "I thought I used to. But you're right, I don't anymore."

He exhaled, closing his eyes for a moment. "That was uncalled for. I'm sorry." The apology in his eyes seemed genuine.

Every part of me froze. Landon *fucking* Urick apologized to me? I didn't know what to do...or say.

So I did nothing, just stared at him and blinked.

"Actually," he went on, "I need to apologize for what I said to you yesterday as well. I was out of line."

It felt like I was in one of those moments in a movie where the person came closer to the screen, but the background went further away. None of this could be real. "What happened? Why are you saying these things?"

The questions seemed to startle him. "Don't you understand what groveling is?"

I narrowed my eyes. "I know what groveling is, and I'm pretty sure we haven't reached that level yet."

His mouth quirked up in the corner and my heart stopped altogether.

Landon was joking and smiling at me. What the hell was happening? I didn't know how to handle it. I could take the anger, I deserved it, but this lighter version of him? It reminded me of the way we'd been together. It hurt too much.

I watched him as he walked around our living room, then circled the dining table.

"Will you answer a few questions?" he asked, scanning the laptops we'd left there, though they'd gone to sleep mode in their disuse.

My world more askew than it was before he arrived, I considered him as he prowled, taking in our living space in a way he hadn't when he'd been here yesterday. "It depends on the questions, I suppose." But after all the lies I'd told for my brother, all the subterfuge, and how he controlled my life, I didn't want to deceive Landon anymore. I didn't want to fight him.

"Ask your questions," I said, moving away from him to the coffee cart against the wall. "But I'm going to need some fresh coffee. I didn't get a lot of sleep last night." Or any at all, really.

He raised an eyebrow, but allowed me to start the coffee maker. "Do you want some?" I asked.

At first if looked like he would refuse, then he nodded, leaning against the concrete wall beside the cart and crossing his arms over his chest. My skin prickled as he watched me go through the motions of filling the reusable filter with grounds, and adding water to the machine. I pressed the on button and turned to him, trying not to react to the intensity of his gaze.

"Still take it black?"

He nodded.

A corner of my mouth turned up. "See, I know you a little bit."

His eyes narrowed, but they held a twinkle too. I cleared my throat and selected two mugs from the shelf of the cart. "How's the shoulder?"

"Fine."

His response was a little too fast, too clipped. I side-eyed him. "You seem to have full mobility." Which was, honestly, very weird. Gunshot wounds weren't an easy fix. He should have his arm in a sling and be stiff for days, if not weeks. "Did you get it checked out?"

"It's fine," he said again. "And you're supposed to be answering my questions, not the other way around."

I focused on the bubbling of the machine in front of me. "I said you could ask your questions." As painful as it would be to answer them. Some things between us I never wanted to revisit again, but I'd do it if it would give him peace. If it made up for some of the shit I'd done. And I was tired, so utterly exhausted, of bottling everything up inside.

There was a time when we were together, I'd thought about confessing everything to him, of revealing the control my brother had over me. Being with Landon was the first time I'd ever felt I had someone in my corner. I'd felt special when I was with him, cherished, and I'd been unable to embrace it.

With this mission to bring Emerson down, came the freedom to live how I wanted. Whatever Landon asked me, I'd answer truthfully.

"How involved were you in Walker's torture and Sabrina's kidnapping? She was the woman he escaped with."

My stomach clenched—the woman he'd asked about earlier. I hadn't known her name, only a number on her cage: eighty-seven. When I'd first seen her, grubby in a torn shirt and jeans, feet bare, I'd almost puked. I'd wanted to let her out right then. But if I'd done that, if my brother realized I wasn't on board with his plans anymore, it would have blown everything apart. I would have never been able to download the contents of his computer and plant the virus allowing Marley access to his server—what we'd planned to do at the MBI building as well. And I definitely wouldn't have been able to help the woman, or anyone else, if our plans had failed.

"I didn't have anything to do with their abductions," I started, not sure if he'd believe me. "I didn't know either of them were in Alaska until a few days before they escaped."

"But you knew they were there and didn't release them."

I shook my head. "At the time, I couldn't." A deep breath made the tension in my neck loosen. "It would have ruined every-thing I'd put into motion. But," I hurried on before he could interrupt. "I did what I could as soon as possible."

"Which was leaving them to fend for themselves."

"Yes. I did that. I had to. There was no way I could bring them with me." I tugged on one of my curls in frustration. "I had a two-seater plane waiting for me in a strip outside of Fairbanks, and only a limited time to get there. If I'd missed my ride, if Emerson had stopped me, everything I'd done would have been for nothing."

It wasn't the only reason I hadn't taken them with me. They were beasts and I didn't trust them, especially after what they'd gone through. Walker had almost shot off my head. I grimaced. "And I already promised myself I wouldn't lie to you, so yeah, their escape was also a good diversion for me to get away."

With the pot done brewing, I grabbed the handle and poured two mugs worth before returning it to the burner. I passed Landon his, meeting his gaze, expecting to see the same sort of anger as yesterday, but it seemed to have fizzled away. He gazed at me with a curious expression, like he was trying to figure me out.

What had Walker told him? "Are they okay?" I swallowed. I'd add the trauma they endured to the long list of all my other sins.

"Yeah," he said, turning away from me with his mug in his hand. "They survived."

There was a finality to his tone, like he wouldn't speak more of their welfare. Understanding I didn't deserve more than that, I took my own mug to the sofa where I flopped down on the thick cushion, a huffed sound exuding from the worn leather.

After a moment, Landon joined me, sitting in the armchair on the other side of the coffee table. Elbows resting on his knees, mug cradled between two hands, he met my gaze straight on. "Why is your brother doing this?"

Nausea swirled in my stomach, the band around my chest tightening. Here it was, time for the *big truth*. I prayed I was strong enough to get it all out. Closing my eyes, I tried to keep my voice level. "It's my fault. Everything my brother has done is because of me."

When I opened my eyes again, it was as though someone had hit the pause button. Landon sat motionless, his gaze fixed to mine.

"Tell me how it's your fault." His voice was quiet, calm, deceptively so.

"I saw all three of you that day." Questions flared in his eyes, and I hurried on before I chickened out. "Those bear attacks. I was seventeen at the time, and you'd already graduated. I was walking in the forest, heard a woman scream, then I saw—" I paused as images from the scene sprang fresh in my mind. As long as I lived, I'd never be able to forget. "I saw your friends change and attack that bear, one into a cougar, the other a grizzly."

The stillness hadn't left him, and I waited for him to speak, to comment, to say *something*. When he didn't, I finished with, "A grizzly and two people died that day."

"The grizzly deserved it," he spat, and I jumped slightly at the force behind it.

"After seeing what it had done to those hikers, I agree with you." I shivered, though it wasn't cold in here. "But I was seventeen, scared, and I ran home freaking out, crying. I told Emerson everything I'd seen. For once, he believed me, said he'd always known something was wrong with our town. Every decision he made after was to monitor, track, and contain people like your friends." Embarrassed by my pleading tone, that I was dying inside for him to understand, I gripped my coffee mug tighter, the heat too much for my skin, but I accepted the sting of it anyway.

Landon glanced away from me, his face ashen like he was going to be sick, his knuckles white on his mug.

This was it. This was the end of every possibility between us. I'd confessed my darkest sin and he'd be done with me. I inhaled a deep breath and held it.

Silence rang between us for long moments, then he met my gaze again. "You were young. It was years ago. You're not responsible for your brother's actions."

Such simple words, but they did something tremendous inside me. My chest felt like it had been cracked open, my innards spilling out onto the floor in sheer relief. I'd been so tightly wound, holding myself unnaturally rigid for so long, those words felt like forgiveness even if they weren't meant that way.

I couldn't speak, and stared at the mug clutched in my hands, trying to regain control of my emotions.

"Why did you want to work for me?"

I swallowed around the lump in my throat and lifted my head. "I never would have applied for the job if it wasn't my brother. Ever since we were kids, he's been dictating my life. It got worse after my mom passed away, and more so when my dad died." I took a deep breath, letting it out slowly. "But everything started, his…" I hesitated, trying to find the right word for it. "Obsession with people like your two friends, that day."

He glanced over his shoulder at where Marley and Alina had disappeared.

"I've told them everything," I said, predicting his question. "I've had to with what we're doing."

His expression hardened. "And have the three of you told anyone else?" The words were strained, like someone strangled him as he spoke.

"No," I said, and some of the tension leaked from his posture.

We stared at each other, only soft murmurs coming from down the hall. I appreciated my friends knowing I needed privacy for this.

"I'm sorry."

Landon's words made me twitch. I frowned. "You've already apologized for yesterday."

He lifted a hand and let it fall. "I'm sorry about what you said just now, about your brother controlling you when you were young and after that. It wasn't right. The adults in your life shouldn't have let it happen. The people around you should have seen the truth." His words left me raw while his eyes stared at me like he could see all of my faults. "*I* should have seen what was happening and done something."

"Why would you have?" Confusion made me shake my head.

His Adam's apple bobbed. "When you worked for me, I should have known something was off, that you were in danger. That he'd hurt you." His last words were tinged with the anger I'd seen yesterday, but this time paired with self-loathing.

I shook my head again, my brain not comprehending his statements. How could anyone have helped me with Emerson? It didn't make sense.

My heart throbbed uncomfortably in my chest, my throat tight. I didn't want to talk about this. "Are you done with your questions?"

Blinking, he took a sip of his coffee before meeting my gaze again. "What was the point of working for me?"

I licked my lips, my toe tapping on the floor. I set my mug on the coffee table. "Like I said, Emerson kept tabs on the beasts who left Goldenlach Ridge."

He winced. "Shifters. They're called shifters."

Shifters. "Right. Okay. That makes sense." I nodded, enjoying the fact I had a proper name for these types of people instead of the one Emerson thought up. "He liked to keep tabs on the shifters, and you were the only connection to two of them."

"Are the people in Goldenlach Ridge in danger from him?" he asked before I was done speaking.

He probably knew more of them living there. "Not in an immediate way." I scrunched up my face. "He has always been more concerned over those who've left town and those he finds in the world on their own, especially if they're in an important position." I grabbed my mug again and took a sip. "Ever since I told him of their existence, he's been able to tell who were beas—I mean shifters—and who were not just by looking at them. I don't understand it really. It doesn't make sense to me, but he's never wrong."

His expression turned contemplative. "Why the collar? With

everything you could have stolen from me, why did you pick the plans for the collar?"

I rubbed the space between my eyebrows, an ache forming. "I couldn't take it anymore. I couldn't be with you and lie to you about why I was there day after day. I lo—" I stopped talking and averted my gaze while my cheeks burned. "I cared about you too much. I'd become dead inside."

Meeting his gaze again, I continued, hoping he hadn't noticed my almost-confession, the words I'd refused to utter when we'd been together because of my deception. "You weren't giving up your friends' locations which was something Emerson really wanted. So I needed to give my brother something that would satisfy him, something which would fulfill my purpose. Because I had to get out." I breathed in through my nose and let it out slowly. "When I found out you were working on projects not on the regular books, I figured it was my chance. I broke into the secondary lab using a keycard I'd stolen from you, and downloaded what I could from a computer."

His expression turned steely during my explanation, but I pressed on. "And it was enough. My brother cut me loose and I went into the military soon after."

Landon rubbed a hand over his face, and shook his head in disbelief. "Why the military?"

"It was another of my brother's edicts." I pressed my lips together and forged ahead. "After stealing from you, he knew I should lay low for a while because you had almost as many resources as he did. He also wanted me to keep tabs on Hayles, though it was rather hard to do when he'd been sent overseas and my battalion remained in Canada."

I noticed the way he tensed at his friend's name, but I kept going. "Emerson thought basic training would be a great learning experience for me. I'd toughen up, turn into one of his enforcer-type people. He was always telling me how weak I was, and this seemed like the perfect solution to him."

"Did it work?"

I let out a harsh laugh. "No. It was the first time I'd been out from under my brother's thumb. Working for you, there'd always been the weekly check-ins, the reminders of *why* I was doing what I was doing. He used my fear, said shifters would hurt us if they knew we'd learned about them."

Landon twitched in his seat, but didn't say anything. I kept going. "I was never allowed to forget my purpose. But with the military, he didn't have control anymore. I wasn't force-fed whatever ideology he wanted me to believe. I realized I had to bring him down."

Landon's eyes never wavered from mine.

"And your two friends? How did you meet?"

"Marley enlisted the same year I did. We were together in basic training, then posted at the same base after, even though she was a cyber operator and I was in the infantry—another of my brother's demands. We met Alina when we had American-Canadian cooperative training exercises. They've been together ever since. My friendship with those two was one thing Emerson couldn't take from me."

"They're lucky to have you as a friend."

"Ha!" The bark came out of me unbidden. "No, they're not. I've signed them up for a life on the run, or worse, if we fail. They should have never agreed to help me."

"They love you."

My stomach flipped. "And I love them, but I don't deserve them."

"You deserve more in this life than you've been allowed, Jolyn." My chest twinged. I would have tried to brush off the comment, but then he asked, "Why are you being so open with me now?"

"What have I got to lose?" I'd lost everything already thanks to my brother: my autonomy, my integrity, and the one person I'd loved. The only thing I had left was my life, and I knew my brother wanted that too.

"Are you happy?"

My stomach twitched. Of all the questions he could have asked after what I'd already told him, he went with that one?

"What is happy?" But I knew. I'd been happy once. With him.

Landon stared at me like he had more to say, but didn't know how to voice the words. I waited, watching him sort through his thoughts.

"We've found something," Marley called from the cockpit, breaking our silent standoff. "You better come in here."

14

LANDON

I PRESSED HER HANDS TO THE WALL, MY BEAR REVELING IN THE *submissive position, and breathed in the vanilla scent at the base of her throat.*

"God, the things you do to me," I groaned against her skin.

Leaning away, I lifted the gray business skirt upward, then stilled. A black lace thong and matching garter belt held up her stockings—I'd died and gone to heaven.

"Did you wear these for me?"

She nodded, her breaths leaving in short bursts. I stroked the blade of my hand over the slip of silk between her legs, her thighs shaking in need. "I love it. You're so damn sexy."

I wanted to tie her up and make her scream with pleasure—but we weren't there yet.

Soon.

Marley's voice came from the tricked-out room full of monitors, startling us out of our staring contest. Our eyes locked on one another, Jolyn and I stood at the same time, the coffee table separating us.

My heart pounded with everything she'd told me. I'd understood she knew about shifters after talking to Walker last night, but having heard her story, of why this was all happening, tilted my whole reality.

I wracked my brain for what else besides the collar would have been on the download she'd stolen. I'd set up that secondary lab for shifters on my staff to work on shifter-related tech. The collar was shifter-specific, but other projects were shifter-inspired. A human working on them would have asked too many questions. Later, I hadn't needed the second lab. We'd made leaps and bounds in the tech community, and any new development from Urick Enterprises was seen as unique innovation, well-padded from anything pointing directly to my kind— like the shifter-proof comm she'd been using earlier. How she'd gotten in and out of a lab run by shifters without being detected was the real miracle.

She'd said her brother knew who shifters were just by looking at them. How was that possible? Had it been a lie to control her? Or was there truth behind the statement? Wouldn't he have told her that I, too, was a shifter before she came to work for me?

From the way she spoke, she remained ignorant. *A blessing or a curse?* Because after all she'd revealed, all her honesty, I was still lying to her.

Even though I'd moved away from Goldenlach Ridge after I'd graduated for school, I'd heard through my mother, or one of her friends, that Jolyn had stopped attending school in favor of tutors her senior year, something about the public system not being good enough for her. Now I understood the truth. It had been because of what she'd witnessed in that forest that day. My heart ached for her.

That day was one of the most tragic of my life. I remembered seeing a flash of color in the trees right after Kane had attacked

Tom, the other grizzly shifter. It must have been her, but I hadn't scented anyone, and there'd been so much going on at the time, I hadn't thought of it further.

Tom had been attacking hikers all spring. No one had known it was him until we'd stumbled across him and his kills. In the chaos of the scene, Kane killed Tom, trampling the already-dead woman in the confusion, and later thinking it was his fault she was dead because he'd once again lost his sense of self.

If that day hadn't happened, Kane, Walker, and I might have been in completely different situations: Walker using his spot-on intuition to do business at my side, and Kane in the development room with his designs instead of hiding away from society. My plan from the time I was fifteen was for the three of us to work together. While we were walking in the woods that day, Walker told us about his plan to join the military. I'd been about to tell him to come to Vancouver with me, to join me in business instead, when we'd heard those screams.

I straightened my shoulders. Jolyn may have set everything in motion, but she wasn't responsible for her brother's actions. She'd been a victim too, and for longer than I'd understood before today. All the time she'd worked for me, I should have realized, and it made me sick to my stomach that I could have done something—that scent of nerves that always hung around her. But she'd *seemed* happy. Now she admitted she didn't know the definition of the word. My chest squeezed painfully.

"Jolyn?" Marley called, and the name made us move.

We found Jolyn's friends sitting side by side in front of four monitors, a bunch of digital file folders on one screen. The fresh paint smell was stronger here than anywhere else, mixing with the ozone from the computers. The pair glanced at me, then Jolyn.

"Do you want him in here?" Marley asked. "It's sensitive stuff."

I prepared to argue my case, but before I could speak, Jolyn nodded.

Marley turned to her screens. "Two big things. One, I found another property in the area. A bottling plant. I need to do some more research, but I think we should check it out. And two, I cracked a bunch of files marked with the name we found earlier, BDX-32. There's a shit ton of stuff about it in our newly acquired intel."

"Like what?" Jolyn asked, gripping the back of Marley's chair while I leaned against the wall so I could see all the monitors at once.

"A lot of sciencey stuff, like what sort of hoops a person would have to go through inventing a new drug and getting it approved by the FDA."

"Sounds like something my brother would have a hand in."

"Exactly." Marley tipped her head at the screen full of file names. "Then I found ones labeled Test Trials. This one has a time stamp from about six months ago."

A grainy video popped up on the middle monitor. It showed a small room, only a bed inside. On the bed sat a woman, her arms wrapped around her shins, her head bent over her knees, wearing a hospital-gown-type of garment. A tray slid under the door with a plate of food and a glass of water. Apprehension rose in my stomach as we all watched her stand, crouch beside the food, and eat.

A heaviness entered my chest. From the way she glanced cautiously at the door every few seconds, it was obvious she was being held against her will and possibly abused. The urge to stop watching overwhelmed me. Deep down I knew something bad was about to happen.

Then it did. She screamed and clutched at her belly as if in pain. She rolled on the floor, kicking her legs. Her body spouted fur, her muscles taking on a different form, until a doe took the place of the woman. Only, this animal didn't have the same vitality. It lay unmoving.

My heart pounded. I waited for the doe to get up, but she

never did. After about a minute of utter stillness, two orderlies came into the room and dragged her out by the hind legs. The video froze on the image of an empty cell, the contents of the tray strewn across the floor.

Bile rose in my throat, the images sinking in. They'd labeled those Test Trials? How many others had experienced the same fate? This could have happened to Walker and Sabrina if they'd been fed a different meal?

Every part of me shook. "Do you recognize this place?" I asked Jolyn, unable to keep the rage out of my tone.

Face pale, her freckles standing out in sharp contrast, she shook her head. "I can't tell from the one room, but if I had to guess, it was where we were last night, where we got these files. It doesn't look like the place in Alaska." She glanced at Alina. "What do you think?"

"Yeah, it could be that warehouse." Alina focused on me. "As soon as we found the offices, we didn't go any further, trying to be quick."

If felt like someone took hold of my chest and squeezed. "What warehouse?"

"We infiltrated one of Emerson's properties a little way outside Detroit to get these files."

My heart jolted. Was this the place Walker had warned me about? If that was the case...I glared hard at all three of them. "That was incredibly dangerous."

They all stared at me with varying degrees of confusion. "You know we were all in the military, right?" Alina asked with her head tipped to the side. "We're trained soldiers. This isn't our first rodeo."

Right. Trained soldiers. But so was Walker, and look what happened to him. Plus, all three of them were human and didn't have the increased speed and heightened senses of a shifter.

I stared at the empty cell on the screen, now paused and flickering. The anger I'd held for Jolyn yesterday had been

completely replaced by fury for the murdered shifter. I ran a
hand over my face, trying to wipe away the death of a defense-
less woman. I needed to get the word out about this BDX-32
stuff.

What if there were still shifters at the warehouse? They could
be dying right this very second.

"I have to talk to Walker, get him to tell Clyborne about this,"
I murmured, grabbing my phone out of my back pocket.

All three women straightened like meerkats who'd heard a
loud noise.

"Did you say Clyborne?" Alina asked.

"Like, as in Clyborne Inc.?" Marley added.

Finger hovering over Walker's number, I narrowed my eyes.
"What do you know about them?"

"We applied there about a year ago," Marley replied, a frown
pinching her brow. "But never heard back. They didn't even give
us an interview when we'd obviously be kick-ass additions to
their crew."

"I applied a second time and same thing," Alina said. "Radio
silence."

"What?" Marley turned to her with a jump. "And you didn't
tell me?"

"Well, I thought if I got an interview, then I'd make sure you'd
get one too."

I crossed my arms over my chest. Walker's whole former team
was employed there, all shifters specializing in covert operations.
"What do you know about the company?" How far did their
knowledge of shifters go?

"They do private security mostly," Marley said, pulling up
Clyborne's official website on one of the screens. Its blue-and-
white-feathered logo took up the center portion of the top
banner, the services the company provided underneath, with
customer testimonials at the bottom of the page. "Anyone who
was anyone in the military got a job there after serving. I've only

ever heard positive things from the employees: full benefits, pensions, living stipend."

Alina shivered beside her. "Talking about it gets me all tingly inside."

I glanced over at Jolyn who'd stayed quiet through her friends' exchange. "And you? Did you want to work there too?"

She shook her head. "I've never been able to look past this job, of bringing my brother down. There's no way I could work at a place like that when he has so much control over me. And now he's trying to silence me, so..." Her explanation tapered off.

Marley reached up to place her hand over Jolyn's. "But once we expose what he's doing to beasts—"

"Shifters," Jolyn interjected.

My chest warmed pleasantly at her correction.

"—then he'll go to prison," Marley finished. "He won't have control over you anymore."

A spike of instinctual fear sliced through my stomach. I held up a hand. "Wait. No. You can't expose what he's been doing to shifters. You can't endanger them like that. There would be others who'd take his place, experimenting and trying to control them." It felt strange not to include myself in their number, but my instincts told me to keep my true nature hidden, even if I was starting to trust these women the longer I spent in their presence.

They all stood there, their jaws slack as they stared at me. Then Alina nodded. "You're right. We didn't think of that."

Marley's brow furrowed. "It makes things more difficult." She glanced over at Jolyn. "How do we make our plan work if we can't expose what he's been doing?"

Her lip caught between her teeth, she stared at me. "I don't know. Part of Emerson's power is how he works in both the shadows and the light. I wanted to expose his shadows to the world, then he'd have nothing to hide behind anymore."

"Sunlight disinfects," Marley murmured, almost to herself.

Alina nodded. "We'd lined up a bunch of media contacts, so

when we got the proof we needed, it would hit the air all at once, all over the world." She leaned back, her chair squeaking beneath her.

If it weren't for the shifter element, the plan would have been a good one. Thank God I'd used my lingering scent from the walk yesterday to return here before this trio put the final part of their plan into action. They might not have been as cruel as Mahn, but the results of their efforts would have been just as damaging.

I rubbed my knuckles against my jaw, thinking. "We might not have all the answers on how to proceed, but we can focus on what we do know. I need to call Walker, tell him about the drug and what we saw on the video." I clenched my hand tight around my phone at the memory of the doe dying in pain. "If it's not where Clyborne planned on heading, it should be. Can I have the coordinates?" I asked Marley.

She nodded, and pulled them up on the screen.

I called Walker. He picked up on the first ring. "Hey, man. Where are you?"

"I had some things to take care of," I replied, wincing when I realized I was keeping information from him.

All three women shared similarly nervous expressions, like they expected me to tell him about this converted warehouse after Jolyn had specifically told me not to. I wouldn't break her trust in me when we'd just begun to mend it. "Look, I've come across some information your friends should have." I quickly gave him the rundown about BDX-32, the video we'd seen, and the coordinates of the warehouse.

Walker cursed. "Yeah, this is something my old team will want to know about. And it definitely sounds like the place where they picked me up. Fuck, Landon. How did you learn about this?"

"That's not important right now."

"Bullshit. But I won't press. Gotta call Lavigne." He hung up and I slid my phone into my pocket. Lavigne had been the head of his special ops team, and I suspected he had a similar position at Clyborne's.

Jolyn stared at me, a speculative gleam in her eyes. "You didn't rat us out."

I shrugged. "Maybe it's because all three of you are right here, and would beat the crap out of me if I had."

Her expression didn't change. "I don't think that's it."

"And what had you said about another property?" I asked, changing the subject and looking at Marley. "A bottling plant?"

"Yeah." She tapped on the screen. "Southwest of here, beyond Belleville." A red marker appeared on her screen surrounded by foliage and nothing else.

I leaned closer. "What do you know about it?"

"Not that much. I found some invoices and some emails mentioning the place. It seemed all very hush-hush, which of course made me dig more. It's too far to send the drone from here."

It could be another place where shifters were being tortured. "We should go check it out."

"We?" Jolyn asked, turning her shoulders toward me.

I nodded. "We could see if it appears active, and call the experts if we find anything." I wasn't going to ask Walker to go check it out, not if it ended up being a wild goose chase. He was safe right now with his new mate and I wanted to keep it that way.

And Clyborne would be busy with the other warehouse. "We need to find out what's happening there, the sooner the better. We do the footwork for Clyborne Inc. while they're busy, and find out if it's another experimentation site."

The three of them all remained silent, staring at me with varying degrees of doubt, when Jolyn finally said, "No offense, but you should probably sit this out."

"How do you figure that?"

"We," she said, circling her arm to encompass her two friends, "are military trained. "You"—she actually pointed at me so I wouldn't misunderstand—"are not. A reconnaissance mission isn't any place for an injured CEO." She held up her hand when I tried to speak. "I know you work out and keep fit, but this isn't a run in Stanley Park. This is basically a military operation. It's best to leave it to the professionals."

I pressed my lips together before saying, "I'm not as useless as you think I am." My shifter senses would be an asset.

"I didn't say you were useless, I said you were recently shot and weren't trained for something like this."

"Fine, I'm not," I admitted, ignoring her first statement but giving her the second. "But I'm also serious about coming along."

At a stalemate, we stared at each other, neither of us giving in. I could tell she wished to say more, to argue, but there was hesitancy too, like she didn't want to fight me. I wasn't too proud to admit I'd use that to make sure I got my way in this scenario.

Alina leaned closer to Marley and loudly whispered, "Is it just me or are they arguing with their eyeballs?"

Her fist on her chin, Marley hummed a sound of agreement.

15

JOLYN

The back door burst open and Emerson staggered inside. I jumped up from my place at the kitchen counter, trying to catch him before he fell. Blood dripped down his face, a huge scratch near his ear.

"What happened?" I asked, leading him to my stool.

"It attacked me. One of the beasts."

"Who?"

He shook his head, not answering as I passed him a glass of water. "We can't stay here anymore. Dad wants us in Toronto anyway."

I blinked, not wanting to process that right now. "But what about the beast? What happened? I thought you went duck hunting with Cory."

He looked me straight in the eyes. "As soon as they understand you know what they are, they'll try to kill you."

I was pretty sure I should be worrying. Taking Landon on this op was a bad idea to begin with, especially when I knew Emerson was in Detroit, but he wouldn't be talked out of it.

Alina, Marley, and I stood by the freight elevator, waiting.

Each of us wore full tactical gear: black bulletproof vests, helmets, night vision goggles, and utility belts chock-full of useful objects. My Glock was in the holster at my hip, and I held a M4 carbine in front of me, the strap over my shoulder. I'd corralled my hair into a ponytail as best I could.

I didn't know why any of us had agreed to take him along. Sure, he was a tall, fit guy, but he wasn't military trained, and Emerson's goons liked to carry big guns. I'd already gotten Landon shot once for fuck's sake.

How was he so mobile after his gunshot wound? The idea of ripping off his shirt to examine it more closely had crossed my mind. *For health reasons only.*

The longer we waited, the more my stomach swirled with dread, making it impossible for me to stand still. I couldn't get the image of the woman transforming and dying in her doe form out of my head. My brother must be stopped, but I also didn't want Landon racing into danger.

Finally, after what seemed an hour, the man in question stepped into the hallway from my bedroom where I'd told him he could change. Marley let out a snort. Alina tittered.

None of us were close to his height. We had no extra clothing for him, and told him he couldn't come with us in a gray suit and glaringly white dress shirt. He'd said he had a change of clothes in his car.

But this...he wore one of his expensive black silk shirts, matching dress pants, and what looked like brand-new loafers. I shouldn't have been surprised. When we were together, I'd rarely seen him in anything other than business attire.

The icing on the cake had to be the Kevlar vest. The way it fit over top of his shirt made the sleeves billow out a bit, lending him a pirate-like appearance.

"This is what you're wearing?" Alina gasped like she was trying not to laugh outright. "A black suit? We're not off to a funeral."

"I was told to wear all black. This is what I have that's all black." He glanced at his feet. "I'm even wearing my new shoes."

"Yeah, shiny as fuck too," Marley grumbled.

He narrowed his eyes at her. "You might laugh, but this is the kind of clothing I'm most comfortable in."

"It's true," I agreed. "He wore loafers as a kid in gym class."

He gave me an odd look. "And here I'd thought you only had eyes for Kane when we were young."

My cheeks heated. "Trust me, the only kid in loafers in the whole school is kind of noticeable no matter who I had a crush on."

That shut him up. He pressed his lips in a straight line.

"This is for you," Alina said, passing him a Glock grip first.

He shook his head, holding his hands up instead of taking it. "I'd rather not."

All three of us froze, matching tension in our bodies. We probably wore the same expressions of shock too.

It was Marley who managed to speak first. "You're coming with us to infiltrate a property with potential hostiles but won't take a gun?"

He tightened the fastenings of his Kevlar vest. "It didn't go well last time."

All three of us stared at where he'd been shot. I glanced at Marley and she narrowed her eyes at me. None of us could explain how quick his recovery seemed. It didn't even look like he wore a bandage under his shirt.

A creeping awareness crawled up my nape, my intuition telling me something was off. I didn't have time to explore the sensation because Alina was handing him a helmet, goggles, and a comm while Marley ushered us all into the freight elevator.

Together, Alina and I closed the outer heavy door, then the inner gate. When Marley hit the down button, the car clanked, then began to move. All that was missing was the canned music to make it awkward as hell. Alina kept glancing at Landon's billowing sleeves out of the corner of her eyes, biting her lip to keep from laughing. Even Marley's mouth was twitching. I shook my head at them both.

Landon took it all like a champ. He'd never cared about what people said about him in school, and I didn't think he cared now. He was who he was. Maybe the one person I could say who seemed a hundred-percent comfortable in his own skin. What you saw was what you got.

The elevator rumbled and creaked to a stop. Marley opened the two metal doors, and we all stepped out into the garage. The space mimicked the size of the warehouse above, and was honestly too big for our uses. Alina's Fiat sat up on blocks while she fixed it, and we'd parked the van near the elevator doors. Otherwise, it housed a lot of the unused renovation supplies we'd stored and some forgotten items from previous owners who'd bought it as a storage facility for their staging business.

Marley clicked the key fob. The Mercedes van blinked at us under the flickering fluorescents. Opening the door, she hopped into the driver's seat, Alina taking the passenger side, which left the bench in the back for Landon and me.

It was a tight squeeze. Normally meant only for one person, the space pressed us against each other. My whole side fired up being in contact with his, especially where the Kevlar didn't cover: my shoulder, arm, and hip.

The engine purred. Marley shifted into drive and headed toward the garage door.

Landon jerked his chin toward the other side of the van. "I'm seeing a lot of Urick Enterprises' tech in front of me."

Alina turned. "We're fans. Good quality at competitive prices."

"Not another advertisement," I grumbled.

"It's the truth," Marley added over her shoulder, the garage door rising in front of us.

I narrowed my eyes at them both and muttered, "Ass kissers," under my breath, which I'm pretty sure Landon heard because he raised an eyebrow.

The van jerked forward. Marley drove up the ramp, then turned right into the darkened road beyond. There weren't a lot of working streetlights on this stretch of road. With the next left turn, the motion pushed me against Landon. My heart sped up at the contact. Was he as aware of me as I was of him?

A slight turn of his body, and suddenly, I was plastered more to his side. I squinted up at him, gauging whether he'd done it on purpose or not. He faced the surveillance equipment, not looking at me, the helmet and goggles Alina had given him clutched in his hands.

"Are you sure you want to do this?" I asked, keeping my voice as quiet as possible so the other two wouldn't butt into the conversation.

He turned, met my gaze, and nodded once. "I sent Walker to do my dirty work, and it was a mistake. I need to do this."

I didn't have the chance to ask him to clarify, because Alina leaned forward, touched the dial for the radio, and rap music began to pump through the sound system.

We left Metro Detroit behind. Our headlights cut a path in the darkness, the oncoming traffic becoming sparser the further we drove. Landon leaned his head against the wall of the van. From all appearances, he rested his eyes, but the movement pressed his side even tighter against mine.

I didn't move away.

God, this was nuts. A few days ago, Landon had been the greatest regret of my life, and now he sat beside me about to embark on a reconnaissance mission.

I let out a slow breath, sinking into the heat of his body. He'd always felt like his own personal furnace, no matter how chilled I'd been. The memory of us cuddling on a sofa watching TV gave me comfort—a warmth to offset the coldness of reality.

Whatever my brother's goals for me working for Landon had

been, there were many good moments, ones I'd taken out like cherished heirlooms and held close to my heart when things got rough. Those first weeks in basic training, the intensity of it compared to the fake life I'd built with Landon, were almost too hard to bear. I'd used those memories to combat harsh military life. But even the good memories weren't enough sometimes.

Thank God for Marley. She saved me from myself too many times to count, knew I was hurting, but never asked for the details.

I turned my head to stare out the front windshield. We passed under a green traffic light and kept going, trees and houses lining the darkened road. It must have rained recently, because the occasional puddle splashed under the tires.

The closer we got to the bottling plant, the more my veins buzzed with the need to move. I might have appeared calm on the outside, but my insides tingled in excitement. Before I joined the army, I wouldn't have considered myself a thrill seeker. Now the pre-mission adrenaline rush was almost addictive.

I guessed Emerson had gotten his way in that regard. He'd sent me to the military to toughen me up, and I had. Now I could take a stressful situation, piece it apart, and keep my head level. My mind went back to our recent op. *Most of the time.*

But with Landon at my side, my focus was split. I didn't want anything to happen to him. Hell, he'd even refused a gun. Instead of centering all my thoughts on what lay ahead, I was concentrating on the man beside me and hoping he came out of this unharmed. And all of those distracting thoughts were detrimental to the mission.

Pushing my internal battle aside, I stared at the surveillance equipment in front of me, ignoring Landon's sharp eyes on my face.

We stayed that way for a long time. The rap music changed from one song to another, ads after that with the DJ cutting in to talk about a music event happening on the weekend. I would have preferred silence, but knew Alina needed the noise to quiet her mind.

After many more songs, Marley took a right off the main highway, then another left. When we arrived at the coordinates we'd preselected, she pulled over to the side of the road in amongst trees, and put it in park.

Alina turned off the radio. "Everyone ready?"

With a nod, I pushed to my feet, my neck bent so I wouldn't hit the roof of the van. Scooting past Landon's knees, I opened the back door, then hopped out with him following.

I straightened, cracking the joints that had gone stiff during the ride, and surveyed my team. This was really a five-person operation, but since we didn't have a fifth, we would leave the van unoccupied in order to approach from two different sides in pairs.

Landon placed the helmet on his head, and if we'd been anywhere else, I might have given in to the chuckle wanting to leave my throat. He really did look ridiculous. Landon and special ops did *not* go together.

The thought sobered me more than anything.

Everyone adjusted their night vision goggles, and with a nod from Marley, we headed through the trees in the direction of the bottling plant, making sure to look out for motion detectors like we'd spotted at the other warehouse.

Moisture dotted the leaves and transferred drops of water to my arms and legs. With every step, I was aware of Landon right behind me. My heart beat in time with my footsteps. I stepped over a fallen log. Frogs jumped out of our way. The trees thinned.

A light rustling sound followed us as we all cleared the foliage. We paused. A building stretched out in the dark, the size of a football field. Everything was dark, not one light to say anyone was home. After giving Marley and Alina a quick glance, we continued forward, then crouched beside a chain-link fence.

Already my senses tingled in warning. I'd thought it would be more like the warehouse we'd infiltrated yesterday, but this place appeared abandoned, no one in sight.

I adjusted the settings on my goggles. No heat signatures lit up beyond the walls.

"Looks like everyone went home for the day," Marley whispered, her focus on the building.

"I guess that follows if it's actually a bottling plant. No one would be here after closing time." I just hadn't expected it to be what it said on paper. When my brother was involved, it always seemed something nefarious lay below the surface. Could this be a normal factory?

"We need to take a closer look," Landon said at my side.

I agreed, but didn't voice it, really wanting him to return to the van and stay out of harm's way.

"No sense sitting around and chatting about it," Alina said, taking the bolt cutters out of her pack to start on the fence.

"Are those mine?" Landon asked, his posture straightening.

Alina only grinned and made the first cut. The *click click* of each steel wire provided counterbalance to the crickets chirping behind us. After making a hole big enough, she returned the bolt cutters to her pack and bent the remaining wire aside.

I glanced at Marley and nodded. Silently, we crawled through the gap and stood. I only waited a second for Landon to get to his feet. Then I was off, jogging toward the north entrance, knowing my two friends went to the south.

Nothing moved. The whole place felt like it had been empty forever instead of since closing time. No one came out of the shadows. No one stopped us. We crossed a parking lot empty of cars, gravel crunching beneath our shoes.

Abreast of the front doors, I paused with my spine to the wall, Landon right beside me. After a deep, steady breath, I tested the door. Locked.

"Keep your eyes open," I said to Landon as I crouched in front of the door with the lock picker Marley had given me. I should have asked if it came from Urick Enterprises.

After a few seconds, the door clicked open. I waited for an alarm to blare, but nothing happened. My instincts buzzed, telling me to beware. I wanted to turn around and take Landon as far away from here as possible.

"We're in," Marley said quietly into the comm.

"Be careful," I murmured.

We slipped inside.

16

LANDON

"I GOT YOU SOMETHING."

Her head snapped up, eyes focusing on me. "You did?"

The light from the sunset made it look like her hair was on fire—an apt description for what she did to me inside. The wind tried to push us over, a usual thing for this bend of the beach in early spring. It would warm up soon.

I slipped my hand into my suit pocket, hesitating only a second before taking out the box and setting it in her hand.

"Why would you buy me something?" she asked, blinking at it.

"I had it made, actually."

She stared between me and the box. Finally, she lifted the lid. "Oh wow." Her eyes flicked up to me, her cheeks turning red, then gazed down at the pendant in the box. "This is beautiful." She lifted the chain. "A crescent moon. Thank you."

I opened my mouth to tell her it wasn't a moon, but a bear claw, then pressed my lips together.

Too soon.

The cement walls and doors sucked out all the light coming from narrow windows near the ceiling. I didn't turn on my night vision goggles, but shifted my eyes to see better, a far superior alternative. I should know, Urick Enterprises manufactured the ones Jolyn and her friends were using, the design attempting to duplicate a shifter's ability.

Scents swirled around me—human—nothing I would call fresh. I followed Jolyn, her body alert, eyes focused over the barrel of her assault rifle as she scanned every direction, clearing each room one at a time. I could tell from the lack of sounds and active scents we were alone in the building, but didn't think she'd take my word for it without a full explanation. And she'd probably want to clear the rooms her way even if she'd known about my talents.

We turned right. Jolyn placed her hand on the first doorknob and opened it. Once determining no people lay in wait, she stepped inside, then glanced at me over her shoulder—and did a double take. I backed off my eye-shift. She might be able to see the yellow reflection behind the lens of the goggles, and I had to remain aware of that. She didn't react further, and the tension left my shoulders.

Entering the office space, a sense of hurry swirled around us, like someone had left quickly. A desktop computer sat unplugged on top of a wood desk. Filing cabinet drawers were left partially open, half-filled with folders. A stack of files towered beside the computer, leaning precariously. Allowing her gun to hang off her shoulder, Jolyn reached for the top file.

I tensed at the sound of quiet feet on concrete. "Someone's coming," I said, placing a hand on her shoulder.

She flattened herself against the wall, and I did the same beside her. A tactical-clad woman stepped inside and lowered her weapon. Jolyn relaxed a fraction.

"We've cleared everything that way," Alina said with a jerk of her head, Marley right behind her. "This place is a ghost town."

I glanced at the women's formidable guns. Were they even legal?

"Find anything interesting?" Jolyn asked, pushing away from the wall.

"We walked through the factory area and it was attached to a lab," Marley said, then held out a strip of brightly colored labels. "They're bottling vitamin water. There aren't any bottles, though, just the labels. It's been cleared out."

Jolyn's gaze flicked up from the labels. "They looked to be moving out of that warehouse the other night, and now this place is deserted?"

Alina shrugged. "The timing could be coincidental."

"I don't believe in coincidences," I said, stepping forward to take the label from Marley. A stylized logo swept across the width —two *V*s mixed with a *W*: Vaunce Vitamin Water.

"I've heard of this stuff," I murmured, frowning. "A major cola company is doing a launch this week. They've been advertising nonstop."

"This factory isn't owned by that company." Marley propped her night vision goggles on her helmet, then bent down to plug in the computer. "It's owned by your brother," she said to Jolyn, striding to the door, then to all of us, "Light incoming."

The two other women took off their goggles, and I mimicked the action right before the lights turned on. We all squinted against the glare.

"Let's see if we can find more information in here," Jolyn said, returning to the stack of folders. "My brother has this place for a reason."

I joined her while Marley sat at the computer and Alina moved to the filing cabinets. Setting the label on the desk, I picked up the next folder—an employee roster dated from a year ago. The next was the same sort of thing. I kept digging.

"Here's a whole section marked SDX-42," Alina announced,

pulling out a thick folder from the middle cabinet. "The stuff we found earlier was BDX-32. Too similar to be unrelated."

Trepidation dried the inside of my mouth. I picked up the label again.

"And some FDA applications and correspondence for the same compound," Alina added, holding another thick folder.

I blinked at the label in my hand, shaking as I read the ingredient list. "It's in here."

"What?" Jolyn asked, lifting her head.

"That compound. The shifter-killing drug. It's in the vitamin water." It was right there, SDX-42, in amongst the monopotassium phosphates, folic acid, and natural flavors.

It's in the goddamn drink. I closed my eyes against the memory of the shifter dying a horrifically painful death. Instead of erasing the image, it changed her face to that of Kane, then Walker, then their mates. If this stuff got out into the world...

I opened my eyes, swallowing. Around me, all three women had frozen, the gravity of this situation sinking in.

Beneath the makeup Jolyn had used to darken her skin, she looked like she was about to be sick. "We need to stop him." She stared at the file she held, and around at the other cabinets full of information. "There's enough evidence here, along with what we've already cracked on the other server, to take my brother down."

"The FBI and FDA will need to be informed," Marley said, plugging a USB drive into the side port. "If people start dropping dead, they'll be investigating anyway. We could help them get the right information."

"Emerson will pay them off," Jolyn spat, her whole body vibrating with anger. I wanted to comfort her, but my own fingers were clenched around the label, mangling it.

"How can he pay them off with something so public?" Alina asked. "As soon as people start to die and they link it to the drink, it will get pulled from the shelves." She looked up from the folder she held and slid another one out of the filing cabinet. "I don't get it. What's his endgame? All of this for a few dead shifters?"

Shaking her head, she stared down at the folder open in her hand. "Hold on. What's this?" Her finger skimmed over the page. "This is a delivery schedule and these dates are current: today, tomorrow. Samples of Vaunce Vitamin Water are being delivered across the country."

"Not only the US," Jolyn said, turning the page in her hand so we could all see. "This says Toronto. Another says Tokyo." The paper crinkled as she set it aside. "This is a worldwide delivery schedule." She kept filing through the pages, her voice edged with panic.

My mind raced. This was a launch of a new product and they were taking it worldwide with free samples. Anyone who tested it was in danger, especially shifters. If they shifted and died as soon as they drank it, then it was mass genocide. This wasn't a few dead shifters. Countless people would die.

"He couldn't have supplied this many locations from this one site." Jolyn slammed the folder on the desk. "He must have other factories."

"Maybe not all of it has the SDX-42 in it." Alina glanced between all of us. "Maybe it's just some of the samples."

I shook my head. "We can't take that risk. We have to assume it's all tainted."

"Son of a bitch," Jolyn muttered, her eyes glued to another paper.

I stepped closer. "What?"

"One of the shipments is going to Goldenlach Ridge. It's set to arrive at the high school tomorrow."

"Fuck," Marley said, her voice barely above a whisper.

I couldn't speak. A school full of shifters. If they all drank the stuff, hundreds would die in that one location alone. Kids. "We need to stop that delivery."

I pulled out my phone from my back pocket and dialed my

mother's number. She could contact the town council, tell them of the danger. Except, the call wouldn't go through. No cell service.

It felt like someone had stabbed me in the chest with a knife. "Let's get out of here. I have to make some calls." Everyone I knew in Goldenlach Ridge was in danger. Walker needed to tell Clyborne Inc. They had connections with the FBI. But first, I had to stop the delivery to the high school.

Jolyn gave me a determined look. "We'll stop it."

I nodded once. "I know we will." I headed toward the door.

"I need ten seconds to finish this download." Marley tapped her fingers on the top of the desk.

"And what about all these files?" Alina asked. "We should take them with us so they stay safe."

"We'll let Clyborne figure that out." I strode into the hallway. "Let's worry about the immediate stuff first."

"Hold up, Lover Boy," Alina called out, hurrying ahead of me. "Let the professionals lead the way."

Swiping the USB out of the computer, Marley joined her a moment later, while Jolyn walked beside me. All three women resumed their tense postures as we hurried through the dark building, our footsteps echoing off the concrete walls.

"Do you know how many shifters live in Goldenlach Ridge?" Jolyn asked, keeping her gaze forward.

I sent her a quick glance. "You don't?"

She shook her head, scanning down the next hallway we passed. "My brother never told me. It was another way he exerted his control. He only said they were everywhere and I should never let my guard down."

What would be the point of concealing this from her after everything? She already knew about us. "About half the population are shifters."

Her footsteps faltered. "Half?" We stopped altogether, and Jolyn peered around the foyer of the building, like she might see a shifter lurking in the corners. Ironic, when there was one standing right in front of her. "Is half the population everywhere shifters?"

Ahead of us, Alina and Marley exited the building. We followed the pair, urgency in our steps. Crisp air surrounded us as the door closed with a *thunk*. "Half is pretty high for a human town as far as I've heard." Marley and Alina were already cresting the hill, and we followed, gravel crunching. "There are some purely shifter communities, but they usually like to stay hidden, isolated. Otherwise, it's shifters on their own, in small family groups. So no, not a lot of the population are shifters."

"How do you know so much about them?" she asked, Alina and Marley disappearing into the tree line.

I paused and turned toward her. If it weren't for the truckload of death heading toward Goldenlach Ridge at this very moment, this would have been the perfect opportunity to tell her what I was, to be honest with her. Even over the course of the day, her attitude toward my kind had softened. She and her friends wanted to help; they didn't want to expose us.

Continuing across the parking lot, I shrugged. "It pays to have friends with connections."

She was going to ask something else when gunshots resounded ahead of us.

Jolyn paused, her face a mask of dread. She spoke into her comm. "Marley. Where are you?"

There was no response, no crackle that the comm was on, or heavy breathing to indicate they heard us. The sick sensation in my stomach twisted and churned. What was happening?

I moved in the direction of the noise, but Jolyn put a hand on my arm, stopping me. "We don't know what's ahead and I don't want you running into bullets."

She was right. Of course she was right. I really did need to leave this clandestine shit to the professionals. I followed her as she skirted the parking lot, leaving my night vision goggles on my helmet. I saw better without them and couldn't waste time pretending.

The sound of an engine gunning it made us whip around. A van barreled down the drive toward the building, a truck following it.

"Titty fucker," Jolyn spat.

We were out in the open, sitting ducks.

The vehicles skidded to a stop near the door, two men in each, jumping out with a general sense of scrambling. They spotted us.

I had no time to think about what I was doing. I turned, snagged Jolyn around the waist, and used my shifter speed to hurry us into the cover of bushes near the fence-line of the property.

Setting her down, I crouched. Jolyn did the same. If she had felt anything different in me or my movements, she didn't speak of it, her focus entirely on the men fanning out to find us in the dark. Their shouts and more voices on their radios bounced off the walls of the building. These didn't look like the same kind of guys who'd fired at us on the freeway. These men wore jeans and T-shirts instead of tactical gear or suits—but they still had guns. Their scents came toward me on the breeze. All human.

"Alina," Jolyn pleaded. "Talk to me."

No response.

"Ideas?" I asked. The men headed our way, about to corner us. If we ran toward Alina and Marley, we'd be exposed. If we stayed here, we'd be dead. Heart pumping hard in my chest, I stared in the direction of where the other two women should be, but couldn't see anything through the trees.

Jolyn stared too, scanned the area with her night vision goggles. I hadn't been able to see anything, and I doubted she would either. She turned back to the factory. "The devil you know," she said under her breath, then reached up and took out her earpiece. "Turn off your comm. We don't know who's listening."

I followed the order, putting it in my pocket, when she added, "I'm giving you cover and we're taking one of their vehicles. Follow me."

Before I could tell her how unhinged the plan sounded with only the two of us, she stood, her gun held in front of her like she meant to fuck shit up.

And she did. Her first shots made the men coming in our direction dodge for cover. Jolyn let out a few more, then she was running through the bushes parallel to the bottling plant. I kept close behind her.

As soon as the building blocked our view of the men, she veered left, cutting across the yard toward the back. We circled it and kept sprinting toward the front on the other side.

If there had been more than those four guys, this never would have worked.

We stopped at the corner of the building. I could hear the men's voices close by—it didn't sound far enough. On the plus side, I could also hear a motor. They'd left one of their vehicles running in their hurry to find us.

Her weapon pointed ahead of her, Jolyn signaled me, holding up three fingers. She curled them down. *Three, two, one.*

She stepped around the corner of the building. *Ratatat.* Bullets blazed out of her gun. Clued in to our location, the men scrambled, trying to get out of the killing field while returning fire.

I ran toward the truck. The door nearly came off its hinges in my haste to open it. I jumped inside. More gunshots echoed—Jolyn aiming at the tires of the van—then she vaulted in beside me.

"Nice of them to leave it running for us," I said, putting it into reverse after securing my seatbelt. The engine roared as I stepped on the gas.

Her door banged shut. "Yes, yes." She buckled up. "No time for jokes. Just show me your driving skills."

Slamming the brakes, I shifted into first gear, and gravel sprayed behind us. *Tack tack tack.* We ducked. Bullets cracked the back window. It fragmented, pieces falling into the rear seat. Jolyn opened her window and returned fire before ducking down again.

My heart leaped into my throat every time she stuck out her neck to fire. If I got shot, I could shift and heal. She couldn't. I gritted my teeth instead of telling her to stay the hell down, but my bear roared, ready to protect. My skin itched with the need to shift and rip apart all who threatened her.

Another van turned onto the property ahead of us, then stopped, blocking the narrow gap of the gate.

"Keep driving," Jolyn shouted. Aiming forward, she fired out her window. The vehicle rocked, the people inside ducking. She might have hit a tire.

There was no way to get through without colliding into their van and slowing down or stopping completely, probably hurting Jolyn in the process. At the last second, I swerved, aiming for the next section of chain-link. The truck jerked and jolted. The airbags blew. I was blinded. The sound of scraping metal filled the cab, and in the next second, a puffing noise. Jolyn stabbed my airbag with her knife.

"Don't stop," she said, turning to fire at the other vehicle.

Tires squealed as I took a left onto the highway. *Twing twing twang.* More bullets hit the side of the truck.

I shifted my eyes and glimpsed the men scrambling around their vehicle in the rearview mirror. She definitely hit at least one tire.

"Nice shooting," I murmured, my heart racing with adrenaline and relief we'd gotten out of there alive.

"Nice driving." She shut the window and settled herself in her seat. "We need to find Marley and Alina."

I nodded, flooring it and keeping my concentration on the road ahead. The asphalt sucked any light from the surrounding area, making it impossible to see without my eyes shifted.

Jolyn reinserted her earpiece and I reached into my pocket to do the same. "Marley. You there?" Her voice was strained with worry above the roar of the wind coming in through the broken back window. "Alina?"

Tension crawled up my spine at the silence on the other end of the comm, my hands tightening on the wheel.

She turned, looking behind us. The road remained dark. Pieces of safety glass fell every few seconds. "Circle to where we parked. We need to find out what happened to them."

I didn't want to do it, just wanted to get Jolyn out of here and as far away from the guys with guns as possible. I also knew she wouldn't leave her friends behind. But what if more people waited for us? What if it was a trap?

The comm crackled, and I jumped from surprise.

"We're here. We're good." Alina's voice came over the line, and I breathed out a sigh of relief at the same time as Jolyn. "Two assholes were waiting for us at the van. We introduced ourselves."

"But you're both okay?"

"Yeah, we're on the road. Where should we pick you up?"

"We took one of their vehicles," she said, glancing at me. "You two need to return to base. We'll meet you there. I don't want to say more because this channel might not be secure."

"Understood."

The comm went silent, and Jolyn ran a hand over her face, smearing her dark makeup until freckles poked through. "We've got to ditch this truck as soon as possible. If those were my brother's guys, and that seems a certainty, it'll have a tracker on it."

"Yeah, okay. Makes sense." My thumbs tapped the steering wheel in agitation.

"Let's look for a Walmart, people always leave cars there. Or somewhere else we can change this for a different vehicle."

As the road behind us remained clear, the tension in my body released little by little. I slowed and took a right, heading north, then accelerated again. Turning on the headlights, I kept my eye on the speedometer, trying to keep close to the speed limit. Now wouldn't be the time to get stopped by cops.

I dug out my phone from my back pocket and passed it to her. "Tell me when we get service. I have to talk to Walker." And my mom.

She nodded, turning it on. "Nothing yet."

Rolling my shoulders, I removed my helmet and set it on the seat beside me. The wind from the back window chilled the sweat on my neck, but it felt good to be rid of the headgear. I glanced at Jolyn. She hadn't relaxed, her eyes darting all around, into the ditches of the road where the headlights bounced off trees and bushes and beyond, then behind us every few seconds.

The reality of what we'd survived sank into my bones. The adrenaline rush gave way to shaking fingers. I tightened my hands on the wheel. My bear was surprisingly quiet, probably the result of being safe for now. There'd been moments where I thought he'd take over completely.

And wouldn't that have been something—shifting into a grizzly while driving a truck. I couldn't think of a worse way to tell Jolyn about the other side of me.

Focusing on something else was probably wise. I cleared my throat. "You admitted to having a crush on Kane, earlier."

A huffy breath left her lips. "After what we went through you want to bring that up now?" She shook her head, like she wasn't going to admit to it, then said, "Big time."

I thought it was all she was going to say on it when she went on. "After he beat up Tom Akins for hitting me, I kind of idolized him." Her posture stiffened. "Until I saw him transform that day."

My stomach squeezed. This had been a bad question to ask. I wanted her to stop talking, but she kept going. "It's kind of like a violent splash of freezing water straight in the face to see

someone change into a bear." She let out an awkward chuckle. "I
never really understood it, how you could be friends with those
who had the potential to rip out your throat in a heartbeat."

The nausea in my stomach returned. She might be more
receptive to knowing there were shifters in the world, but it didn't
mean she'd left all her prejudices behind.

"But now," she added, "I don't know how it's any different
than regular people. Emerson doesn't blink when he hurts someone. Your friends probably aren't even close to the same as him."

"They aren't psychopaths, no." I couldn't say more, my throat
too tight. No matter how much I cared about Jolyn, I realized I
could never be completely honest with her about who I was. I
tried not to think about what that meant.

My heart aching, I pressed my lips together and took another
right, hoping we'd see that Walmart. The sooner we got rid of this
truck, the better. And we needed to make those calls.

Movement in the rearview mirror caught my attention. I stiffened, shifting my eyes again. *Bloody hell.* "I don't think we'll need
to ditch the truck."

Jolyn turned to me. "Why is that?"

"There's someone following us."

17

JOLYN

"You've finished your degree, now's the time to find a job."

"But at Urick Enterprises? It makes no sense. He'll know I'm there for you. He'll see right through me."

"Then it's your job to convince him otherwise." Emerson gripped my jaw between two fingers, forcing me to meet his eyes. "We need to learn how much he knows about these freaks. There will be something there, either in his personal or business life, for you to find. Keep your eyes and ears open."

I ripped my chin from his grasp. "I'm telling you, he won't hire me."

I turned around, but saw nothing behind us. "How do you know?"

"They have their lights off."

It didn't answer my question, but I wouldn't discount his words. If I didn't trust my teammates, then I shouldn't have gone on a mission with them.

And I did trust Landon, didn't I? After everything, he'd been nothing but solid today. I understood his earlier anger. That he'd been able to overlook what I'd done, *that* was the real mindfuck.

"We need to lose them," he said, putting more pressure on the gas pedal.

I nodded, glancing behind me, still not seeing what he was seeing.

"Any ideas?" he asked.

I faced forward, scrambling for what to do. There weren't any cars ahead of us. "We can't lead them back home." I turned in my seat again, but it was only blackness, highlighted red by the glow of our taillights. "I don't want to drive into any populated areas if they're going to start shooting at us."

"Won't they be more likely to shoot at us if we're in a less populated area?"

"It's a chance we'll have to take." I wouldn't add to the innocent blood I had on my hands.

The car jolted forward as Landon pressed the accelerator. I looked through the rear window again, but couldn't see anything, not even when a car going in the other direction lit up the highway. I glanced at him, wondering how he saw the tail. And earlier, when he'd scooped me up and ran to the tree line at the factory, he'd ran quicker than I'd ever thought possible. It may have been my adrenaline or his, but everything had seemed to move in fast-forward for a few seconds.

Another car appeared in front of us down the highway. Landon switched to his low beams but the other car didn't. It kept coming closer, the glare of its headlights blinding in the dark.

"Landon," I said between clenched teeth, a word of caution, alarm bells blaring in my head.

"Yeah." His hands tight on the steering wheel, he slowed our speed. Muscles flexed as he leaned forward like he was trying to see the vehicle better.

My instincts were spot-on. At the last moment, the car veered into our lane, a head-on collision imminent. A scream escaped my throat as Landon swerved to miss them. At our speed, the whole truck shuddered, rubber tires resisting the sharp turn.

Bang. The other vehicle hit, the force snapping me backward. Stars shot behind my eyelids, my temples throbbing. The world flipped. A crunch of metal, a spray of glass, then pain spiked through my shoulder and side. The airbags didn't go off—I'd already cut them away once.

The scent of burnt rubber surrounded me. That scraping sound continued, asphalt beside my face, through the window, the truck on its side as it skidded down the road.

Another *bang* came from all around us. Another hit. I thought I heard Marley in my ear, but couldn't be sure. The comm fell out as the car somersaulted. Weightlessness consumed me for a moment. Then my head and body pounded to the sound of more scraping and glass, followed by silence. The truck had settled upside down, my neck pressed against the ceiling, my body bent in half.

Twack twack twack twack. The noise of an automatic weapon being emptied into the front of the truck echoed inside the cab. It sounded like they aimed for the engine. Were they trying to blow us up?

The glare of another vehicle's headlights illuminated the cab. Disoriented, I searched for Landon, then realized my feet pressed against his chest.

"Fuck." I tried to move away from him, give him space. He didn't stir. "Landon?"

Twack twack twack. I jerked on instinct, trying to secure a safer position. My buckle wouldn't budge. I reached for the knife tucked in my utility belt and felt the comforting coolness of the polymer handle. My right side stung, but I couldn't worry about the injury right now. In my scrunched, upside-down position, I nicked the skin of my lower back as I pulled the knife free. I cut myself loose.

Oof. I fell sideways, and blood trickled into my eye. "Landon?"

The hail of bullets slowed as I felt for his face. "Landon," I whispered again, close to his ear.

A hot breath warmed my skin before I settled my palm against his cheek. My hands shook with relief that he was still alive. I tried to support my weight on my knees, didn't want to hurt him, but the confines of the upside-down vehicle didn't help.

Shouting resonated from outside, echoing strangely in the space of the cab. *Where's my fucking gun?* Both the M4 and my Glock were missing. If I could find one, I could fight instead of feeling like a wounded fish in a barrel trying to protect another wounded fish.

I need to be a fish with a gun. A hysterical giggle escaped my lips. *Get it together, Jolyn, get it together.* Great, now I was talking to myself. Not good. I must have hit my head harder than I thought.

In my search to find my weapon, my hand sank into something hot and wet. "Shit. Landon."

Panic crawled up my throat, the band tightening around my chest until I could hardly take a breath. His legs were crushed between the seat and steering wheel column, blood seeping from somewhere. I resisted the urge to shake his shoulders to wake him, in case he had a spinal injury and I'd end up exacerbating it. But I wanted him to open his eyes, talk to me, to tell me he was okay.

Knife in hand, I cut Landon's seatbelt. He didn't fall like I did, his legs too stuck.

Gravel and glass crunched beneath footsteps as someone neared. I clutched the knife in my hand, ready to defend to the death. Another vehicle roared close, its light illuminating the cab fully for the first time.

Blood dripped down the side of Landon's neck. So much blood—a fatal amount. His whole neck and side of his vest were coated in crimson. A bullet must have hit him somewhere above the Kevlar.

A sob escaped me. I pressed my hands to his throat, praying I covered the wound. "I need a doctor!" I screamed, not caring what they did to me, but Landon required medical attention *now*. He was going to die.

The people talking outside quieted. Warmth squished through my fingers. "Call an ambulance!"

Someone laughed.

Fury overtook every other emotion. If I had to fight everyone single-handedly to get Landon some help, I'd do it.

A pair of footsteps got closer, then stopped on the other side of Landon's window. A man crouched down to stare at me, Cliff, MBI's head of security. A handgun dangled casually from his fingertips. "Your brother wants to have a few words."

He made it sound like he was going to say a eulogy at my memorial. Knowing how homicidal my brother could become when he didn't get his way, it was probably a good guess.

I waited for him to fire, but a sharp pain poked my ass. Someone laughed again. Still holding Landon's wound, I twisted, my shoulder screaming at me to stop. A syringe stuck out of my butt cheek. They'd shot me full of something—something that made my eyelids feel like hippos were pulling them closed.

We're dead.

18

LANDON

When I'd asked her out, I'd thought she would refuse. I couldn't have been more pleased she accepted.

We stood on the threshold of her apartment, a bachelor suite in a nice part of town. It was our first date, so I wouldn't ask to go inside. But I couldn't leave her just yet.

I lifted her hand to my lips. "Thank you for a lovely time."

"It was fun," she replied, her voice a little breathless, and cheeks flushed pink. Nervousness mixed with her vanilla cake scent.

Fun. It wasn't a raving endorsement, but maybe I could turn that around. The knuckles of my free hand brushed her cheek. "I've always wondered what your freckles would taste like."

Her eyes widened, cheeks flaming from pink to red. Every time I could make her blush, I felt victorious. My bear agreed.

She remained immobile as I leaned closer. Her pupils dilated. When my lips skimmed her cheek, she inhaled sharply. My eyes rolled back in bliss.

She tasted of perfection.

"Doesn't matter, really. He'll probably bleed out by the time we get there if he's not dead already. Mr. Mahn didn't say anything about doctors."

Voices dragged me out of a refuge I would've rather stayed in.

"He didn't say anything about taking the dude at all. Just the woman."

This place... Dear God, I hurt all over. I didn't know where I was, but it was dark, and my body felt broken in a hundred places. There was a disconnect to my legs, but they still managed to hurt like a son of a bitch. The Kevlar I'd worn had been removed, giving me room to breathe, but every time I did, points in my neck and hips stung and throbbed.

"Whatever. Mr. Mahn can do what he likes with him. Hell, we can dump him out the back after we take off again if he wants. But if it turns out he wanted the guy and we left him behind, some of us might not live to regret it."

A crust over my eyes kept me from opening them fully. Razor blades had taken up residence in my throat. I felt as weak and lightheaded as a newborn cub.

The hum of an engine told me we were in a vehicle of some sort, and from the way it dipped and swayed, I'd guess an airplane in the process of landing. Beneath the smell of my own blood were the scents of animals—possibly wolf—stagnant around me, and below that...a shifter. Part of my brain perked up. Was that Walker's scent? Was he close by? No. How could he be? We'd been in a collision, Jolyn and I.

Where was she? Was she okay? I didn't scent her among the rest of the strange smells.

I extended my hand, the snap of pain through my elbow telling me something was broken. My wrist hit something hollow, like wood. Yes, like a box or crate, or coffin. My fingers brushed above me, trying to push up the lid, but it was stuck. I was definitely inside something.

Ignoring that messed up fact, I sank into as much of a shift as

I could in my weakened state, each molecule transforming, renewing. Usually, it meant a feeling of relief because I'd pushed being in my human form too long. But agony ripped through me. I didn't know if any part of me remained unbroken. I reached for my belt, needing to loosen it to give my bear room. Every movement created more pain.

The engine noise got louder. I jerked forward as wheels connected with pavement. A groan left my lips as my skin and muscles stretched and contracted, a lava-hot sensation running along my bones. Sparks shot off behind my eyelids, my head pounding a torturous rhythm. I finally tugged my belt free and it clattered to the bottom of the box. The more I shifted, the smaller my container became as my bulk expanded to fit the bear who lived inside me. Tearing noises sounded loud within the confined space as my shirt burst at the seams to accommodate him.

My legs hurt the most, the sensation excruciating, like I'd broken several bones in a small space. Then came the heat in my throat and head. A bullet left the meat of my shoulder where it curved into my neck, then another squeezed from the muscles at my hip. Eventually, the burning of my wounds faded as my flesh knit back together.

The plane stopped and the voices receded. Now that I'd given my bear leeway to heal, he wanted to break free, to smash this box and find Jolyn. But someone could be close by with a finger on a proverbial, or literal, trigger. I had to stay in charge.

Breaths left me in harsh gasps. With my healing completed as best as I could manage, I used the torn remains of my shirt to wipe the crust away from my eyes, and tried to get my bearings.

A few slivers of light broke through the slats of the box around me. I leaned closer, trying to see what lay beyond. Movement caught my eye, someone pacing not far away. No, *something*. The scent of wolf—a real one, not a shifter—came at me again, mixed with other smells and manure. I made out silver bars, that of cages, and tilted my head trying to see more. Animals in cages? Where the hell was I?

I sat back on my haunches, remembering what Brooke had told me of her and her sister's capture. There'd been animals on that plane too. A monkey she'd said? I couldn't remember any other specifics. Was I on the same plane?

From the snippets of conversation I'd heard earlier, we were on our way to see Emerson Mahn. *Fine with me.* I was going to tear out his throat the second I saw him. I didn't feel bad about planning someone's murder, not this person.

Where was Jolyn? I scooted as far down the box as I could, searching for a wider gap in the slats. I still couldn't see her. Did they take her somewhere else? Did they leave her behind? Was she dead? My stomach squeezed with possibilities, each worse than the last. I wouldn't accept any of it. She must be close by.

Placing my hands flat against the wood, I tested its strength. Yeah, my bear would have no trouble demolishing this crate if we'd been at full strength, but if I attempted it, would I have enough energy to shift back?

I needed to be smart about this, use my human intelligence instead of my bear's brute strength. Voices moved toward me again. I held still, listening, trying to catch something that would tell me what was going on around me, maybe even hear the melodic sound of Jolyn's voice.

A *thunk* resounded in the small space around me as something hit the box, followed by a creak of wood. I tensed, grabbing my fallen belt, and readied myself to fight.

Bright light flooded my confines, disorienting me. Before I could spring and attack, a stab of pain hit my nape. Fire cascaded through my limbs; my muscles froze. The rapid *tick, tick, tick* of a Taser filled my ears as I fell into the crate, helpless.

"Get a collar," a voice said, force behind the words.

I must have blacked out, because the next thing I knew was the sensation of something encircling my neck. I lashed out, swatting at a metal bar. *Click.* I couldn't swallow from the tightness around my throat. I reached up to yank it off, encountering cool metal and buttons. An image of the collar Brooke had dropped on my desk a few days ago flashed in my mind. I'd had a hand in its construction. *And now I wore it.*

A deep voice laughed a distance away. Squinting from the glare of the overhead lights I surveyed my surroundings. Five men crowded around the crate, one of them holding a pole extending to my neck, like something a dog catcher would use. A new wave of rage swept over me, my muscles bunching. I dove at them, using my legs to push out of the box, only to be kept at arm's length. A second man grabbed the pole to help. Both of them strained as I reached to rip into their throats.

I started to shift out of instinct, needing to kill these men who already knew to put a collar on me. Blinding pain flashed through my body, stabbing me in the stomach.

Walker had told me about the collar, but nothing could have prepared me for the anguished reality. Crippling agony dropped me to my knees. With a shove, the men holding the rod pushed me away, the collar separating from the pole.

I gripped the metal at my throat, trying to pull it away from where it strangled the most. Another laugh, and I turned, searching for the person who I would kill first—a twenty-something with anemic skin, his ball cap on backwards.

They were all human, not a trace of shifter on any of them. Two wore tactical gear, another two were in jeans and T-shirts. My focus zeroed in on the person in the middle of the group, the one wearing a designer suit similar to the ones I favored: Emerson Mahn. His strawberry-blond hair glinted in the light from the fluorescents, his face smooth-shaven. Remnants of the boy he'd once been etched his face, but his eyes were hard, emotionless. He looked at me as if I were nothing to him, an insect under his boot instead of the CEO of a multimillion dollar company.

I clenched my jaw, my hands tight on the collar. "Take this off of me."

His mouth upturned at the corners. "I don't think so."

The plane lurched forward, everyone bracing their legs in reaction. I used the distraction to lunge at him, to attack. The pain spiked again, dropping me over the edge of the crate. The wood cutting into my stomach was nothing compared to the electrical shock of the collar. Hat-backwards guy laughed again.

I gasped, taking in deep breaths. Minutes passed before I was able to collect myself, to face Mahn again.

"Where's Jolyn?"

Features tightening, his eyes darted to the side, an involuntary reaction.

I adjusted my kneeling position to get a better look, the wood pinching into my kneecaps. More cages came into view, some with animals, one with the monkey Brooke had mentioned. And in one of them lay Jolyn, unconscious, her hands and clothes covered in blood.

I shot to my feet. "Get her out of there!" My bear raged inside me, frantic to break free and destroy the people who did this. The collar spiked anguish through my body every time he tried to take control. I doubled over, unable to breathe.

That laughter again. I curled my hands into fists. If my bear gained control, I could rip them all apart, tear them to pieces, spill their blood like they spilled Jolyn's. My bear agreed wholeheartedly.

The pain ramped up, dropping me to my knees. I tried to inhale, to clear the haze from my vision. I needed to remain calm, to not give them an excuse to use the collar against me. Lifting my eyes, I met Mahn's gaze. His expression had hardly changed, eyes cold. He felt nothing at seeing someone in agony.

"What do you want from me?" I gritted between clenched teeth.

His eyes crinkled. "To find out how sister dearest likes

regaining consciousness in a cell with a beast. She's desperately terrified of you lot, did you know?"

My already nauseous stomach twisted and clenched.

He turned and strode away. "Deal with him," he said over his shoulder.

One of the tactical guy's faces filled my vision, a remote in his hand. "Sleepy time."

Pain ricocheted through my body as the light faded from my eyes.

19

JOLYN

"I CAN'T DO THIS ANYMORE," I SAID INTO MY PHONE. "HE WANTS TO take me out, like date me. I can't keep lying to him. I'm not good at this."

And Landon didn't deserve my dishonesty. Ever since I started working for him, he'd been nothing but kind, making sure I had everything I needed—not only at work, but at my new apartment too. He was sweet, and courteous, and hot as hell. When I was with him, I had a hard time remembering my purpose here. Because I wished it were real.

"It's perfect. Date him."

Emerson's words were like a splash of cold water. He couldn't mean...

"Do whatever it takes." The band around my chest tightened, my stomach churning with nausea the more he spoke. "Learn as much about him and his friends as possible. You do everything in your power, or don't bother coming home."

I stared at the wall in front of me, not seeing it.

"Oh, and you should probably go on some type of birth control."

The call disconnected. I couldn't move, my phone shaking in my hand.

Consciousness trickled in through the cracks in my brain, slow and thready. Fear settled in my stomach before I opened my eyes. Something bad had happened, but I couldn't remember what. The scent of stale bodily fluids and dirt surrounded me, a chill hung in the air along with an unsettling silence. There was something familiar and comforting too—the crisp scent I associated with Landon.

I shivered like I'd once been warm, but the warmth had left me recently. My face pressed against soft fabric, hardness beneath it. I opened my eyes and focused on the hand in front of my face pressed flat against concrete. Everything in here was layered in shadows. I waited for my eyes to adjust. The cold floor spread before me, ending in a solid metal wall, the corrugated kind Emerson liked to use in his facilities. Pushing up with my hands, I turned my head to see an identical wall opposite it. A wad of black material separated my cheek from the concrete.

The sense of dread in my chest intensified, the tightness making it hard to breathe. *Where am I?* I trembled harder, the freezing air seeping into my bones. I wore the long black T-shirt and cargo pants I'd had on under my tactical gear when we'd gone to the bottling plant, but my vest, belt, and weapons weren't weighing me down.

The memories of that op tumbled through my mind. I lifted myself more. Landon's scent came at me again, from the wadded, blood-encrusted fabric below my face. My breath quickened. A concrete wall faced me, a gap at the top letting in a small amount of light. What looked like metal tracks ran along the floor and ceiling from one corrugated wall to the other.

"Are you all right?"

I turned at Landon's voice, relief making me weak. *He's okay.* I'd thought...

Through the shadows, I saw that he sat on the other side of the room, bare-chested, his back pressed against the wall with his legs bent, elbows resting on his knees. His pants were torn to shit, covered in blood, the lighter color of his skin visible between the ripped seams.

Those last moments in the truck bombarded my brain, my breath leaving my lips with each new memory. We'd been hit. They shot at us. The image of Landon's broken body seared my eyeballs. He'd been bleeding, near death. He shouldn't be alive and sitting ten feet from me using a calm tone.

I'd been hurt too—pain in my shoulder, blood on my face. I reached up and felt silk beneath my fingers. A scrap of Landon's shirt was wrapped around my arm. It ached like a motherfucker, congruent of a recent injury, while Landon appeared as though he'd been fully healed for days. *The wound on his arm.* The one I'd helped Alina stitch up...I couldn't see it. *What is going on?*

"You had some metal and glass in your shoulder," he said, voice even. "I took the shards out and bandaged it. You also had a head wound. It seems to have stopped bleeding now."

His assessment of my injuries distracted me from his. Why was he talking that way? Why was he way over there and not next to me? We'd gotten past the distance between us over the past day, hadn't we? Why was he acting like a stranger again?

"Where are we?" My voice came out a croak.

"I was hoping you'd know." His voice remained steady, like he measured his words. "Your brother brought us here on a plane."

Then we weren't in Detroit anymore, couldn't be at that other warehouse. I wracked my brain, thinking through my brother's other properties. *God, no.* A cold, concrete holding room? The compound in Alaska was destroyed. So it could only mean...

"I see you might have an idea."

Groaning, I adjusted my position until my spine pressed against the unyielding concrete opposite him, then pushed my blood-matted curls out of my face. "It's too gruesome to voice." I felt down my pant legs, searching for weapons they might have missed, but found nothing. They'd taken them all.

"I'd rather know," he said after a beat, stretching his legs forward.

That's when I noticed a flash of something metallic around his neck. The shadows had hidden it before. A chilled sensation sped through my veins as I stared at the collar. I pushed with my legs, used the wall at my spine to stand. A collar would be pointless on a human.

My heart pounded so hard in my chest it was the only thing I could hear. Blood pumped, making me lightheaded.

All the weird things I'd noticed over the past few days, hours with Landon, hit me upside the head: super speed, glowing eyes, fast healing. Why hadn't I seen it before now? My brain had created rationalizations because I hadn't wanted to accept the truth.

Mouth quirking at the corner, Landon lifted his hand to touch the collar, then let it fall in his lap. "A gift from your brother," he said without humor.

"No." The word whispered between my lips, a prayer that none of this was really happening. First Kane, and now him?

Landon stiffened, his jaw clenching, but didn't move as my heart raced faster in my chest. Hands fisted, he stared at me, every part of him tense. I wanted him to deny it, to tell me the stupid thing wouldn't work on him. He remained silent, the truth shining in his eyes.

He was one of them, the beasts, the shifters I'd feared since I was seventeen years old. For most of the past decade, I'd participated in my brother's plan to expose and contain their kind—it had been one of the things we'd agreed on in the beginning. I'd seen what they could do to humans. Bile rolled in my stomach and up my throat.

"I would have tried to take it off," he said, his tone remaining calm. "But then remembered it'll explode if tampered with."

It was true. Emerson had told me the same thing.

My stomach bubbled with acid as Landon stared at me. I'd worked for him, dated him, made love with him.

All this time and I'd never known. He'd kept it from me. The truth stabbed while the rational side of my brain told me he'd been smart to do so. What would I have done with that information four years ago? Told my brother? Kept it to myself?

I closed my eyes and returned to that time. With Landon, I'd been happy. It had felt like he was the only one who truly understood me, even while I deceived him. If I'd known then...

No. I wouldn't have betrayed him. I wouldn't have revealed his true nature to my brother. I would have protected his secret because back then, I loved Landon, *still* loved him. And I probably would have abandoned my brother's plan to protect him. I would have told Emerson I'd found nothing and taken whatever twisted punishment he thought up if it meant keeping Landon safe from his notice.

I tensed, a sickening truth swirling in my gut. My brother *would* have known. He always knew who the shifters were just by looking at them, and we grew up with Landon. When Emerson sent me to Vancouver, he'd known who he was sending me to.

And he did it anyway.

He'd wanted to be proven right. He'd wanted Landon to do something bad to me because of his nature. Emerson had put me in harm's way on purpose, not caring what happened to me. Everything he did was an experiment of one kind or another. *Set up the pieces. Watch them fall.*

I pressed my palms flat against the cold wall, trying to regain control of my emotions. Across the space, Landon stood to his full height and rolled his shoulders back. I drank him in, the expanse of his bare chest, the width of his shoulders, every part of him familiar, but now I was looking at him with new eyes, new awareness. There was an animal hiding beneath his skin.

It didn't matter *what* he was, because he was Landon. I knew

him—or, at least I used to. The essence of the man hadn't
changed with whatever animal he could transform into. He could
be a mouse or a snake. It didn't matter.

Actually... My eyes drifted upward to the gap where the roof
met the ceiling. If he were a small animal, or a bird, he could get
us out of here if it weren't for the collar.

"I don't suppose you can change into something to fit through
that?" I asked, gesturing to the gap.

His body stilled, then relaxed as he shook his head.

So, not something small. It had been worth a shot. My
curiosity bloomed at which animal he could be. Would he tell me
or keep it private? There was no reason for him to trust me. I
pressed my lips together.

He ran a hand over his face and met my gaze. "Can you tell
me where we are?"

"The arena. The place where my brother takes shifters to be
hunted by his rich acquaintances." And he'd brought Landon
here. I tried to swallow around the dryness in my throat. "He sells
them off to the highest bidder, usually in the millions."

His muscles flexed with each word I spoke. "And you allowed
it?"

"I only found out about it last week!" I pushed off the wall,
then stopped, ashamed of what I'd let happen right under my
nose. "I didn't know about most of what my brother was up to
until I returned from service."

Landon let out a frustrated breath. "Sorry." He nodded, then
ran a hand over his jaw. "I should know you wouldn't condone
something like this."

Should he know that? I'd done things for my brother I wasn't
proud of, things I never wanted to voice. Some concerned
Landon, but more had to do with others. He didn't know me, not
truly, not the way he should for how much I cared about him. If
we got out of this alive...maybe he'd give me the chance to fix
that.

I could hardly dare to hope—especially because we were here.

"This place..." I contemplated our cell, the band around my chest squeezing painfully. "No one ever comes back from here. The guys working for my brother called it a one-way ticket."

Landon stared at me, grim resolve in his features, fingers twitching at his sides. Then he looked away, exhaling, to pace the length of the wall.

I watched him for long moments, then took a step forward when he paused. "Why didn't you tell me?" I tried to keep the hurt out of my voice as best I could. It was a foolish emotion to have, given the circumstance that sent me to him.

His eyes bounced down to my neck. "I did."

I lifted my hand. The necklace he gave me hung on the outside of my shirt. I'd always thought it was a crescent moon, but now that I was looking at it in the shadows of this room, the light glinted off the sharp edge. I inhaled a quick breath. He'd given me a claw—a large one. *A real one.* Was this *his* claw?

My stomach flipped, eyes snapping to his hands hanging loose at his sides.

It's amazing really. They'll grow their skin back if you allow it, even a limb, but that takes longer.

Nausea rose in my throat just as it had the day I realized what my brother and Allan had been doing to shifters while I'd been away in the military. They'd kept that remote location in Alaska to experiment on the ones he couldn't "employ."

I pressed my thumb against the sharp edge of the claw, ran it along to the point, something I'd done often to give me comfort. There were only a few animals I could think of that would have a claw this large. Dear God, what kind of shifter was he? A mystical sort of sensation grabbed hold of me. My brother's words from a long time ago flitted across my brain. *Are they all just regular animals, or will we someday discover something extraordinary? A unicorn perhaps?*

I lifted my gaze to Landon's. Would he turn into a mythological creature like a griffin or a dragon? My heart pounded. Would he tell me if I asked?

Swallowing against the dryness in my throat, I opened my mouth, then closed it again. I could barely make out his lifted eyebrow in response. My gaze jumped to the gap at the top of the wall. It had darkened since I'd woken up. "What time is it?"

His hands twitched at his side. "I seem to have left my watch in my other suit." I shook my head, not appreciating his attempt at humor. "Sunset, I think." His voice cracked on the last word.

That meant a whole day had passed since the crash. My stomach rolled, the tightness in my chest squeezing to maximum. It meant all those deliveries scheduled for today would have come to pass. Landon glanced away from me, blinking.

"God, no." His family would all be shifters too, his mom, cousins, everyone. "I'm so sorry."

I couldn't stand being apart any longer. I rushed toward him and wrapped my arms around his torso, squeezing him tight. My cheek pressed against the soft hairs of his chest. His heart beat steady beneath my ear. Taking a ragged breath, he hugged me to him. My mind raced, trying to find hope in this bleak situation. "Maybe Marley and Alina stopped the deliveries somehow."

"Maybe," he allowed, but I heard the defeat in his voice. "Those kinds of thoughts are the only thing keeping me sane right now."

I squeezed him harder. As his hand roved up and down my spine, the crisp scent of linen surrounded me, comforting in this horrible place and circumstance—familiar. My body recognized the warmth of his.

I inhaled another deep breath. "Were you holding me earlier?"

"Yes. It's cold in here." He said it like he needed an excuse. "But I didn't want you scared when you saw the collar."

I tipped my head to see his expression. "You don't scare me."

With slow movements, his hand cupped my jaw. I leaned into the touch, shivers cascading through my neck. We stood that way, the wind picking up outside, then he leaned forward and pressed his lips to my forehead. I closed my eyes and melted.

Clank clink. I jumped away. The metal door beside us began to lift. Dim sunlight shot beneath the door to highlight our feet, then shins. Side by side we faced it, Landon's shoulder grazing mine. I took a deep breath. Whatever my brother's plans for us were, we were about to find out.

20

LANDON

She twisted the handle on the window, cracking it open with a protesting groan of wood and paint. With a shake of her hand, she dropped the ladybug on the windowsill.

"Are you going to let all the spiders go free now too?" I teased, coming up behind her.

She spun around, a sheepish expression on her beautiful face. "Well, spiders are one thing. But ladybugs wouldn't hurt a fly."

"Just aphids."

She laughed. "Smarty-pants." She tossed me a look over her shoulder before returning to her desk.

My bear panting, I barely resisted the urge to follow.

The thick, corrugated metal wall trudged upward. A red light flashed in the corner of the room, highlighting us both in an eerie mix of crimson and shadows. Fresh air spread inside our holding cell, dispelling the dank and the scent of scared and enraged shifters. The cold breeze brought goosebumps to my naked flesh.

Beside me, Jolyn stood in what I could only call a fighter's stance, waiting for what lay on the other side of those doors as battle-ready as she could—a different woman than the one I'd fallen in love with, but no less extraordinary.

Despite our situation, my chest swelled with hope. She hadn't panicked when she came to terms with the fact I was a shifter. She hadn't screamed, hadn't fainted. After a hundred emotions had played over her face, she'd taken a step toward me, not away. I'd seen all those questions she'd wanted to ask in her eyes, and hoped like hell I'd get the chance to answer them.

The wall clanked its way upward an inch at a time, revealing a grassy clearing and a forested area beyond it. I lifted my arm to block the ball of light sinking behind mountains in the distance. The door stopped, and Jolyn and I glanced at each other. The look on her face said she knew as little of what was about to happen as I did, and was just as apprehensive.

Clank clack. We turned simultaneously. The other metal wall pressed toward us, moving on metal tracks as slowly as the door had opened. If we stayed still, it would push us out. *Nowhere to hide.* If I were a lone shifter taken here for sport—*goddamn it,* I couldn't finish the thought. The terror mixed in with the other shifter scents, lingering and faint, told their stories.

From what Walker had said, the video footage we'd seen, and now what Jolyn had told me, I held no illusions of what was about to happen to me. Mahn had brought me here to die.

Shoulder to shoulder, Jolyn and I stepped into the clearing before the moving wall could spit us out. Trees stretched before us, a mix of pines, birch, and bushes. Shadows gathered between the trunks as they swayed in a chill breeze. This forest was silent, no singing birds to make it a welcoming place. I glanced over my shoulder. A twelve-foot metal fence jutted out from both sides of our holding cell. From the hum it gave off, it was a pretty safe bet it was electrified. Yards beyond that, a cinder-block wall stood another ten feet tall. Both barriers continued outwards as far as the eye could see. Beyond them, mountains.

A building similar in construction to the one we'd left, squatted fifty feet away, a bunker of sorts. Instead of a metal wall, a wide window spanned its concrete construction. I couldn't see inside, the dark glass reflecting our images and the forest back at us. Jolyn stepped closer to me, her shoulder touching mine, and we faced the second building, knowing someone must be inside.

The window became translucent suddenly, the interior visible. It didn't make me feel any better about our situation. My heart pounded hard in my chest, stomach twisting in knots.

"Welcome to the arena," Emerson Mahn said with a flourish of his arms. His voice echoed from a loudspeaker mounted on top of the building. He'd changed out of his suit, and now wore camouflage fatigues the same color as the forest around us.

Four men flanked him, the same ones who'd been on the plane. Each held a weapon of some type, ranging from assault rifles, to shotguns, to simple handguns.

My accelerated heart rate increased in tempo when I noticed the four shoulder mounts—trophy heads—at the back of the room: a lynx, cougar, elk, and wolf. I tore my gaze away and focused on the monsters who held our lives in their hands.

They all stood behind a desk, one door on the wall behind them. Television monitors filled one side of the room, at least a dozen of them. I could see our images on some, each from different angles. The screens changed to new views every few seconds. This whole place was wired.

"Beautiful trophies, aren't they?" Mahn gestured to the shoulder mounts. "They were the first four beasts we hunted here, and I keep them close as a reminder of how far we've come. Isn't that right, Jo?"

Beside me, Jolyn stiffened. Rage-induced acid boiled in my stomach. I couldn't see a way out of this. They had total control. I couldn't shift with this collar on and I was still weak from blood loss. I had no weapons, only my wits.

"I hope you have your affairs in order," Mahn said, voice mild.

"I'd hate for your board members to be scrambling once you disappear." Then he let out a sharp half laugh. "Maybe I'll make a bid on your company if your shares go public. A fitting end, I should say."

I disregarded his words, scanning the faces of my would-be executioners, eyes settling on the hat-backwards asshole who'd laughed every time they'd shocked me on the plane. Besides Mahn, I owed him the most pain.

Jolyn stepped closer, her pinky finger skimming down the length of my hand until it hooked against mine. I gave it a gentle squeeze and noticed a slight relaxation of her shoulders.

She'd been expecting rejection, and maybe a week ago I would have turned my back on her. But not now. Not when I understood everything, how this psychopath had controlled her life, the narrative she'd accepted regarding shifters. She hadn't been able to break free of the cycle of abuse until recently, and I was so proud of her that she had.

"You did know me," I said, glancing at her necklace. Even if I hadn't told her about my shifter side, I'd always given her all of myself, no holding back. My bear was a part of me, but he didn't control me. The year we were together, she *did* know me.

Jolyn tilted her head to meet my gaze. Most of the dark makeup she'd worn yesterday was wiped away, her freckles standing out in stark relief against pale skin. The blue of her eyes pierced me, searching. After a long moment, she nodded, like she was satisfied with what she found.

Then she faced her brother, her shoulders squared. "You knew about him all along, didn't you?"

"Of course," Mahn replied. "I've always been able to clock them from a mile off, you know that." Then he stared straight at me. "Did she tell you it was she who put it all in motion? That without her, I probably wouldn't have figured it out?"

He smiled at Jolyn, but it never reached his eyes. "I've always wanted to ask, did you enjoy your time with a beast? Did he bite,

Jo? Did he scratch? How was it to have an animal's cock inside you?"

If I hadn't wanted to tear him apart before, I did now. Nothing would satisfy me and my bear except him dead at our feet, lifeblood leaving his body.

"You're sick," Jolyn croaked.

"Maybe. But it's all for research, the greater good. You know that. You used to agree with me."

She swallowed and shook her head, her fingers tight against mine.

"Ah well. I suppose I shouldn't be surprised by your lack of participation. You've always been a weak disappointment."

I didn't want him to focus on her. "Where are all your mind-controlled shifters I've heard so much about?"

His eyes narrowed. "They keep dying on me, unfortunately. Not that it matters. They would have ended up here anyway. It's just money." He glanced between us.

I stepped forward, blocking his view of his sister. "How did you control them, make them work for you?"

This was the first time true enjoyment entered his eyes. "There are many differences between humans and beasts, and the one I like the most is an animal's need to please its master once tamed. In some, I could exploit that quality with the right combinations of conditioning and pharmaceuticals. For others, it never worked." He shrugged. "We never did find out why, despite my cousin's extensive research."

My hand curled into a fist, needing to strike. He said it like it was no big deal, as if mind control was a side hobby.

Then his face hardened. "Your friend Walker Hayles was especially difficult to convert. Usually, cougars were some of the easiest. Did he brag about what he did to my cousin? That he jumped on him in his beast form and ripped out his intestines to feast? I saw it all."

Though my stomach rolled at the description, I wouldn't hold it against Walker. If he'd done that, then it was probably a mercy compared to what had been done to him. I kept my face blank, not reacting.

"See?" He said it like I'd confessed something. "You're just like them all—bloodthirsty and brutal to the core. Wolves in sheep's clothing, all lying in wait until you can make your move in the most gruesome way possible." He looked at Jolyn. "I was always truthful about what they could do."

I took another step forward, blocking her completely.

His eyes narrowed on me. "Why did your kind kill my mother?" He'd kept his tone mild in comparison to his words.

I didn't have a clue what he was talking about. What did I know of their mother? She'd been in a wheelchair for as long as I could remember, then died when Jolyn was only twelve or so. Did I hear how she'd come to be in that wheelchair? A car accident, perhaps? Nothing to explain his question.

His expression turned stony. "I'm sure you and your friends would have heard about her accident." He spit out the word. "Wouldn't there be one of you bragging how you'd used claws to push her car over the edge of the ravine? Wouldn't there have been laughs about how moronic humans were, how stupid? How many beasts were in law enforcement at the time to keep it under wraps? How many corrupt ones still remain?"

I shook my head. We would have all been kids at the time. I had no clue if any of what he said could be true.

"Of course. You beasts always stick together, don't you?" His lip curled in disdain. "Always trying to get the upper hand. Jockeying for positions of power." His gaze raked me up and down. "You're no different. You climb the corporate ladder, place your spying technology in businesses around the world. You sit down at the table with normal people, smug in your differences, and plot our demise. More and more of you emerge around the world as leaders. Someone needed to put a stop to it."

A chill ran through my body. I'd known he was deranged

from Walker's recounting and Jolyn's fear, but I hadn't understood how far his paranoia ran until now. He saw all of us as the enemy no matter what kind of person we were. There would be no reasoning with him, but would I be a fool not to try?

I raised my voice. "We found out about the vitamin water. Why do this so publicly? People will connect it to you. You'll go to prison, probably the death penalty for mass genocide."

He didn't appear fazed by the fact. "Perhaps. Or perhaps not." The corner of his mouth curled upward. "It was never about me going free or escaping consequences. If your kind are revealed and most of those eliminated, then my purpose on this earth is fulfilled. It doesn't matter what happens to me."

A true megalomaniac. A breath shuddered through my body just as Jolyn stepped up beside me again, her hand hooking into mine, giving me a squeeze.

Mahn's eyes narrowed on our joined hands, then he glanced at his companions. "I think we should get this show started, don't you?"

Murmurs of assent and nods answered his question. Hat-backwards asshole chuckled. I glanced at Jolyn, then at Mahn, realization dawning. He wouldn't *hunt* his sister, would he? He couldn't be that twisted. But he hadn't given her another option. He meant to keep her here in this arena. *Fuck me.*

Mahn picked up a remote and waggled it toward us. "If he doesn't rip you to shreds, Jo, I'll hunt you both."

21

JOLYN

IT WAS TOO DARK, THE FOREST CLOSED IN ALL AROUND US. I SQUEEZED Landon's hand tighter.

"Are we lost?" It was about the sixth time I'd asked, and his answer was always the same.

"Nope." But this time he added, "Cabin is right up ahead. And when we get there, I'm going to run you a bath, massage your feet, and make you spaghetti carbonara."

As lovely as all that sounded, I just wanted the first part, the cabin. Once we were back, he could ignore me for the rest of the night as long as we were out of this dark, creepy forest. I swore as soon as the sun set, eyes stared at me from the shadows.

We turned a corner, and there ahead was the cabin, dark because we hadn't left any lights on.

I let out a relieved breath, a new bounce in my step now that we'd returned.

"See," he said, pulling me close. "Just around the corner."

"I have no clue how you found this place. I was sure we were lost."

Grinning, he kissed my forehead. "I could tell. Sorry I kept you out so long. You're a trooper. We should have headed back earlier."

I tried to laugh off my earlier apprehension. "Well, now that we're here, I'm looking forward to that bath and spaghetti."

Emerson pressed a button on the remote.

Landon gasped, his hands flying to his neck. I jumped back, my heart galloping. His skin rippled and seemed to grow, hair erupting along his arms and chest. A tearing sound echoed. What remained of his pants, then underwear, ripped away as his body swelled.

The transformation didn't stop. The fur grew longer, the muscles bulkier. His face...my God...his face stretched and warped, canines growing over the top of his lips. My heart lodged in my throat. Each limb filled out until he landed on all four paws with a huff of a breath, the grass in front of him bending at the force of it.

The moisture in my mouth dried up; my throat clenched tight. A one-ton grizzly bear stood in front of me and I had nowhere to hide. The air around me stilled in anticipation of what came next.

The bear tossed his head, then stared at me with dark brown, almost black, eyes. *Those eyes.* They were Landon's eyes, and they were fixed on me. I held myself immobile, waiting for him to make a move. Then he bowed, breaking eye contact.

You did know me.

Those were Landon's words from minutes ago. He'd been telling me our past wasn't a lie, the same as I had told him. But he was also telling me *this* was him. Inside the bear, it was Landon.

He lifted his gaze, but remained where he was, watchful, waiting. Swallowing around the lump in my throat, I stepped forward. Oh God, he was so big. On all fours, his shoulders came up to mine. He could crush me if he wanted to.

I reached toward him. His snout lifted, touching my fingers. A sharp inhale squeezed my lungs. His breath was warm on my hand, his nose damp. He moved his bulk forward, his cheek brushing my palm. I stroked up his neck. A huge huff of breath escaped him, shuddering through me from the weight of it. Another step and his shoulder bumped mine gently.

This was Landon. He might look different, but it *was* him. Even though he was something other than I expected, I felt the same things I did yesterday. I still loved him.

The collar he wore cut into his auburn and black fur, matting a large swath of it against his body. It looked painful. My eyes burned. That collar wouldn't have been choking him if I hadn't stolen the plans. I wanted to weep for what I'd done. And if I hadn't told my brother what I'd seen that day in the forest, Landon wouldn't be hunted.

My arms wrapped around his neck, and I buried my face in the soft and wiry fur of his shoulder. "I'm so sorry."

I didn't know if Landon understood words in this form, but he leaned into me enough for me to believe he returned my hug, forgiving me. My throat ached with the need to cry.

"Touching." Emerson's angry voice cut through the moment, causing me to jerk straight and spin around. He stood behind the safety glass of his bunker, a disdainful curl to his lips. "Since he seems to be one of those beasts who don't attack when a human sees what they are, I guess we'll move on to the audience participation portion of the agenda."

He'd always pushed that narrative, that each time he'd used deadly force, it was because the shifters attacked first. I never should have believed him. Landon's intelligence shone through his eyes. He remained self-aware.

The sun set behind the mountains, drenching the arena in shadows. I'd been thinking at least we had that on our side, but with a flick of Emerson's wrist, floodlights turned on everywhere, blinding. One light in particular cast a circle around me and

Landon like a circus act. I leaned into his side, comforted by the warmth and weight of him.

"I'll be nice and give you a five-minute head start." Emerson's voice was as hard as I'd ever heard it. The sound of Cliff's shotgun being cocked reverberated through the speakers.

My brother would kill us both. With joy. *So fucked up.* My heart raced. We were out-manned and out-gunned with no backup in sight.

"Clock's ticking." Emerson stared straight at me when he said it. "I'd suggest moving unless you want to be slaughtered here." The guys behind him vibrated with anticipation, wide grins splitting across their faces.

Clenching my fists, a frustrated noise escaped my throat. I spun around, ready to run with Landon. He'd lowered onto his belly behind me. At first I thought he was giving up, then he tossed his head at me. He wanted me to climb onto his back.

A thrill shot through me, one incongruent with the occasion, but no less profound. *I'm about to ride a bear.* How many people could say they'd done that?

My chest tight with fear for both of us, I took a fistful of Landon's scruff and swung my leg over him like I would a horse. I sank into his fur, my legs spread wide to accommodate the breadth of his shoulders.

As soon as I settled, he was off. His movements rocked me forward and back. My arms squeezed him tight, my shoulder pulsing where he'd bandaged it. *Don't fall off.* Wind whistled past us, my hair coming out of its ponytail a tendril at a time. I never would have thought a bear could move so fast. We trundled through the brush like a locomotive without brakes, crashing sounds echoing behind us. Stinging branches lashed my face. I tucked down, flattening against him, protecting my body as best I could.

More than ten minutes must have passed by the time we

arrived at another wall. I didn't know how fast Landon had been running, but it felt fast. *This place could be a thousand acres.*

We could use it to our advantage. A big space kept us safe from the hunters. Landon circled around, surveying where we'd come from.

"We need a spot to hide, somewhere we can maybe ambush them one at a time." If they all kept in a group, then we didn't stand a chance. I rubbed a hand over my face. "But with all those cameras everywhere, I don't think hiding is a real possibility." Especially with floodlights lighting the place up like Vegas.

But what other choices did we have? We could run, try to evade, but they'd eventually find us. Our efforts would only gain us more time.

Landon huffed out a breath and turned, trotting parallel to the wall. I wanted to argue his choice to go *toward* the hunters, but there really wasn't any point. They'd know where we were no matter which way we chose. And that meant...

My heart began to race optimistically for once. I gave Landon's fur a tug and he slowed down. "There were only five of them."

He turned his head a bit to indicate he was listening.

"Did they leave someone in the bunker?"

He held still beneath me, then jerked his head up and down. Yeah, that's what I thought too. Two groups of two, and one left at the bunker to report our whereabouts. "So one guy is alone."

Another bob of his head up and down. *Okay, we need to do this smart.* "He can't know we've circled back to him or they'll all come running at once." My heart raced. "Go deeper into the shadows. Let's see if we can spot some cameras."

As unlikely as our survival seemed, I wasn't giving up hope, and I'd take any advantage we could get. It would be nice if we could take out some of those floodlights too. We trudged deeper into the brush, the artificial light not really reaching this far. It gave some privacy, but I wasn't delusional enough to think they didn't have cameras in the shadows.

After a few minutes of walking, a red light glowed in one of the tall pine trees about twenty feet up. *If they'd been smart, they would have concealed those lights.* I'd never been more grateful for someone's oversight as I was in this moment. Red lights stood out in the dark. Or maybe they didn't usually do this at night.

I leaned over Landon's shoulder. "Camera up ahead," I said quietly.

He paused, then lifted up on his hind legs like he wanted me off. I shimmied, landing on the hard ground with a thud. He ran straight at the trunk, like he would try to knock it down, but instead scrambled up it. Bark and pine needles sprayed downward. Once he was high enough to reach the camera, he ripped it free of its mount, then slid down the tree, not in the least bit quiet, breaking branches echoing all around us.

If they didn't know where we were before, they certainly did now.

I crept forward in time to see him pounce on the camera again and again with his front paws, effectively burying the pieces in the dirt.

"I think that should do it."

He huffed a breath, then crouched so I could climb on. My shoulder twinged. "One down, a hundred more to go." When he huffed out another breath, I said, "Let's get out of this area."

He took off at a run, me holding on for dear life until we saw another red light in a tree. He did the same thing again, climbing up to knock it down, then pouncing the shit out of it. It would have been cute if we weren't running for our lives.

We continued onward, not taking any particular path, but circling to the beginning a little bit at a time. For a guy who never went in the military, he knew how to vary his route. I kept my senses open, watching as best I could for signs of the hunters.

We passed a thicket of tall bushes, and I saw something that made me speak up.

"Stop." A pile of good-sized rocks lay beside a tree. Someone had put those there. Someone running for their lives? I swallowed. If it were a shifter stuck in animal form, they'd have trouble throwing rocks no matter how determined.

I jumped off Landon and shivered as I left his warmth. The temperature dropped by the second and I only wore one layer. Trying to ignore the cold, I picked up the fist-sized rocks, shoving them into the empty pockets of my cargo pants. When those were all stuffed full, I made a cradle with the bottom of my shirt to carry more.

Once loaded up, I climbed onto Landon's back. He shot off, clearing the area before one of the hunters could find us. The burden in my shirt made it hard to balance. I gripped his fur tight, losing a couple of the rocks as he dodged around a tree.

He slowed. At first I didn't know why, then I saw all the flies buzzing around one area on the forest floor.

"Dear God," I breathed. *So much blood.* If flies were still after it, it wasn't that old. Nausea burned my throat. I flattened myself against his hump, squeezing as tight as I could. I'd give my life before I'd allow Landon to have the same fate. The oppressiveness of the area bore down on me. I had to get out of here. "Let's see if we can take out some of those floodlights," I said in his ear, my stomach churning.

He skirted the blood, heading to one of the brighter portions of the arena. We paused in the shadows, listening. I couldn't hear anything but the soft puffs of Landon's breaths and the beating of my own heart.

I slid off, dropping my rocks in a pile to peer up the floodlight thirty feet above. It wasn't a secret I was no major-league pitcher, but I didn't think I had a bad arm either. Back in the army, when we had downtime, a couple of the officers would play catch—rain, snow, or shine—and Marley and I would often join them.

Keeping to the shadows, I lined up my aim, and threw the rock as hard as I could. It went wide. I turned to grab another rock, and found Landon trying to palm one with his ample paws. A bear didn't have the thumbs to grip a rock.

I threw two more before I connected. *Crack.* The glass casing smashed, shards raining down on the outer wall. But the bulb remained intact and glared down at us. Tension crawled up my shoulder blades. They definitely heard that. But I didn't want to leave a job half finished. I picked up another rock and threw it as hard as the previous one. It missed.

Heart pounding with the possibility a hunter would come upon us at any moment, I took a deep breath, aimed, and threw one more. *Smash.* It connected with the bulb in a satisfying spray of glass.

Landon snuffed at my hand, and I instinctively turned my palm toward him to nuzzle. "Yeah," I breathed. "We need to move."

Picking up the last two rocks off the ground, I climbed onto his back. He took off like a shot, making me hold on tighter, and aimed toward the bright light across the arena.

Something must have alerted him to slow, because after a minute, he moved into the shadows of a thick collection of bushes, then stopped. Rocks in hand, I slid off and crouched where he'd hunkered down. I shivered, blew on my hands to warm them, and he pressed his body closer.

Nodding my thanks, I scanned the area for cameras, but didn't see any glowing red lights pointed in our direction.

I tensed at the sound of rustling leaves followed by the crunch of footsteps. Without making a sound, I adjusted my position to see better. Two hunters walked by, not twenty feet away, their focus ahead. One wore tactical gear, the other had his hat on backwards.

A radio crackled. "They should be close by."

The one in tactical gear lifted his radio to his mouth. "What do you mean 'should'?"

"They've taken out a few of the cameras but missed more. Lost them for a moment, but they were headed in that direction. Over."

"I don't like working with generalities, Dicky," the guy said into his radio. They trudged forward, snapping twigs beneath their booted feet.

"That's the best I've got." There was a pause on the other end of the radio. "If you guys can't find them in the next hour, I'm leaving this fucking room. Boring as shit staring at these TVs."

The guy with the backwards hat cursed. "If he's going to run around half-cocked by himself, then we need to..." The voices trailed off as they continued toward the light we'd taken out.

When they were far enough away, Landon ambled to his feet. A rock in each of my hands, I straddled him and wrapped my arms around his neck as best I could. He shot off, taking a more direct route toward the starting bunkers. We stopped outside the circle of brightness given off by the four floodlights around the main building. The interior was visible, the window translucent.

After watching for a beat, noticing how the man clicked through the camera feeds looking for us, Landon rounded the outer edge of the clearing until we could see the door on the one side. There was no knob, only a keypad. And the glass in the window itself was probably bulletproof. My rocks would have very little effect.

How could we get inside? There were probably motion detectors hidden around the bunkers. I didn't think we'd tripped one, though, because Dicky hadn't come running out. Keeping an eye out for something similar to the ones Alina and I had found at that warehouse, I slid off Landon's back. The rocks felt heavy in my hands as I weighed our options.

"If he's as eager as he sounds," I said quietly, "then maybe he'd come out without signaling the others if you looked weak."

Landon turned his head to me, a skeptical expression on his face. I don't know how I understood it to be skeptical, but if he'd been in his human form, I was sure his eyebrow would have been raised. But I knew what he was thinking. It would be absolutely idiotic for Dicky to come rushing out here on his own.

I shrugged. "It's all I've got." Hopefully we could count on Dicky being an idiot.

With a jerk of his head, Landon indicated the door on the side of the building. "I'll wait out of sight, you do your thing, and I'll come up behind him?"

The grizzly bear in front of me nodded.

"It's a plan." Rocks tight in my hands and keeping to the shadows, I skulked toward the door. When I reached the pine tree closest to the building, I tucked out of sight.

Landon burst through the tree line on his hind legs, his paw over top of his heart. He weaved side to side like he was drunk, or been stabbed in one of those movies where it took the villain an hour to die. With an exhausted breath, he fell to the hard ground in the middle of a beam of light, the grass bowing away from him at the force of it.

A bit much.

But it worked! Dicky ran out of bunker, a shotgun at his shoulder.

My chest squeezed at the thought of him firing, but I ran toward the door, stuck one of my rocks in before it could close, then followed behind him as silently as possible.

Focused over the barrel of his weapon, he aimed at Landon's head. My heart beat loudly in my ears as I crept closer. Landon lay silent and still on the ground, not even the rise and fall of his chest to indicate life. "Hiya, Dicky," I said, stopping behind him.

He spun around. Rock in hand, I whacked him across the temple before he could aim at me, then followed through with an uppercut. *Thud.* He fell to his side, blood trickling down his cheek, eyes closed.

Landon stirred and rolled to his feet. He sniffed at Dicky as I pushed him enough to pull the shotgun from where it landed beneath his prone form. The soft rise and fall to his chest indicated he was alive. It meant he could wake and cause trouble. Better to put a bullet in him now and be done with it.

Except I'd never killed a person, and he was unconscious. My brother might not think twice about it, but I still had a soul.

"Help me get him inside," I said to Landon, then moved to grab Dicky's feet.

With another huff of breath, Landon took his shoulder in his huge jaw and dragged him backward to the bunker.

"That'll do it." I jogged ahead, scanning the area for any more of Emerson's thugs, and held the door wide.

Landon almost didn't fit. It took him three tries to scrape through the door, his rump wider than his shoulders. Dicky's head was smacked repeatedly on the doorjamb before getting inside. I tried not to notice.

Making sure the door locked behind us, I assessed the TV monitors. As each screen flashed a new image, I noticed a location tag in the bottom right corner: Northeast #23, Southwest #15. An image of the pair of hunters we'd passed on the way here came up on a central one. From what I could see, they were near the light we'd taken out: Southeast #5.

A feed popped up with Emerson on it. I tensed. He skulked through the brush, keeping to the shadows. My stomach twisted. I wanted to vomit. My brother hunted me for sport.

Landon huffed, drawing my attention. His paw lay on Dicky's chest, and he had a "get on with it" expression in his eyes.

"Yeah, okay." I moved to the cupboards underneath the monitors. When I opened the first one, the stench of old blood wafted out to me, making my already nauseous stomach turn over. Inside were rope and bungee cords along with rust-covered pliers and shears. I didn't want to imagine what those tools had been used for.

With Landon's help, I pushed Dicky onto the desk chair, then wrapped the rope as tight as possible around his shoulders. Before I could finish, Landon nudged Dicky's hand so it lay in his lap. The effect made it look like Dicky was jerking off on the job.

"Always embarrassing to get caught with your pants down." Through the window, Dicky would resemble someone lolled in post-ejaculation bliss. "Come on." I moved to the back wall, ignoring the shoulder mounts of the wolf and elk head staring down at me, and heard Landon follow.

We had to find a way out of here. I wasn't positive if we were in Alaska, but the terrain felt right. My brother and his goons had talked about taking their prey to the arena by plane, and wouldn't have had to do that if it were close to the other compound.

In the corner, a thick metal door was inset in the wall, a keypad on its side. For shits and giggles, I tried the last four-digit code I'd been given at the compound. The light remained red.

I aimed Dicky's gun and let off two shots on the knob. *Shit, that's loud.* I spun around, looking for any movement beyond the window. Nothing stirred. Turning back, I rattled the knob. It fell off, but the door didn't budge—probably had numerous bolts like Marley's doors. The only way through would be if we knew the code.

"No dice with the door," I murmured to Landon. "We could have used your keypad hacker." I scanned around for other options. Even though the bunker was defensible, I didn't like the idea of sitting here waiting—too passive, and they had more weapons than we did—and everyone out there probably knew the code to the door. They could also call for reinforcements. Maybe more were already on the way.

My internal clock counted down. They'd find out what we'd done to Dicky soon.

The radio on the desk crackled. "Where are they now?"

Tension crawled up my spine at the sound of Emerson's voice, the band around my chest squeezing tight. We had to put a move on, to get out of here before they cornered us and we eventually ran out of bullets. They had us outnumbered four to two, and could overpower us if they used the right strategy.

But I had a gun now. We had a way to defend ourselves. And the hunters wouldn't have Dicky tattling our location every five minutes. We'd evened the playing field.

Landon huffed his way in front of the monitors, staring hard as they changed from view to view. My eyes went to the collar around his neck. I needed to get him out of that thing. It would have a tracker on it. I could see my brother not using it immediately because it would spoil some of the fun, but he would eventually.

I took a moment to search the desk drawers and other cupboards for the remote. Nothing. The next time my brother's image flashed on the monitors, I noticed it tucked into his utility belt. He stopped walking and held his radio to his lips.

"Dicky, come in."

A frown furrowed his brow before the camera changed to another view.

"We've got to go before someone comes and investigates," I said, turning to Landon. He stalked toward the door leading to the arena and pawed at it.

With a last glance around, I snatched Dicky's radio. Then, with a deep breath, I opened the door and stepped outside where my brother was bent on killing me.

22

LANDON

"I HAVE TO BE HONEST, I'M HESITANT TO BRING YOU ON BOARD WITH *your connections.*" I stared at her over my desk, trying to keep my heart rate level with the girl of my dreams sitting across from me. Even though she looked frazzled, maybe even a little tired, she'd grown into her womanhood and shed the last vestiges of her teenage years.

On paper, she was a perfect fit for Urick Enterprises: double business and economics major, graduated top of her class from University of Toronto. I loved seeing ambitious young adults making waves in the business world. But she squirmed in her chair, her eyes leaving mine to stare at her thighs. My statement had made her uncomfortable.

I knew, then, I shouldn't trust her, but my resolve changed the second she lifted her gaze and said, "I would like to stand on my own two feet, away from anything connected to my family."

Real emotion shone from her eyes, and I scented her fear. I'd been keeping loose tabs on her over the years, told myself I wasn't being a stalker because I'd never act on any of the information, and knew her father had passed away a couple of years ago, putting her brother in charge of Mahn BioIndustries.

If I could help her out of a difficult situation, I would. My bear demanded it.

Stepping out into the clearing, it was the first time I could breathe properly since setting foot in that hellhole of a bunker. The whole room stank of dead shifters. The scents strangled me, making me want to tear into the humans who'd done this, to track down each rich, demented asshole one by one and let my bear loose on them. *Let's see how they like to be hunted.*

Jolyn scanned the area around us, her eyes level above the gun's sight. Ever since Mahn forced me to shift, my bear had been howling a constant tune: mate.

He'd always wanted me to claim her, but until today, I hadn't understood that my connection with her went deeper than love. In my bear form, we both knew. I'd never been around her as my animal to recognize that truth. Now he wouldn't shut up about claiming her.

Need her! Now!

I reined him in again. What we *needed* was to get out of this clearing, kill the people hunting us, and get the hell home. *Then* I could process all of this. I chuffed, grabbing her attention, and lowered my body so she could climb on. Her touch calmed me. As soon as she settled, the length of her newly acquired weapon pressing against my hump, I took off, heading south.

I ran for a few minutes before slowing, and stopped in a darkened patch of bushes.

"Why here?" she whispered as she hunkered down beside me.

Inappropriate amusement shuddered through me. She kept asking questions like I could answer her, revealing just how much she accepted this version of me. I responded the only way I could, nudging her shoulder, licking her cheek, then perking my ears to the south where the pair of men we'd heard earlier were returning. I'd watched them double back on their route on the TV monitors, and predicted this would be close to where they'd walk again.

Jolyn pressed a hand to her damp cheek. "Kissed by a bear," she murmured.

Affection bloomed in my chest. I didn't have time to repeat the gesture, because feet tromped through the woods toward us. I tensed, bracing my paws against the needle-covered ground.

"Dicky isn't answering." This was the laughing, hat-backwards guy, his tone now nervous. *It should be.*

"Probably wants to make it more challenging for us." They emerged from the trees side by side, each holding an assault rifle in front of them. "Lasts longer that way."

"Or he followed through on his threat early and went Rambo on us, but I don't know, man. Something coulda gone wrong." The volume of their voices increased with each step.

"Look, this is our one chance to do this." They were right in line with us now, not ten feet away. "It's always the rich pricks who get the privilege. Shut up and enjoy the ride."

More grumbles followed. I waited until they'd passed us by before moving, creeping out of the shadows to follow, Jolyn right beside me. Adrenaline sharpened my senses. I made sure to take each step with care, being as quiet as possible.

"You're scared of some girl and a beast that could be zapped to death if Mr. Mahn presses the right button?" The one guy adjusted his black cap. "Come on, dude, keep going. If they don't turn up soon, he'll use the locator beacon on the collar."

I'd been prepared for that, had seen the tracker on Brooke's collar when she'd given it to me. But hearing these assholes talk about a kill switch so casually...I bared my teeth.

We stalked the pair until we were right behind them. I glanced at Jolyn, waiting for her to fire. Even though her feet moved forward with each step, the rest of her seemed in a trance. *She won't shoot someone in the back.*

Conflicted emotions tumbled through me. This was a life-

and-death situation, but I was proud of my girl for having a conscience, unlike her brother.

No help for it. I chuffed a loud breath.

The pair jerked, then spun around. I pounced on hat-backwards guy before he could lift his gun. My teeth sank into his throat, blood rushing into my mouth. He got off some shots, but they went wide. His scream turned into a gurgle.

More bullets sprayed toward me, hitting the dirt first, then piercing my flank. I roared, turning to face the threat. Beside the guy wearing tactical gear, Jolyn appeared to have frozen, her eyes glued to the remains of my gruesome attack.

I couldn't help her accept what I'd done right now. Diving forward, I swiped my paw, knocking the gun out of the man's hands, then struck again, clawing a fistful of skin off his face. A scream ripped through the air as I followed him to the ground, the sound cut short as I tore out his jugular. More blood shot into my mouth.

Silence echoed around us. Not even the wind moved, as though we were suspended in the eye of a storm. I let go of the dead body, his head thudding against the ground. Ambling to a nearby bush, I wiped some of the blood off my face.

When I looked up, Jolyn's eyes were transfixed on the men at her feet. "The couple in the forest," she murmured. "They screamed like that."

My heart lurched in my chest. I'd been there that day too. I'd seen what Tom Akins had done to those two hikers up close. They'd been innocents and didn't deserve their fate. But these two on the ground didn't deserve her sympathy.

I chuffed, trying to get her attention.

She flinched, snapping out of her daze, but avoided looking at me. Crouching, she picked up the gun the one man had dropped. "More weapons are always good," she murmured, checking it for ammunition. Then she paused, staring down at her hands. Blood speckled her skin. She wiped them on her pants.

I huffed another breath.

"I know," she said, peering into the shadows of the forest. "We need to keep going."

Frustrated, I chuffed even louder, the leaves on the hard-packed earth twirling out of my way. Finally, she turned to me. The glassy quality of her eyes from moments ago was replaced with grim determination. She nodded once and took a step toward me.

Prepared for her to climb on my back, I lowered to my belly, but a spear of pain shot into my stomach. I roared, my entire body shaking. This felt worse than all the other shocks I'd experienced combined.

My legs collapsed beneath me and I rolled to my side, trying to curl inward. I couldn't escape the agony. Blinding light lanced through my brain, the most excruciating thing I'd ever experienced in my life.

I thought the torture had stopped when a fresh wave cascaded through my body. I roared. My teeth, claws, and fur all sizzled with electricity within a never-ending loop of anguish. I couldn't get away from it.

From a distance, I heard Jolyn scream "Stop!"

My chest clenched at the torment in her voice. She shouldn't have to see any of this. Not what I'd done to those men, not what I'd do to her brother once this pain stopped. When I'd known her before, she could hardly hurt a fly.

Through the anguish, I rolled, trying to get my bearings, to see anything—to protect my mate. Fire rippling through my body, I dug my claws into the dirt, then pulled. I needed to get to Jolyn.

Feet shuffled ahead of me, an altercation, and I lifted my head enough to see Jolyn locked in a struggle with the last of Mahn's men. I roared to protect my mate, but was useless at the receiving end of this debilitating pain.

The pair separated, the man now with her shotgun in his

hands. He swung it like a baseball bat. *Whack!* It hit her across the face. She collapsed. I roared again, the sound scratchy and wrong.

Jolyn didn't move for the longest time. Moisture streamed from my eyes. *It can't end like this.*

23

JOLYN

HEAD BENT, I WALKED THROUGH THE SECURITY GATE AT PEARSON *International Airport. My heart pounded painfully with each step. The necklace Landon had given me a few months ago lay against my sternum, the weight of it burning me in my shame.*

I didn't think I'd ever be whole again. I'd done what my brother wanted, and it only cost me my soul. Landon hadn't deserved any of it. He'd only been sweet, sexy, and supportive with me.

The USB drive burned a hole in my pocket. I didn't know what I'd downloaded from that secret lab, but it would have to do. I wasn't returning to Vancouver ever again. I couldn't keep lying to Landon, someone who I cared about—who said he loved me. He deserved a life partner better than me, one who would give him everything.

A sob stuck in my throat, I strode through the last door. And there stood my brother, one of his security team at his side. It had been over a year since I'd set foot in Toronto, and I couldn't say I missed it, especially not having my brother constantly looking over my shoulder, micromanaging my life in his threatening way.

Stopping three steps away from him, I pulled out the USB drive and extended my arm. "Here," I said, hating myself and what it represented.

Instead of taking the blasted thing from me, Emerson captured my wrist in a pinching hold, pulling me closer. I did my best not to react, but tears pricked my eyes.

This horror would start all over again. I'd pretended I could have a normal life this past year. Immersing myself in Emerson's world once more made me want to vomit. I'll never be free.

"You did good, Jo." He took the USB with his free hand. "Now it's time for the next chapter."

"What?"

He slapped a brochure for the Canadian Armed Forces in my palm. "You're going to be following in Walker Hayles's footsteps."

Facedown in the dirt, my cheek and eye throbbed where Cliff had struck me, my skull buzzing like he'd cracked it open. I gulped breaths, then spit blood. This was it. I was down for the count.

Landon's anguished roar cascaded over my bruised body. *No.* I couldn't quit. Not now. Not when I still had breath in me. I'd vowed to defend him to the death. I wouldn't break that promise.

Cliff's shadow lay heavy across my back. I adjusted my weight, grabbing a handful of dirt to throw in his face, and my stomach pressed into something hard.

My eyes flew open. A few feet away lay the man Landon killed, gaze frozen in his death stare. His throat gaped open, a second mouth, oozing blood on the ground. But it was his assault rifle beneath me that made my heart pound in my ears.

A shotgun cocked, the sound bouncing against the trees. In one movement, I grabbed the gun, my finger on the trigger, and flipped over. *Clack clack clack clack.* Blood sprayed from Cliff's neck and face. I didn't release the trigger until he dropped to the ground.

I gulped breaths, my hands shaking around the gun. Landon's moans snapped me out of my daze. Dropping the weapon, I crawled toward him, desperate to help. The collar was still shocking him. His body shook. Moans erupted through his mouth.

"Oh, God. Landon." Once beside him, I clutched at the collar. A sharp, heated spike of pain shot through my fingertips. I gasped, shaking out my hand, then looked over at Cliff to see if he had a remote. There was nothing on his belt except another gun and a radio.

My brother had to be close by. He wouldn't do this without a way to enjoy it.

"Stop!" I screamed to the sky. "Stop! You can have me. You can kill me. Just stop hurting him."

Landon made another horrible sound, one of protest. He pressed his face into my stomach, like he wanted to push me away. But I held tight, resting my face against his soft ear, trying to take his pain. "I'm not leaving you." Tears leaked from my eyes.

He moaned, his paw stretching against my hip, another shove. I squeezed him harder.

"Your affection for that animal is truly touching, Jo." My head snapped up at my brother's voice. He stood behind Landon, a ridiculously large gun, a Desert Eagle, in one hand, the remote in his other. "You know they call it bestiality for a reason."

I snarled at his amused tone. "Turn this off. Let him go." Landon continued to moan in pain. "Please," I begged. "I'll do whatever you want."

There was a moment where Emerson considered me, his thumb caressing the buttons on the remote. Then he sneered. "Don't say I've never done anything for you."

Abruptly, Landon's body relaxed. His shoulders shuddered a breath. I stroked a hand down his snout, trying to ease his anguish. His tongue licked my palm, residual trembles vibrating from him to me where my thigh connected to his shoulder.

Weakened, he could hardly lift his head when Emerson stepped into his line of sight, speaking directly to him. "You try anything, and I'll press the kill switch." His gun trained on us, my brother's thumb hovered over a red button at the bottom of the remote.

The band around my chest squeezed so tight I could barely breathe. I didn't care what Emerson did to me anymore, didn't care what I needed to promise, just wanted Landon safely away from here. I'd bargain with the devil himself if it meant Landon lived. I pressed my face into his neck.

"Why don't you admit your feelings, dear sister." Emerson's voice cut through the dark. He walked around us, circling behind me. "Isn't that what a pathetic person does at death's door? Admit you want to fuck a beast."

Glaring at him over my shoulder, there were hundreds of things I wanted to say about his deranged beliefs. I swallowed those words, and instead focused my attention on Landon. Those almost-black eyes looked upon me with sadness and defeat.

"I love him," I said, and watched his eyes clear, becoming brighter. "I've never stopped loving him."

Pressing his snout into my palm, Landon closed his eyes and huffed a long breath.

Emerson kept circling, coming closer. "Disgusting," he murmured, his Desert Eagle aimed at the back of Landon's head. "It'll have to be a Romeo-and-Juliet-type love affair, because you both know too much." My chest rose and fell with erratic breaths while he continued to speak. "Can't have him going to all his business friends and telling them what happened here. And after your treachery, Jo, a bullet to the head is too kind for you."

The sound of a helicopter in the distance made us all tense. Mahn looked to the east.

With a scream, I launched myself at him. *Boom.* The massive gun went off like a cannon, making my ears ring and my brain buzz. The bullet went wide. The sound of tree trunk exploding echoed as I grabbed the scorching barrel of the gun. I kept hold of it as my brother pushed me aside. I landed on my back, pain shooting up my skull. But I'd gotten the gun, and now aimed it at Emerson's head from my position on the ground.

A sudden stillness descended over the three of us, a standoff. Emerson had his thumb over the red button, Landon froze in a half crouch, and my finger rested lightly on the trigger of the Desert Eagle.

Apprehension passed over Emerson's face for a half second before he smirked. "You're not going to kill me." His words were muffled with my ears still ringing from the gunshot.

The helicopter neared. Was it more of his people or someone else? He didn't seem worried.

"How can you be so sure?" I asked, my chest heaving, but I kept my aim true.

"You've never had the balls." His thumb twitched over the red button.

I didn't think twice.

Boom.

The sound of the Desert Eagle reverberated through the trees, making my tender eardrums ache. The kickback pushed me against the dirt. Emerson's head exploded, brain matter spraying the trees around him, the rest of his body crumpling in a heap.

I blinked, not comprehending what I'd just done.

A roar of pain from Landon snapped me out of my shock. Had my brother hit the kill switch?

"Landon!"

Gun still in my hand, I rolled to my knees and crawled toward him. Agonized roars whimpered from his lips. His body shook with pain, like he was being electrocuted.

Need the remote. The helicopter was almost on top of us now, searchlights sweeping around the arena. I changed directions, heading toward the decapitated body of my brother. Vomit climbed up my throat. I crawled through blood and gore and found the remote beneath his hand. Fumbling, I pressed the off button.

Landon's moans stopped. I glanced at him, and he lifted his furry head. *Thank God.* I touched the control that said Release and heard a click. Scrambling to my feet, I ran over to him, sliding to a stop in the dirt on my knees. As quickly as I could, I removed the collar from his neck, careful of the skin rubbed raw beneath.

Immediately, he began to change. I sat back on my haunches, body shaking with adrenaline. Fur dissolved into skin; muscles adjusted in size. With my lips parted, I watched as bullets were pushed from his thigh and buttocks. His bulk shrank until his hands and knees smacked against the hard-packed dirt.

Naked, gasping for breath, and fully human, Landon lifted his head to meet my gaze. I reached for him, but stopped when he asked, "Was it true what you said?" His voice shook with emotion.

I dropped my arms, not knowing what he meant.

He cleared his throat. "You love me?"

The whole time we'd been together, I hadn't said the words. Even though I *had* loved him, still did, I hadn't wanted to add it to the layer of deception I'd already created, like it would have made my sins even worse.

I swallowed around the lump in my throat and nodded. "Since before our first date, I've loved you."

The sound that left his lips was primal and raw, creating goosebumps across my skin. Before I could protest, he stood on shaky legs and swept me up into his arms and started walking.

"What are you doing?" I automatically linked my fingers around his neck. After the trauma he'd experienced, there was no way he should be holding me like this. "Landon?"

The *whop whop whop* of the helicopter kept getting louder. A searchlight skimmed by us. My stomach twisted. Was it more of Emerson's men? We should be grabbing those weapons we'd left behind, preparing to defend ourselves, but Landon kept up his determined pace with me in his arms, striding away from the carnage I'd created. He didn't stop, didn't pause for a moment. Every part of him seemed focused ahead. I became extremely aware of his naked state, and my bedraggled one.

Adrenaline ran amok through my body, confusing my emotions. I peeked over Landon's shoulder to where we'd left four bodies, now hidden by darkness and trees. I'd blown my brother's head off. Though it should have horrified me, the truth hadn't sunk in yet. Emerson had done truly sickening things. If I needed to shed a tear for him later, I'd do it in private, but for the first time in my life, I couldn't feel the tight band around my chest.

I tucked my face into Landon's shoulder, just below his ear. "What's happening? What are we doing?" I didn't understand my emotions, why I wanted to crawl inside his skin and never leave.

"Need you alone." His voice came out rough, causing shivers to climb my scalp. "Need to make you mine."

I lifted my head to stare at him, my heart racing at his words and the determined expression on his face. Did he also feel this strange sensation of wanting to be as close as possible?

Whatever he planned, I didn't think he'd have time to do it. Not with the helicopter circling around near the bunker clearing. It lowered, hovered, then turned into something out of a training exercise. People rappelled down ropes since there wasn't enough room to land safely.

Landon veered to the left, away from the bunkers.

"Landon!"

The shout came from one of those who'd dropped in. Landon stopped, turning toward the voice. The sounds of people running through the brush proceeded them. Five individuals jogged toward us in full tactical gear. The one at the front took off his helmet: Walker Hayles.

But when he got closer, Landon growled at him. *Actually growled*—in human form.

"Whoa, dude." Walker held his hands up in surrender fashion. "I get it. Not touching her. We just need to make sure the both of you are okay."

Landon looked down at me. His eyes scanning over where Cliff had hit me with the gun. It pulsed, but after everything, it wasn't important. I'd heal.

"I'm okay," I said, not wanting him to put me down.

"Where's Emerson Mahn?" one of the other men asked.

"Dead," Landon gritted out, pointing his chin toward where we'd come from. "With three others."

Two of the guys jogged off in that direction.

Walker took another tentative step forward, his hands up by his shoulders. "What do you need?"

"For us to be left alone." Landon's voice still didn't sound normal.

"Okay. All right. We can do that. And I'm going to get you some clothes."

Landon would have taken off again, but I placed a hand on his bare chest to stop him. "What about those delivery trucks?" I glanced over at Walker.

"We were told about those by some friends of yours. We can talk more when this"—he circled a hand to encompass the pair of us—"is taken care of."

He'd scarcely finished speaking, and Landon was off again, running through the trees and bushes like he had as a bear. The sounds of people and the helicopter faded the further he went, until it felt like we were the only ones left in the world. And for once, birds chirped from above.

Landon slowed, then set me on my feet next to a thick tree. Warm arms came around me, turning me to face him. I didn't know if I'd ever seen such a stark expression on his face before and my insides squirmed in anticipation.

"I need you," he said, his voice rough. He stepped closer until our chests nearly touched, then scraped the stubble of his beard against my cheek. His hands dove into my hair, freeing it from what remained of my loosened ponytail.

Shivers exploded over my skin, my scalp tingling. I couldn't speak because of the emotion clogging my throat. No one had ever needed me before Landon. And I'd nearly ruined everything between us by following my brother's wishes.

"I want to claim you." His words whispered past my ear and my heart leaped into my throat. What did that mean? It had to be a shifter thing. Nervousness spread through my belly.

But I trusted Landon. I may have abused that trust long ago, but he'd always been solid, never hurting me, always my soft place to fall. If he needed this, then I wanted it too.

"I want to be claimed," I said, embarrassed at my breathless voice.

His eyes widened, then narrowed. A wild, triumphant look spread across his face. He crowded me until my spine pressed against the tree. Heart beating a staccato rhythm in my throat, I grasped his shoulders, my fingers cool against the warmth of his skin.

His arms tightened around me, giving me a hug that touched the ragged parts of my soul. Tears pricked my eyes. I'd missed this so much, the simple affection, the intimacy we'd created.

"I want to forget," I said, and I meant what had just happened, but also the entire fallacy I'd had to live because of my brother. I didn't want to think of any of it. I only wanted it to be Landon and I together, two people who loved and needed one another going forward.

Landon's arms flexed around me. "And I want to remember."

My heart somersaulted in my chest.

Then he lowered his cheek to mine. "I can scent your desire," he murmured against my throat. "And your apprehension. Why are you scared?"

He could smell my emotions? I flushed. How many times had he known what I was feeling when we'd been together before?

I shook my head, not wanting to think about it. "I'm not scared of you," I told him again. After what I'd seen him do with claws and teeth, I probably should have been, but this was Landon. "I just don't know what claiming means."

His stubble scratched my jaw, his nose to my cheek. He pressed his face into my neck where it met my shoulder and inhaled. "I want to mate you. Bite you. Claim you so all shifters know you're mine and I'm yours—a commitment for as long as you'll have me."

My core clenched at the word "mate." That sounded...nice. And important. *Significant.* I wanted that too. Arousal pooled between my thighs.

"Am I supposed to bite you too?" I'd never been into kink, though I knew Landon leaned that way. I had wanted to follow him, but couldn't. Not when everything about kink was about trust and I'd lied to him every day.

He pulled away slightly, a small grin on his face. "If you like." He pressed his forehead to mine and inhaled through flared nostrils. "You smell amazing. After I claim you, I'm going to eat your delicious pussy."

Dear Lord. This claiming was getting better and better. "Yes, yes." I patted his naked shoulder, his skin hot beneath my palm. "I want that too. Let's get to it. Claim me."

It was like I'd flipped a switch. The Landon who was toying with me, making me shiver against a tree with his gentle touches, turned into a wild, untamed thing.

He gripped the hem of my shirt and ripped it open. I gasped. The one side fell away, the other held on by the bandage he'd made earlier. Cool air tickled the flesh my bra didn't cover, but I wasn't cold. I burned up inside from the expression on his face.

Before I could take another breath, he spun me to face the tree. My pulse skyrocketed. Rough bark scratched my palms. His chest pressed against my spine, protective, warming me. His skin felt amazing and I closed my eyes to soak up the sensation.

His lips brushed the shell of my ear. "I'm going to take you hard."

A moan escaped my lips as liquid heat pooled between my thighs. My pussy clenched. His one arm wrapped around me, separating me from the tree and pulling me against him. "My bear needs it," he said, his mouth at my throat, the words guttural. "I need it."

Teeth scraped my sensitive flesh. I pressed my legs together, embarrassed at how wet I was becoming. "Tell me you need it too." His other hand fumbled with the clasp of my cargo pants.

I dug my fingernails into the bark of the tree. "Yes, I need it too."

Releasing his hold, he moved quickly, yanking my pants over my hips. They dropped to the forest floor from the weight of the rocks inside the pockets. My black satin underwear went next, settling around my ankles. Cold air swirled between my legs before he was there again, his cock hard between my ass cheeks.

Breaths left my lips in little puffs of anticipation.

"Hard, Jolyn. Tell me you want it hard."

I didn't recognize his voice. "Yes," I agreed, wanting it so much.

His hands spanning my hips, he lifted me, adjusted our positions, and entered me in one swift movement. Stars sparked behind my eyelids. My body welcomed him, slick and ready. I groaned at the stretch, the way he filled me up. He moaned in an echo of pleasure, then held me there, the pair of us getting used to each other after years apart, the sensation both familiar and new.

His mouth pressed against that same space at my neck. "If you hadn't run from me, I never would have let you go."

My lips parted. I didn't know what to say. Not when he was inside me and it felt like the best thing I'd ever experienced.

He pulled out and thrusted. Sparks exploded in my eyes. It felt *so good*, so right, and I never wanted it to stop.

"More," I said, pushing against the tree to increase the friction.

He gave it to me, pulling out and thrusting with force. His teeth scraped the place where my neck met my shoulder. A moan reverberated through his chest into my spine. My eyes rolled back in their sockets.

He pounded inside me over and over again. I usually couldn't come without clitoral stimulation, but I felt my orgasm building. His cock touched the magic place inside me until I couldn't think, could only feel my body disintegrating into a million pieces.

"I love you!" The words ripped from my throat, half plea, half promise.

His teeth sank into my flesh, a sharp pinch that brought pinpricks of tears to my eyes. Something changed inside me, something profound, a connection I couldn't define. It pushed me over the edge and I came so hard my teeth ached. I screamed his name and lost myself to it. Pleasure wasn't a good enough word. It was existential joy, a perfect moment in time I never wanted to end.

He kept pumping inside me, frantic now, my stomach pressed against the bark of the tree. I could only hold on as shudder after shudder wracked through my limbs. Then he let out a great groan, one worthy of a bear. It reverberated through his teeth into my shoulder.

The world around us paused. Time didn't matter. Our location didn't matter. Euphoria and being joined together in more ways than one were the only things of significance.

My senses returned in a trickle of sight and sound. The sky brightened and the birds sang a morning tune. Far off, voices conversed in baritones.

Still inside me, Landon wrapped his hand around my belly and pulled me away from the tree to hug me against his chest. He let go of my neck. I gasped at the separation and turned my face to lean into him, my new wound twinging. His scent surrounded me: musk, crisp linen, and outdoors.

We remained that way for a while, each of us catching our breath. Then he bent his head and ran his silky tongue over his bite marks. New shivers swept over my skin.

"I need to clean you up." Gradually, inch by inch, he pulled out.

I gasped, not wanting him to leave me, but he turned me around with gentle hands. My discarded clothing separated my bare feet from the forest floor. I had no idea where my boots were.

When I saw the look in his eyes, my chest warmed.

"I love you, Jolyn." His hand slid over my hips, then down my bottom. "I've loved you since I was twelve years old." He pulled me up against him, my inner thighs cradling his cock. Fire glinted in his eyes, possessive.

My heart raced. He'd loved me that long? I wound my arms around his neck, my bra-covered breasts pressing against the muscles of his chest. "I won't run away from us. Never again."

24

LANDON

I SHOVED MY HANDS IN MY POCKETS AND KICKED A ROCK WITH MY *loafer. I hated recess. I was always on my own. I didn't want to play basketball, or wrestle, or do all the other things most shifters my age wanted to do.*

A flash of orange hair paused my steps. Jolyn. She was two years younger than me, but I'd had a crush on her ever since I understood what crushes were. Her eyes shone with fierceness even though she was quiet most of the time.

She stopped when a group of older shifter boys said something to her. The posture through her spine told me it wasn't anything good. I knew those types picked on the weak because they thought they wouldn't fight back.

"Keep walking," I whispered to no one, taking a step toward them.

She didn't keep walking. The group laughed. Tom, a councilman's son, said something else. She spun around, curls bouncing, and launched herself at him.

Dammit. I ran toward them. A tiny human girl taking on a shifter? Didn't she have any self-preservation instincts?

By the time I got there, Tom had pinned her beneath him and punched her in the face. My bear bellowed inside me. I lunged, but others grabbed me, holding me back. He wouldn't stop hitting her.

A roar made everyone freeze. In the next instant, a blur attacked Tom, ripping him away from Jolyn. Another roar, followed by the hitting of flesh against flesh.

I blinked, trying to process what I saw. It was my cousin, Kane, the aloof guy who'd moved here a month ago. Our mothers had wanted us to be friends, but we hadn't yet clicked. Due to his size, I'd pegged him for being an asshole like most of the shifters around here.

Guess not. *He pummeled Tom like he didn't have another purpose in life. Everyone gathered around wore the same horrified expressions. Kane had roared and looked like he would shift at any moment.* Forbidden. We couldn't expose ourselves to humans.

A collective breath left us when two teachers pulled the boys apart. Screaming and shouting made words indistinguishable. Someone crouched by Tom to see if he was still alive. Two teachers dragged Kane to the school, even though he struggled like he wanted to finish off Tom completely.

My eyes went to Jolyn. Her face was bloody and bruising, but she was breathing. I stepped toward her to help, but her brother was there, yanking her to her feet. He spoke in angry tones.

I tried to get her attention, to see if she was okay, but she only had eyes for Kane as the teachers took him away. I'd never seen such adoration in someone's gaze before.

My chest hurt. It should have been me who saved her.

With a groan, I captured her lips with mine. Jolyn tilted her hips against me, searching for more friction, inviting. My cock rubbed between her pussy lips, but as tempting as she was, I didn't adjust to the angle that would submerge me inside her. My tongue licked into her mouth. She took it all and moaned for more.

I ripped my lips away from hers. Mouth descending her body,

I hungrily nibbled her throat, then the valley between her breasts. I bit at her juicy nipples through the black satin of her bra, and her grip tightened on my head as her knees buckled.

Those fingernails in my scalp created pleasurable electricity all across my skin. I moaned in approval. Lower my lips journeyed, over her sweet stomach to the juncture of her thighs, until I was on my knees before her. I inhaled the honey scent of her desire as she trembled against the tree. Sliding my hand up the smooth skin of her leg, I lifted it until her knee hooked over my shoulder, opening her to my gaze.

"Need this," I growled. "Need your scent all over me."

Her entire body flexed with want. The fragrance of her desire surrounded us. Fingers digging into my scalp, she jerked my head toward her pussy.

I moaned, loving the aggression, and licked her from ass to clit. Her supporting leg buckled. I kept her stable with a hand on her stomach and explored every inch of her folds before settling on her clit.

Every pant and moan that fell from her lips fueled me to create more. I wanted her to melt with pleasure. I'd known her body intimately before, but this was a new pairing in so many ways, no secrets between us now.

She screamed my name, her whole body shaking. I sank two fingers into her moist heat, coaxing while I sucked her clit in my mouth. Her body bucked and pushed against me, and I didn't stop until I'd wrung every drop of her orgasm out of her, nonsensical noises escaping her lips.

Keeping my mouth against her delicious flavor, I retracted my fingers, then gripped her hip to hold her steady. Slowly, she relaxed her body. With my one hand on her stomach, I supported her weight as her leg slid over my shoulder. I leaned back, looking up at her pale face in the dim light, her hair wild, an orange beacon in the dark.

I stood, keeping my hands on her hips, then captured her lips in a searing kiss. She shivered. I ran my hands over the flesh of her arms. *Too cold out here for her.* But I also didn't want to let her go. I pulled her close, sharing my body heat, needing her against me after everything.

When she shivered again, I looked down to examine her face.

She cleared her throat. "So that's a claiming."

"Yeah." My hands stroked her shoulders, then the silky skin of her back. I never wanted to stop touching her. "I plan to do a lot more of it later."

A grin spread across her face, and she nodded. Voices were getting louder, and she broke my gaze to look around the forest floor.

"Here," I said, bending to scoop up her clothes. Taking a knee, I helped her step in her satin underwear first, then her cargo pants. Her destroyed shirt hung off my one arm, and I pulled it over her shoulder. "Sorry about that." I'd gotten a bit carried away at the beginning there.

She shook her head at the apology.

Next came her boots. I wasn't even sure when she'd lost them. With Jolyn leaning against the tree, I helped her with first one, then the other, and stood.

Crunch. We both froze at the sound. At least one person moved through the trees toward us. Straightening, I stepped in front of her, blocking anyone's view of her disheveled state.

"I should be in front of you," she murmured quietly. "You're the one completely naked."

I grinned down at her as she moved beside me, her chin lifted. Bushes rustled, and Walker came into sight flanked by two of his buddies from Clyborne Inc.—I had to assume that was who they were from the helicopter and tactical gear.

Keeping my eyes on the trio, I reached to the side. Jolyn's small hand gripped mine a heartbeat later. In the pre-dawn light, her skin tone resembled an overripe tomato. I gave her hand a reassuring squeeze. None of these guys would care about what we'd done. They'd understand I did what I had to in the high emotion of the moment. I wore her scent proudly, wanted it on me for days so every shifter we encountered would know she was mine.

But as a human, she didn't understand that, and telling her not to be embarrassed probably wouldn't help.

I pulled her closer. The urge to growl at everyone had passed, but it didn't mean I wanted to be far from her. Satisfied I'd claimed our mate, my bear lay docile and content inside me.

Walker stopped a few feet away and tossed an armload of clothes at me. "I'm tired of seeing your naked ass."

"Thanks." I let go of Jolyn's hand only long enough to pull on the black cargo pants and runners a size too small, then slipped the T-shirt over her head to cover her ripped one. What she really needed was a thick jacket, something to keep her warm, but this would have to do for now. I tucked her into my side, then faced the others. They'd all taken off their helmets.

"This is Verdugo," Walker said, tilting his head at the man on his right. About the same height as Walker, he had a stockier build, olive complexion, and carried the scent of a wolf.

"And Lavigne." Walker jerked his chin to the left. The black man wearing wraparound sunglasses—odd choice at this time of the day—possessed a feline scent I hadn't encountered before.

Curiosity made me want to ask questions, but they could wait. I stuck out my hand for each of them to shake. Jolyn did the same.

"Do you all work for Clyborne Inc.?" she asked, before returning to the circle of my arms.

Lavigne sent her a grin. "At your service."

I hadn't met any of Walker's military friends before, but knew a bit about them from what he'd told me after being discharged.

"You both good now?" Walker asked me, but his eyes scanned the forest.

I nodded, rubbing my hand up and down Jolyn's arm.

"Good. Because these guys have a lot of questions and I think only you two can answer them." He cocked his head toward the bunkers. "Let's talk."

We followed Walker through the trees, toward the brightest of the floodlights. "How did you find this place?" I asked, our footsteps crunching on twigs and dead leaves.

He glanced at us over his shoulder, slowing. "I got a tip from some friends of yours that you might be heading to Alaska." He faced forward, walking more beside us now. "I called Clyborne, and once we knew where to look, we found it on satellite images." He let out a bark of a laugh. "Did you know this place is almost a perfect circle? It's basically a huge bullseye saying 'Hey! We're here!' But the only way to get to it is by aircraft."

The noise ahead of us got louder. I gripped Jolyn's hand tight as we strode into the clearing. Clyborne's people had ramped up their activities into a full-scale operation. The bunker where we'd arrived was open wide on both sides, revealing a tarmac where a second helicopter had joined the first. People streamed through, some in tactical gear, others looking like scientific personnel.

Four body bags were lined up between the bunkers. Jolyn's gaze lingered, and I swept my hand over her spine. She'd killed her brother defending me. There would be no easy way to move beyond that. Whatever her journey to healing might include, I'd be with her every step of the way.

Dicky wasn't far from the bodies, trussed up like a rodeo calf with a gag in his mouth. I guessed no one wanted to hear his shit. His eyes widened when they landed on us, and he thrashed against his bindings. I didn't know if he was trying to get away from us, or avenge his friends, and I didn't care.

Walker stopped in front of the second bunker. A table had been set up, items on it set out like evidence, everything tagged.

"We found this," Verdugo said, lifting the collar.

My hand went reflexively to my throat. "They forced me to wear it."

"It's the same type they used on Walker," Lavigne added.

"Yeah," I agreed. "The initial design came from my company, but Mahn made modifications."

"Do you know how he got the design?" Walker asked.

Beside me, Jolyn stiffened.

"No," I said, keeping my friend's gaze. "But I'm happy to send Clyborne Inc. everything I have on it."

"Appreciate it," Lavigne said with a nod.

"What about the vitamin water?" Jolyn asked, her hand flexing in mine. "We need to stop those deliveries."

"Taken care of," Lavigne replied.

Relief spread through me, and I felt Jolyn relax as well.

"Those friends of yours," Lavigne went on, "also told us about the SDX-42 compound that affects shifters, and the distribution schedule. By the time they'd gotten a hold of us, they'd already started a news story about poison in Vaunce Vitamin Water. Networks around the world have been blasting about how unsafe the new drink is for the past five hours."

It seemed the media network Jolyn and her friends had set up paid off.

"Thank God," Jolyn murmured, then straightened. "Wait. You guys know about shifters?" Her gaze bounced between Lavigne and Verdugo.

They smiled at the same time.

Understanding dawned in her features. She glanced from the pair, to the people coming in and out of the bunker, to Walker, then to me. I lifted my eyebrows and nodded.

Before she could ask questions, our attention was captured by a light buzzing sound. A small plane wavered in the breeze as it lowered to the tarmac outside the arena.

"Who is that?" I asked.

"Not one of ours," Verdugo said while Lavigne stepped aside to speak on his radio.

I raised an eyebrow at him.

"But I'll find out." Verdugo backed away, then jogged toward the open bunker.

Jolyn wriggled beneath my arm until she faced Walker more fully. "I'm sorry about what happened to you, Walker." Her tone was determined. "I'm sorry for what my brother did to you and for not setting you free sooner."

I pulled her close to kiss her temple.

Walker nodded his acceptance of the apology. "None of it was your fault. I appreciate what you were able to do."

Now wasn't the time to go into how much her actions spurred Mahn on his sadistic quest. There would be a time and place for it, and I knew Walker would see it the way I did. She may have outed our species, but she hadn't been responsible for her brother's actions.

An awkward silence descended between us. "Where are Kane and the sisters?" I asked him.

He turned to me slightly. "Safe in Detroit at our hotel. Clyborne was going to send someone to keep them company since I insisted on coming up here with my old team." He ran a hand over his head. "I have to admit I was conflicted to leave Sabrina behind, but she ordered me to go. And I sure as hell wasn't bringing her after what she'd gone through."

"Ordered?"

He grinned. "Pretty much."

"Hey! Stop that!" An angry voice cut through the early dawn.

We turned in the direction of the bunker.

"Unhand us, you brutes! Didn't your momma teach you not to manhandle a lady?"

It was Alina, looking ready to kill, both figuratively and literally, in her tactical gear. Verdugo held her by the elbow, an assortment of guns tucked under his arm. Marley was a pace behind, her expression resigned as another of Clyborne Inc.'s people escorted them toward us.

"They're with me," Jolyn said, extricating herself from my arms to run to her friends.

My first instinct was to not let go of her, my second to follow. I swallowed down both, my bear unhappy with me. Walker gave me a knowing smirk and I had the urge to punch him.

Jolyn told Clyborne's people to let them go, then embraced each friend in turn. They were full-on tight squeezes, each of them clearly relieved the other was all right.

Alina swatted Verdugo on the arm, but he wouldn't return her guns.

Deciding I'd given my mate enough space, I strode over to the group and wrapped my arm around her waist, gratified when she leaned into me.

"How did you find us?" Jolyn asked.

Marley glanced around, her eyes hesitating on the body bags, then the table full of weapons and other gear, before settling on the two of us. "Landon's tracker was still working."

It took a second for her words to sink in, then I stiffened. "You had me tagged?"

Jolyn peered up at me with a grimace. "Your wallet."

My lips parted. She'd been tracking me?

Then her eyes narrowed. "Don't look at me like that. It was worthwhile in the end, wasn't it?"

I duplicated her expression, but wasn't able to argue. I'd been keeping tabs on her for years, then sent Walker to find her. Glancing at Marley, I said, "I haven't seen my wallet since yesterday."

"Mahn has a plane parked on the tarmac," Walker interjected, taking Verdugo's place when he moved off toward the bunker. "Your stuff could be there."

"Probably a safe bet since I was shipped in a crate."

"That's a fun ride, isn't it?" he replied, his tone dry.

"The best."

"We would have been here sooner," Alina cut in, "except

when we realized your brother had gotten both of you, we called up your friend Walker. The douchebag thanked us for the info, but wouldn't take us along for the ride."

"That would be me." Walker waved at them.

Both of Jolyn's friends narrowed their eyes, unimpressed.

"So we had to rent a plane, obviously," Alina continued. "We stocked it for war, then because the plane's so small, we had to stop about a hundred times to refuel."

"Five times," Marley offered.

"Close enough. And now we're here." She turned to Jolyn fully, her eyes sad. "I'm sorry we didn't get here in time to help you." She gave her friend's elbow a squeeze.

"Well, the Clyborne guys didn't get here on time either, so you're doing all right." Jolyn stepped out of my arms and gave her friend another big hug. "It's amazing you traveled this far for me."

"Are you kidding?" Alina held her at arm's length and gave her a little shake. "Of course we did. We wouldn't leave you in a —" She stopped speaking, dropped her hands, and spun to stare at Verdugo walking away with her guns. "They work for Clyborne?" She chased after him. "Hey! Who do I see about my application?"

25

JOLYN

Two paper grocery bags balanced in my arms, I kicked the door to our condo closed with the heel of my shoe, then noticed Landon's loafers left haphazardly by the door.

"Hello?" I called, striding through the foyer to place the bags on the kitchen island. When I didn't get a response, I poked my head down the hallway. "Landon?"

"In here," he answered.

Tossing my keys beside the groceries, I kicked off my flats and padded down the carpeted hallway, my fingers trailing along the wall below the photographs I'd hung last weekend, ones we'd taken in Stanley Park about the same time we decided to buy a new place together.

The sound of the TV pulled me through to the den where I found Landon lounging in his favorite spot on the sofa, a glass of scotch in his hand. On the flatscreen, a news program flashed pictures of my brother. I tensed.

"...the CIA and CSIS's cooperative investigation into the corrupt dealings of formerly renowned CEO Emerson Mahn of Mahn BioIndustries. His untimely death due to a hunting accident triggered a full-scale probe into the affairs of MBI, which traced through multiple shell companies to find numerous black market transactions. Several more people have been detained for questioning. Jolyn Mahn, only surviving heir to the Mahn empire, has not been implicated in her brother's corruption and has been said to be cooperating fully with authorities. We're following this story as it develops. In other news, will Jinka Cola Company rebound from its disastrous launch of vitamin water? We'll be asking the experts right after this."

Landon clicked it off and rolled to his feet to stalk in my direction wearing the suit he'd put on this morning to go to the office.

"I won't be sad when this story dies for good," I muttered.

Standing in front of me, Landon cupped my jaw in his hands, affection in his gaze. "Don't count on it." He brushed the hair away from my forehead to trail a finger along my cheek. Shivers cascaded down my neck. "It's a scandal for the ages. Drugs, guns, mobsters, corrupt officials—everyone who had a finger in Mahn's pie is going down. There isn't an end in sight to those who would confess what they'd been a part of. And with Clyborne taking care of the shifter side of things, we can keep knowledge about us safe."

I understood even if I didn't like it. Now that the media attention on me had died down once they realized I knew little of my brother's dealings, it was starting to feel more like background noise.

"How was your day?" he asked, giving me a kiss on my forehead.

"Stressful." As every day was now. Dismantling Mahn BioIndustries was taking longer than I'd anticipated, but I wouldn't be preserving any part of brother's legacy. Instead, I was using its equity to start trust funds for those affected by his actions, his victims and their families. From the outside, it looked like I was cannibalizing the company. The shareholders who hadn't jumped ship as soon as my brother's heinous activities were revealed to the world were frothing at the mouth.

"You know you don't have to do this." He straightened the lapel of my suit jacket.

"Actually, I do." I wouldn't be able to live with myself otherwise. But most days, it was more difficult than I'd ever imagined.

I was in touch with Astrid Clyborne daily as she helped track down the shifter families affected by my brother's twisted agenda. Emotionally, it was a lot. She'd offered up her team psychologist for me to speak to more than once. I was almost ready to take her up on it.

But the process of helping those my brother hurt was also rewarding. And I had Landon to come home to. He had a way of making me forget everything else—even if it only lasted until the next morning, when I'd start the process all over again.

"Did you hear from Marley or Alina today?"

I tilted my head at him, my eyes narrowing. "Yes." I dragged out the word. "They have follow-up interviews with Clyborne." Now that Astrid knew they were aware of shifters and were trustworthy, she was more willing to consider them as future employees. And I may have put in a few good words, like how much she'd be missing out if they weren't on her team. I pursed my lips. "How did you know that?"

"I might have heard something through the grapevine."

"Walker is a gossip to the nth degree."

He grinned. "Maybe. But if he keeps me in the loop, I won't complain."

I smoothed the front of his dress shirt. "You're home early. I thought you wouldn't be back until after supper because of some big meeting."

He pulled me closer. "Yes, well. I kept thinking about you, couldn't get you out of my head, really. No point having a meeting I wouldn't pay attention to. I rescheduled."

"Mmmm," I agreed, my core warming from the heat in his eyes. "It pays to be the CEO." I cleared my throat. "And what was it you were thinking of, exactly?"

His eyes became hooded. "I kept seeing you on all fours, on our bed, spreading yourself open for me."

My inner thighs tingled from the picture he'd created. "That sounds...hot. Was there more?"

He nodded, guiding me backward toward our bedroom. "You touched yourself and kept saying wonderful, dirty things."

I swallowed. "What kind of things?" My voice came out a squeak.

"How you wanted me to fuck your mouth and pussy, and play with your ass."

"Dear lord, your imagination is just a-going, isn't it?" The backs of my knees hit the bed. I hadn't realized we'd traveled that far, my attention solely on Landon and his primal eyes. Sometimes I swore I could see two parts to him, that his bear would sometimes try to take control—like right now.

He removed his tie, slowly, the soft sound of the silk against his collar loud in the silence. Folding it in half, he let the expensive material dangle over his fingertips.

I licked my lips. "Who gets to be tied up this time, you or me?"

"Neither." The silk whispering through his fingers, he wrapped the tie around my head as a blindfold. His scent lingered, filling my nostrils, the material pressing gently against my cheeks and forehead, then firmer as he tugged it tight.

With my sight gone, my other senses heightened. A gentle finger traced my lips, cheekbones, and hairline, before traveling downward over my blouse. He squeezed my breasts, then brushed my nipples. They hardened for him, everywhere he touched coming alive. He moved, the hushed sounds of his clothes created images of what he was doing in my mind. When there was total silence, my stomach clenched in anticipation.

Something pressed against my lips. "Open."

I obeyed, and a finger entered, perhaps his thumb. He stroked the tip of my tongue. I tried to pull him deeper.

"Uh, uh. No sucking yet. You're going to have to be good to get your reward."

I smothered my smile.

His movements stilled. "Someone's looking smug."

This roughness in him was all a game. And I loved it. Every time he took control like this, I burned up inside, wanting more. When he passed his thumb over my lips a second time, I tried to give it a good, long suck.

His fingers disappeared from my mouth. "If you're naughty, I'm going to have to tie you up."

My heart pounded. I liked the idea, but then wondered if having two senses taken away would be too much. He touched my lips again, and I held my mouth open, letting him explore where he wanted without my interference.

"Good girl."

Pleasure whipped through my body at the praise. This was our time, our secret, our special headspace. No one else was invited. We both wanted to be here, wanted to make the other person feel good.

He undressed me, opening the buttons of my blouse one by one. Chills exploded across my skin wherever his fingers grazed. The silk tickled over my arms, then fell to the floor with a soft *whoosh*.

My skirt came next. His arms reached around me, my satin-covered breasts brushing against his shirt, nipples pebbling. There was a moment of fumbling as he struggled with the clasp, then the zipper loosened and the whole thing slid down to puddle at my feet.

Fingers caressed my hips, then lower, hooking into the garter belt I knew drove him wild. If his eyes flared when I was fully dressed for work, I knew he was thinking about the lingerie I wore underneath.

Lower still his fingers traveled. I felt the garter clips release one by one, then he rolled my stockings down my legs. He tapped my foot, and I stepped out of them, then stood tall in only my thong and bra, waiting, the world black around me. I could hear movement, but didn't know what he was doing, only got the impression he stopped close in front of me.

"I'm going to need you to turn around." His rough voice made goosebumps explode across my arms.

I did as he said. His fingers on my hips straightened me. "Hands on the bed."

Falling forward without the use of my eyes disoriented my equilibrium, and I gasped in relief when my palms hit the bedspread.

"Face down."

I lowered my head, but kept my ass tilted upward. A growl emerged from him, one that curled heat inside my stomach. He skimmed my thong down my legs. "Spread yourself for me."

I reached back and did as I was told, exposing myself to his eyes. Cool air swirled against my pussy lips. *I wish I could see him.* His hungry expression always did wonderful things to me. But knowing he was focusing on me, devouring me with his gaze while I lay docile, made up for it. My stomach swirled with need.

Then the air changed, turned warm, and I knew his face was close to me, his breath on my skin. I inhaled in anticipation, expectant of what he'd do next.

"So pretty and pink," he murmured, his words hot against me, but he didn't touch.

With a hush of fabric, he moved off, and I felt the lack of his body heat as air rushed in to take his place. I heard rustling, thought maybe he was undressing, but remained in the position he'd put me in, even though the desire to peek under the blindfold and see if I was right was almost too much.

The mattress shifted, and I envisioned him moving closer, crawling toward me on his hands and knees, that predatory look in his eyes.

"Were you going to ask me something?" His voice came from above my head.

My lips curled. It had been his fantasy, but I was on board with it. "Will you fuck my mouth, Landon? Pretty please?" For emphasis, I dropped my jaw.

He cursed softly, and I did my best to hold back my smile because it really wrecked the effect if he thought I was laughing.

Landon's crisp scent surrounded me as he moved closer. Something smooth outlined my lips, then brushed against my tongue. In my awkward position, I leaned forward as far as I could and took him deep in my mouth.

He groaned, the sound thrilling me, making me suck harder. I took every inch he could give me as he pumped his hips, until I was holding still, allowing him to use me at whatever pace he wanted. His gasps and sounds of pleasure made my pussy wetter. I wanted him to come in my mouth, but he was calling the shots this time.

His hand tickled down my spine toward my buttocks, then over, stroking my crack down to my clit. I moaned, my mouth full of cock.

"What a good girl you are to keep yourself open for me."

Whenever he talked like that, my whole body hummed. It was almost too much: his words, the way his fingers lazily toyed with my folds, and the thick feel of him thrusting down my throat.

He pulled out and leaned forward. "Do you have something to ask me?"

Lost in bliss, I'd almost forgotten the point of his imagination game. Catching my breath, I said, "Will you fuck my pussy, Landon? Please?"

His hand cupped my jaw and I leaned into the soft touch. "Since you asked so nicely."

The mattress sank to one side, then warm hands gripped my hips. He drove into me with one, solid thrust. I couldn't stop the groan that left my lips, and braced my hands against the bed. He rocked into me, steady and strong, each stroke kissing my G-spot perfectly.

"Just. Like. That." Each of my words came out a half groan as he slammed harder inside me. He leaned forward, curving over my spine, and pressed a hand between my legs. Fingers slid along my pussy lips until he found my clit. Circular movements drove me higher, until fireworks shot off behind the blindfold. Shudders wracked my body, every muscle flexing.

Through my tremors, he straightened. His fingers coated in my juices, he played with my back hole while pounding into me. My pleasure spiked. His fingers circled, then penetrated in shallow pulses. I panted at the intrusion. A low moan started in the back of my throat, then erupted from me as another orgasm took me under.

With one last powerful thrust, he followed me over the edge, coming inside me. His fingers bit into my hips, then he let go, collapsing forward and taking me with him until we were curled on our side with his cock still filling me up. Hands stroked over my hip, tickling the sides of my breast. I inhaled gasping breaths, my heart rate slowing. His lips passed over the mating mark he'd given me three months ago, and a new wave of erotic shivers swept through my body.

The mattress moved again as he adjusted his position, the blindfold slipping from my eyes. I blinked at the bright lights in the room, not realizing he'd left them on. He'd gotten quite a show.

His lips slid over mine, then my eyes and forehead. When he leaned away, he gave me a tender smile. "Well done."

I grinned, the praise warming me in secret places, then tugged the tie from his fingers. "My turn."

EPILOGUE
JOLYN

One Year Later

THE WARM WIND BRUSHED MY CHEEKS, RUSTLING THE PINE NEEDLES and leaves of the trees edging the lake. A ripple shimmered across the water, drawing my gaze to the two ducks lazily kicking their webbed feet below the crystal clear surface. Sighing, I closed my eyes and leaned back in the beach chair I'd set up on the dock, pretending I was suntanning even though I'd covered every section of exposed skin my one-piece bathing suit didn't cover with SPF-60 sunblock.

Tap tap tap. The sound of a hammer hitting a nail broke through the calm. I cracked one eye open and watched the two ducks startle and fly off. With a sniff, I adjusted my beach hat and closed my eyes again.

Tap tap tap.

"You two are missing the view."

I lifted my head at the sound of Brooke's voice and side-eyed Sabrina. Wearing a transparent wrap over a blue bikini, she faced the same direction as me, enjoying the calm of Kane's lake in the middle of nowhere. The corner of her mouth quirked up, she shook her head, then lay back in her chair, soaking up the rays.

I'd never been to Saskatchewan before, always flew over it to get somewhere else, but now I understood what I was missing. I couldn't think of another place calmer, or more private.

Landon and I arrived yesterday by float plane. Kane had erected a large canvas tent for us, complete with a queen-sized portable bed on a frame, rugs covering the dirt floor, and a hose hookup for running water. All in all, a pretty sweet wilderness setup. He'd assembled a similar arrangement for Walker and Sabrina on the other side of the cabin, giving us all a small amount of privacy.

I resettled. "Just because my eyes are closed, doesn't mean I'm not enjoying the view."

"Not that view." I raised up a little bit to glance at Brooke over my shoulder. Her chair faced the opposite direction. "*That* view." She pointed toward the cabin.

I followed her line of sight to find our three men working on an addition to Kane's cabin. Architectural plans were spread out on a picnic table, a pile of lumber heaped beside it. While Landon and Kane scratched their heads about something on the schematics, Walker seemed to be the only one doing something.

Tap tap tap. Another nail went into the wood extending from the side of the cabin.

Sabrina and I looked at each other, and like we'd came to the same decision, stood and moved our chairs on either side of Brooke.

Things between Sabrina and I weren't perfect. When she'd been caged in my brother's lab, I hadn't helped her immediately. An underlying tension ran between us, unseen, but there. I knew she understood if I'd helped her sooner, none of what came after to take my brother down would have happened, but it didn't change the fact that she'd been inside the cage while I'd been on the outside looking in.

Clyborne Inc.'s psychologist said it would take time to heal all the wounds. I had to be hopeful they would, in fact, heal someday.

"We have a problem," Brooke said suddenly.

I sat up straight. "What?"

"You don't have a drink in your hand. Major fail on my part." Flicking her blonde hair over her shoulder, she hopped up and bounced to the mini kitchen she'd set up at the top of the dock. A big tub of ice held numerous kinds of liquor. "What'll you have? A martini, rye and soda, cosmo, Sex on the Beach?" She waggled her eyebrows at me. Her bright pink bikini contrasted with the greens, blues, and browns in the landscape.

I grinned. "Martini, please. Make it dirty."

"Coming right up."

Ice tinkled as Brooke scooped some into a shaker—a strange music in opposition to the calm surrounding the lake. Beyond her, our men argued over the renovation plans, Walker appearing the most frustrated, Kane the calmest but stubborn, and Landon somehow the referee between the two.

Warmth spread through my chest at watching him. I loved him so much. Some days I didn't know how I got out of bed, because I just wanted to wrap myself around him and not let go. There was a point in my life where I couldn't see even a day ahead, that my purpose was to take my brother down and that was it. Now I couldn't envision a day without Landon right by my side.

Brooke extended my martini to me, complete with olives. "How are you enjoying the 'roughing it' lifestyle, Jolyn?"

I laughed, taking the drink from her. "I don't think it's actually called 'roughing it' when you've set up a lakeside bar."

"Of course it is. If you don't have a flush toilet, it's roughing it."

On the other side of her, Sabrina pshawed. "If you have a roof, it's not roughing it."

I tipped my glass toward her in agreement.

The three of us sat there, each with our drinks in hand—Sabrina's, a cola; Brooke's, a two-toned fancy cocktail complete with an umbrella—and watched as the men tried to decipher the architect's plans.

The sun climbed above us, heating my body. I toed off my flip-flops and sat cross-legged.

"Ten bucks says Kane's going to take his shirt off first," Brooke said out of the blue.

I smirked at her. "Are we talking American dollars or Canadian?"

"American."

"Hmm. Pretty rich, but I'll take that bet. Landon's going to be first."

We both looked at Sabrina at the same time. "Yeah, yeah. I'll take the bet with Walker. For the record, I think it's going to be Kane too."

"Can't pick my man," Brooke replied, taking a sip of her over-the-top girly drink.

Movement by the cabin earned our attention. It appeared the men were back in action, sorting through lumber and taking it to different parts of the space they'd cleared for the project.

This cabin wasn't in a tropical location by any stretch of the imagination, but as the sun crested over us, the temperature rose. Until, finally, Landon unbuttoned his shirt and slung it to the side.

The pair of sisters hooted and hollered at him like he had performed a top-notch strip show—but I was the one who got the five-dollar bills thrown at me.

"Thank you very much." I tucked the cash into the top of my bathing suit. Holding money seemed the only thing it was good for. I might have gone swimming, except both sisters said I'd probably get hypothermia. These northern lakes didn't warm up much.

"Damn," Brooke murmured. "Landon is more cut than you'd expect under all those suits."

"Mm-hmm," I agreed. When the quiet continued around us, I popped open one eye.

Landon was perfect. And he was mine. I had the mark on my neck to prove it. Satisfaction warmed me further.

Sabrina lifted up off her chair to see me around Brooke. "What are you going to do next, Jolyn?"

Now that I'd finished setting up all the trusts for Emerson's victims, I'd had a lot of time to think about that question. "I want to go back to school."

Brooke groaned. "That sounds dreadful."

"Actually, I've always loved school. I was just never allowed to study what I wanted. This time I'm going to become a veterinarian. I think I'll specialize in dangerous animals."

The two other women snorted, then laughed at the same time. The effect was rather melodious.

I liked it up here, but I was also excited to have my own vacation spot. Dismantling Mahn BioIndustries was an ongoing process. Selling it to the highest bidder wasn't enough for me. It would still be MBI with a different name. I didn't want any of it to survive.

But there was one property I wasn't selling—our family home in Goldenlach Ridge. The monstrosity was in the process of being torn down. I didn't have many happy thoughts associated with the place, the only ones being from before my mother had her accident. I wanted to reclaim the family land, build a home I'd be proud to invite our friends to, and conquer the bad memories.

"There he goes," Brooke murmured.

Kane took off his shirt. The two women beside me hollered again. I laughed, delighted by their enthusiasm. Besides Marley and Alina, I'd never had close girlfriends, and these two were always entertaining.

"And you, Sabrina?" I leaned up to see her better. "What are your plans?"

"We're staying where we are for the time being. Both of us like my place in Michigan, and I love my job."

"Alina said she saw Walker at Clyborne's HQ."

"Yeah," Sabrina said, peering up at the sky. "I'm not sure how I feel about it yet. He's not supposed to be taking dangerous jobs, but he feels like he owes her, so..." Her voice trailed off and she took a big swig of her cola like it was something stiffer.

I wasn't sure what to say to comfort her. Marley and Alina loved their new jobs, but they sometimes did dangerous things. After everything Sabrina and Walker had been through, I didn't blame her for not liking it.

"They're whispering," Brooke said under her breath.

"What do you mean?" It wasn't like we could hear them from this far off. But with their shifter ears, they could all probably hear a normal-volume conversation.

"Kane purposefully turned his back so we wouldn't see what he's signing," Brooke explained.

I squinted at them. If they were whispering, it meant they were up to no good. Those three friends together were nothing but trouble. They didn't connect in person all that often. With Kane and Brooke spending half their time here, Landon and I in Vancouver, and Walker and Sabrina in Michigan, the trio had to coordinate to make time for each other.

"That looks like quite the addition," I said, noting how far they'd laid out the wood.

"Yeah, it's kind of ambitious, but this way we can have visitors in the winter too. And there will be a real bathroom with a real shower." She sighed, adjusting her position in her chair. "The hot water heater gets delivered next week."

The only way to describe her expression was "pure joy."

Chewing the last of my olives, I set my martini glass aside and inhaled a deep breath. I could see why she liked it up here.

We lay in companionable silence until the world around us became way too quiet. The hair on the back of my neck stood up. I lifted my head and blinked. "Uh, guys? Where did our men go?"

The sisters sat up in a flash, their bodies tense as they scanned the area. "Shit," Sabrina breathed, standing. "Get off the dock."

Before I could spring to my feet, a blur of movement caught me off guard. Three fast-as-lightning shifters jumped off the rocks beside us and barreled along the dock with huge grins on their faces. Landon's strong arms came around me. Then I was flying.

Splash. We all hit the water at the same time. They weren't lying about the cold. It took my breath away. How the water could be so freezing when the sun was so hot was beyond my comprehension.

Gasping, I surfaced, only to find two bears and a cougar running away, soaked, into the forest.

"Cowards!" Sabrina sputtered, slapping the water in agitation, but she was grinning all the same. "Come," she said to me, and tilted her head to the ladder on the dock.

We swam to the edge and climbed out, all soaked and shivering. Exuberance rolled off both women as much as the water dripping from their bodies. They wanted to give chase.

"Go on," I said with a smile, brushing my soggy hair out of my eyes. "Don't let me hold you back."

With a hoot, the sisters ran, tearing off their bikinis as they shifted mid-leap. I might not be a hundred-percent comfortable with spontaneous nudity, but I was getting used to it. And witnessing a shifter transform never failed to make me breathless.

Then I was alone. With a sigh, I lounged in my chair, content to dry in the sun.

A crack of branches alerted me to someone's presence. I

turned to find an immense grizzly with auburn and black fur breaking through the tree line, his eyes focused on me.

"Well, hello there," I said, turning away from him and closing my eyes. "Come to apologize?"

Clomp clomp clomp. There was nothing stealthy about his approach. If he intended to throw me in again, he was going to be sleeping under the stars.

The world around me quieted. I opened my eyes, expecting to see a bear, but Landon stood before me wearing nothing but a mischievous expression. "I've been bad."

I returned his wicked smile.

Thank you for reading! Did you enjoy? Please add your review because nothing helps an author more and encourages readers to take a chance on a book than a review.

And don't miss more of the *Goldenlach Ridge Shifters* series coming soon and find more from J. E. McDonald at www.jemcdonald.net

Until then, check out McDonald's paranormal romantic comedy series starting with GHOST OF A BEGINNING! Turn the page for a sneak peek!

You can also sign up for the City Owl Press newsletter to receive notice of all book releases!

SNEAK PEEK OF GHOST OF A
BEGINNING

2009

A screech of metal wheels against the tracks, and Grace's head jerked up with a start. She'd almost forgotten where she was. Exhaustion made her want to close her eyes again.

"Next stop: Russell Square." A woman's voice came over the PA system, her British accent soft and measured. The voice was what lulled Grace to sleep in the first place. That, and the rhythmic rocking of the train.

So tired. She hadn't slept on the ten-hour flight from the States, either from excitement or guilt. Before she'd left home, she hadn't been sleeping well either. So far, she'd been awake for over twenty-four hours. Her body was done with it, a slight shaking in her limbs, her eyes gritty and sore. Even though she was only twenty-three, she'd never felt so old.

Note to self: get a full eight hours of sleep at the first opportunity.

Rubbing a hand over her face, she attempted to regain her bearings. Her ten-gallon backpack was secure, squeezed between her knees, and the train car was almost empty. One family sat a few rows down, two parents and two kids. Their auras were a mix of blues and reds and pinks, flexing and bending with each other. A family who got along, loved each other. Whole.

Swallowing, Grace looked away.

Others had come and gone on the train since she'd gotten on at Heathrow Airport. She remembered a group of teenagers, all with their cute accents and clothes that seemed out of place by a few decades. An eighties revival she had heard.

Where the hell is Russell Square? Her eyes went to the route map across from her. She'd missed her stop, intending to get off at Piccadilly Station. Now she was well beyond that area in a city she'd never been before, in a different country, on a different continent. How could she be so careless as to fall asleep?

The train slowed and the wheels screeched again. Her body rocked against the back of the seat. The family stood.

"Russell Square Station. Mind the gap." The doors opened.

Grace grabbed her backpack, slung the heavy beast over her shoulders, and followed the family out. One man in a business suit headed onto the train, his aura a mix of yellow and green. If she'd had more sleep, she'd be able to ignore the auras better, but when he passed her by, she stepped away from the press of his colors to avoid the guaranteed headache. The doors of the train hissed closed behind her.

She glanced up and down the platform as the train moved slowly away. Why was everything so empty? She would have assumed London would be busier. The family ahead of her walked to the right, through an arched doorway and up a stair-case with arrows pointing to street level. They seemed to know where they were going, even though they didn't have British accents. Tourists from somewhere, Canada maybe. She checked her watch still set to Wickwood time, and did the math. Six a.m. Sunday morning. *No wonder.* Everyone with half a brain was still in bed sleeping.

The station had an antique feel, different from where she'd gotten on at the airport. Here, the white and green tile shone glossy and bright. The black lettering on the wall spelling "Russell Square" looked like something from another century, filling her with a sense of wonder at how time worked. How many people had stood exactly where she stood? How many of them no longer walked this earth?

She'd been to New York once, and so far the subway system here felt cleaner than there. The Tube, the Underground, that's what they called it, not a subway. All the words were different here, charming in their own way. She wanted to learn everything there was to know about London, to immerse herself and learn the locals' slang, their quirks, and everything that drew people to this place.

I have the time. Her return ticket home wasn't for a month. A pang hit her in the chest. She'd never been away from home so long before, but there was no way she was turning around now, not after everything.

Only the echo of the train hissing and squealing away remained in the tunnel along with her. Grace followed where the family had gone, the station now eerily quiet. The staircase to ground level wound its way upward, narrow, with the same white tile on the walls as the platform.

Up and up she climbed, her backpack heavy on her spine. She couldn't remember ever being so tired, and all these stairs weren't helping. Realizing she should have checked for an elevator or an escalator instead of taking the staircase, she stopped.

A gust of wind pressed against her back, like someone came up fast behind her. The fluid sensation made the fine hairs over her body stand on end. Heart pounding, Grace spun around. *No one there.* She was alone. The air settled as fast as it stirred up. Her heart raced like she'd been chased several blocks. She pressed a hand to her chest. The wind probably had something to do with the way the staircase connected to street level, but a new urgency, a sense of needing to get away, made her keep going upward instead of turning around and finding an elevator.

Gripping the straps of her backpack tight, she climbed the steps faster than before, even though her legs shook with fatigue. When it felt like she'd never get to the top, her feet hit the concrete of street level. One long, relieved breathed escaped her lips.

Fresh air smacked her face as she stepped outside, damp and crisp. The street was as quiet as the subway. She couldn't see the family who had ridden on the train with her. The antiquated red facade of Russel Square Station rose up behind her. Cars parked along the street in one direction on both sides, a lot of the models European, nothing like she'd see in the states.

What was she doing here? The events of the past week tumbled in her head. With every word her mother had spoken, the angrier Grace had become, the need to put space between them outweighing everything else. Looking around her, she realized a trip somewhere closer to home would have been a more sensible idea.

Instead, she'd secretly planned her escape, not breathing a word of it to her brother, Zack, or her mom. Only Cassie knew where she'd gone. Her roommate might have raised her eyebrows a lot over the past week, but she'd been supportive, as best friends should.

The niggling guilt Grace felt on the flight over the Atlantic Ocean burned in her chest now. She'd never done something so rash before. She was a dependable person, the one people looked to when things needed to get done, not the impulsive person who went on clandestine trips across the ocean with barely any preparation.

Nerves jangling in her stomach, she scanned the street. A convenience store took up half the block across from her, two red phone booths in front of it. The store wasn't open yet, too early on a Sunday. Letting out a slow breath, she tried to remain upright. Her legs still shook. She needed to find a place to crash for a couple hours. Anywhere would do. But first, she should make a phone call. She owed her family that much.

Grace crossed the quiet street and shouldered open the door to the phone booth. At least she remembered to buy an international calling card before she left. With difficulty, she removed her backpack and put it on the ground between her feet before digging out her wallet from a zippered pocket.

Hands trembling with fatigue, she punched in the number on the back of the card, waited for the prompt telling her how much time she had left to use, then dialed Zack's cell number.

Her younger brother answered on the third ring. "Hello?" His deep voice rasped with sleep. "This better be important because it's one in the morning."

"It's me."

"Grace." Her name came from the other end fast and clipped. Something rustled on the other end of the line like he was getting out of bed. "I've been trying to call you all day. Where did you go? Cassie said she didn't know, but I could tell she was lying."

The sickening sensation she experienced at her mom's revelations surged again, making her jaw clench. Silence rang between them as Grace gathered her thoughts, her explanations for why she did what she did, why she didn't tell anyone where she was going. Her anger and disbelief had fueled the way she'd frantically planned her escape, the flights, the work visa application she hadn't heard back from yet. She'd told Cassie she might not be able to afford going to Mexico in the fall after this, that she might not come home at all.

When her guilt swelled again, she forced it down to answer. "I'm in London."

A beat of silence, then he said, "Please tell me you mean Ontario."

She swallowed. "England."

More silence followed by more rustling. A heavy exhale sounded on the other end. "Shit, Grace. What the hell?"

She didn't have an answer for him. Maybe after doing everything expected her whole life, she was owed something impulsive. Crossing an ocean without a word to her family might have been excessive, but she'd always wanted to come here.

"Why haven't you answered any of my calls?" A defeated tone laced Zack's words.

Flinching at another surge of guilt, she said, "Sorry. I left my cell phone at the apartment." She hadn't wanted the roaming charges. She'd once heard of someone being billed for two hundred dollars for answering the phone for five minutes.

"How are we supposed to get ahold of you then? To make sure you're okay?"

Grace lifted her head and scanned the street. "I'll let you know when I get settled. Maybe I'll get a pay-as-you-go phone here or something." Her eyes landed on the building next to Russell Square Station. The small white sign said "Hotel," a wooden placard beneath with the word "Vacancy." It was the only yellow-trimmed facade in a strip of white ones, all with the same amount of windows, the same arched doorways. Someone had converted a row house into a hotel. Relief shuddered through her. She was only steps away from a bed and a few hours' sleep.

"Look." Zack's voice cut into her thoughts. "Mom told me what she said to you, and I know it might be hard to understand, but—"

"Don't." She cut him off. She couldn't do this, not now with her brain barely functional.

"But I want you to know I've—"

"Don't," she said again, making her voice hard. Mom was bad enough. She didn't want Zack to make it worse. She'd fled the country for a reason and didn't want her first phone call back to be about everything she'd left behind.

Ghosts. What a bunch of bullshit.

A resigned sigh reverberated through the line. "How long do you think you'll stay?"

Even though her return ticket was in a month, it could be changed if she found work and her visa was approved. When she bought her ticket, the travel agent had told Grace a return flight would make it easier to pass through customs. She'd been right. "I don't know."

"But you'll be back in a week or so, right?"

"I don't know."

"Grace."

She bristled at the hard edge in his tone. Just like their dad when he'd wanted them to listen. The thought had her heart lurching in her chest. "Tell Mom I'm fine. I'll let you know where I end up. Bye."

"Grace, don't you hang up on me—"

She hung up.

Still clutching the receiver, she let out a slow breath. Zack cared, she knew that, her mother too. But she needed to do this for herself. She needed the space to clear her mind. Space enough that she'd traveled ten hours on a plane.

With a fortifying breath, she left the phone booth. Foot and street traffic had picked up some during her conversation, but not a lot. Securing her backpack onto her shoulders, she crossed the road toward the "Travellers Hotel" sign. And with every step away from her conversation with her brother, she tried to rid herself of the betrayal she felt, wondered if she'd ever be able to forgive her mom and Zack for the secret they'd kept from her.

Don't stop now. Keep reading GHOST OF A BEGINNING.

Thank you for reading the *Goldenlach Ridge Shifters* and find more from J. E. McDonald at www.jemcdonald.net

Be sure to check out McDonald's paranormal romantic comedy series starting with GHOST OF A BEGINNING!

You can take the girl out of Wickwood, but you can't take Wickwood out of the girl.

At twenty-three years old and fresh out of college, Grace Liller takes a last-minute trip across the ocean to flee her family's… oddities. She might see auras, but that doesn't mean she has to accept the strange things her mother told her. Hoping to find an escape in London, England, instead she encounters Sam Thomas, a young man avoiding problems of his own.

While Grace needs normalcy, Sam craves adventure. His parents have his life laid out before him, years of working a stable job at their law firm. But after living his life as dictated by them, he desires less stability in his life.

When Grace and Sam become roommates, they start to realize they might be exactly what the other is searching for. But can the mystery in their building bring their two very different worlds together? Or will the haunting tear them apart?

Please sign up for the City Owl Press newsletter for chances to win special subscriber-only contests and giveaways as well as receiving information on upcoming releases and special excerpts.

All reviews are **welcome** and **appreciated.** Please consider leaving one on your favorite social media and book buying sites.

Escape Your World. Get Lost in Ours! City Owl Press at www.cityowlpress.com.

ACKNOWLEDGMENTS

This is a bittersweet moment. For the past two years, the Goldenlach Ridge Shifters have consumed my life. There is satisfaction with its completion, but also a bit of sadness to leave it behind.

It seems a long time ago I sat on a beach in Northern Saskatchewan, and gazed over the water of a tumultuous lake during a chilly afternoon in May. Heart heavy with grief, my mind searched for ways to escape. I stared and stared at the rugged but beautiful landscape. I thought of my friends in the south, how different their beaches are, how they'd be sunny and full of people in bathing suits, instead of just one person sitting by themselves and shivering on cold sand. I asked myself, what would happen to a person dropped in the middle of this landscape without any clue as to where they were? How would they survive? A seed sparked to life in that instant. Everything about the Goldenlach Ridge Shifters blossomed from that one moment.

That seed turned into a snowball and grew quickly. I'd already had shifters on my brain, and they inserted themselves into the story with ease. By the end of the week, I'd already had the first quarter of *Captive Wilderness* written in my head. It was a story that wanted to be told, and I couldn't seem to stop it. I was ever so glad when I pitched it to my editor that she agreed with me. I believe *grabby hands* was the first thing she said :)

Which brings me to my first thank you.

Thank you, Heather McCorkle. I might have grown that seed on the beach, but it would never have blossomed without you putting shifters in my head to start off with. Thank you for all your support throughout the writing of this whirlwind of a trilogy. Your influence makes every book special.

Thank you to City Owl Press for being such a solid publisher. There are a lot of horror stories out there with small presses, but Tina and Yelena, you run a tight ship. You really care about your authors as well as bring new opportunities to the table whenever possible. Our successes are your successes, and us authors couldn't ask for a better dynamic duo.

And to those who work behind the scenes at City Owl, thank you! To MiblArt and their fantastic covers, to Danielle doing all she does, and to the amazing copy editors.

Thank you to all the readers and fans of both the Wickwood Chronicles and the Goldenlach Ridge Shifters. Your enthusiasm keeps me going.

Thank you to the book reviewers and bloggers. You dedicate your time and energy to lift others, and are the unsung heroes of the industry.

Thank you to my amazing beta and ARC readers. Releasing a book into the world is a big deal, and I'm lucky you're all a part of my fantastic team. Your support means everything!

Thank you to my family, from my parents to all the cousins who cheer me on. You really are the best.

A last big thank you to my husband and three daughters. You are my rock and my soft place to fall. You make me laugh and drive me a little nuts. You're supportive through every up and every down. I love you.

This trilogy may be completed, but this world hasn't disappeared from my head quite yet. Does that mean more books?

Perhaps...

Because we never know what the future holds.

ABOUT THE AUTHOR

Photography by Zehra Rizvi

J. E. MCDONALD was born and raised in Saskatchewan, Canada, The Land of the Living Skies. As a child, she was either searching the clouds for identifiable shapes, or star-gazing way past her bedtime. She's an anti-morning person who wakes up at 5am to write. Needless to say, coffee is a morning requirement. She cut her teeth watching Star Trek, James Bond movies, and reading the Harlequin novels her mother left in the bathroom—which resulted in an extremely skewed sense of sex education by age eleven. All of these factors contribute to her love of writing paranormal romance with humor, mystery, and lots of spice. J. E. resides in Saskatchewan with her husband and three daughters.

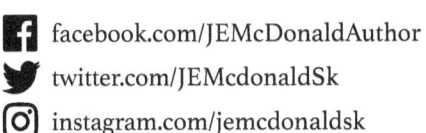

facebook.com/JEMcDonaldAuthor
twitter.com/JEMcdonaldSk
instagram.com/jemcdonaldsk

ABOUT THE PUBLISHER

City Owl Press is a cutting edge indie publishing company, bringing the world of romance and speculative fiction to discerning readers.

Escape Your World. Get Lost in Ours!

www.cityowlpress.com

facebook.com/YourCityOwlPress

twitter.com/cityowlpress

instagram.com/cityowlbooks

pinterest.com/cityowlpress